- [Without Rest] -

WITHOUT REST

A tale of love and madness

by

Published September 21, 2020 by Daniel Strasel

Library of Congress Registration Number: TXu002201519

Library of Congress Control Number: 2020915882

Synopsis:

When he confronts the Truth,
a lovesick god has all of his dreams
turned into nightmares.

 HTTP://www.Mirroranium.com 

ISBN: 978-1-947052-96-3

 - [Without Rest] -

"Beauty is truth, truth beauty,"—that is all
Ye know on earth, and all ye need to know.

John Keats, -Ode on a Grecian Urn

From The Back Cover

In a moment of passion, a lovesick god willingly fails and breaks the divine law. Desperate to nourish and cultivate his renegade love, he searches for the answers to the questions on his heart. Told that he must go to the darkest place in all creation, and that *only there* will he gain what he needs in order to succeed, he does not hesitate in beginning his dread adventure. When he later finds himself in such a place, he does indeed achieve the means to win his love forever…although he did not fully understand the cost.

In the mortal realm, an unlikely group of would-be heroes find themselves hunted by powers they cannot possibly hope to overcome. Captured and taken to a place where sanity is a commodity, they keep their spirits high by helping those around them as they look for a missing companion. While they are searching, they discover—much to their surprise—that they are in the middle of a secret fight amongst the gods.

In the end, love is both triumphant and forsaken in this charming, yet mordant tale of gods and heroes.

Other books by Daniel Strasel:

THE TERRORS OF WONDER
ISBN 978-0-9859964-4-4

A tragicomedy about truth, identity, and leadership. A prominent young child with disturbing visions must overcome an intimate enemy or be lost forever.

GOD, MAN, AND THE MACHINE
ISBN 978-0-9859964-3-7

A story of symbols; a book of philosophy and fiction. An uninteresting man of mistaken importance struggles to understand his role in life.

Stegosaurus the Triceratops
ISBN 978-0-9859964-6-8

A book made to create great conversations: ethics of work, principle, helping, and leadership. A stuffed toy dinosaur encourages others by expressing care.

Visceral Outcries of a Social Moron
ISBN 978-0-9859964-5-1

A short and fun book of poetry and commentary.

For Daniel's complete portfolio please visit Mirroranium.com

- [Without Rest] -

TABLE OF

- [Without Rest] -

CONTENTS

Part 1:

- [Without Rest] -

GODS

PROLOGUE

"People hate prologues," Mue[1] said right after he read the first word. "Nobody wants to have to read through a prologue—"

"But it's a—"

"Don't interrupt. Nobody wants to read through a prologue that's just some big information dump. Nobody wants to be inundated with some possibly random factoids and instances of historical deviation, nor do they want some teaser pre-chapter with some teaser characters. Who *are* these characters, anyway—and who cares? *When* will the prologue make sense, *Marvin*? Halfway through the book? Three quarters? Will it *ever* make sense? I tell you, don't waste time with some impish prologue, just start with chapter one."

"But it's a *play*," Martin complained, "and my name is *Martin*."

"What?" Mue said, blinking. "*What's* a play?"

"The book you are holding…it's a play. The prologue is an orated narrative. Nobody is *reading* anything; people just listen and watch. *I* know that nobody has enough time to actually read, so I figured a play would be quicker than a book."

"So," Mue said, scratching his cheek. "You have someone *narrating* a prologue before the play?"

"Yes, and sometimes *during* as well," Martin nodded. "There will be other actors, of course, singing and acting and whatnot."

"*Singing?*" Mue said, reading the title of the manuscript again. "*The Vile Shepherd*—and there's *singing?* Is this some kind of musical horror?"

"No, it's a play—unless you know someone that could write music for it, then maybe it could be a musical. It's not really a horror story, but there are perhaps some horrific elements or moments. Perhaps if you were to simply *read* it—"

"Yes, well, very good…but I'm skipping the prologue."

"You can't skip the prologue!" Martin insisted.

"Why?"

"Well for one, it won't make as much sense if you don't understand the characters that are introduced in the prologue."

"Hmm," Mue said, frowning and slightly shaking his head. "Well, alright, summarize the prologue for me real quick."

Martin was not happy.

---

[1] pronounced "moo".

"Okay, well," Martin began, his eyes rolled back momentarily as he mentally weighed out what would be the bare essentials. "Let's see, the viewer needs to know about Hypnos—"

"*Hypnos?* Bit of an odd name, don't you think? Surely there's a better name than *Hypnos.*"

"Yes, well, I didn't make it up; he's the Greek god of sleep. *Anyway*, once upon a time, Hera—she's the queen of the gods—begged Hypnos to do a very dangerous favor for her. Hypnos agreed upon one condition: he wanted the hand of Pasithea—she's the goddess of rest—in marriage. Hera agreed and delivered Hypnos his bride following his success."

"Wait, so this Pasithea just gets *sold* to Hypnos?"

"Kind of, yes. It's exactly the kind of problem you would expect it to be. Perhaps if you *read* the prologue—"

"No," Mue sniffed. "Spare me. Continue."

"Fine. Anyway, Hypnos later approaches Aphrodite—she's the goddess of love—"

"Yes, that one I knew—"

"Don't interrupt," Martin said, smiling so that Mue could not see him. "Hypnos approaches Aphrodite and asks her to send one of her *erotes*—those are winged gods of love. See, they look like a cupid, but they're not children, rather, naked adult winged males—"

"*Whoa*," Mue interrupted. "Whoa, whoa, whoa. Listen, I can't let you put on a play with *naked* actors—"

"No, the *actors* won't be naked—I didn't put anything like *that* in there, I just wanted to accurately describe the erotes to you. At any rate, Hypnos needs help because his wife doesn't love him—"

"I'll *bet*. I wouldn't either if I were *sold* into a marriage."

"You're missing a lot. There's a whole section where Hypnos candidly confesses his love for Pasithea, and how he yearns for her genuine affection. You see, his want for the love of his wife has consumed him. Poor Hypnos. It's really quite endearing. Anyway, Aphrodite agrees and sends *Pothos*—the erote of 'yearning love'—to go and shoot Pasithea with one of his *love arrows* so that she will fall in love with Hypnos—"

"What?" Mue looked momentarily disgusted. "That's awful! First she's sold into marriage and now she's being brainwashed, er *heartwashed*? The *Vile Shepherd*, eh?" Mue started flipping through the pages. "Alright, sounds okay. I'm ready to—*holy*…how long *is* this prologue, anyway?"

"Just long enough," Martin answered resolutely.

"Haven't you ever heard of 'show, don't tell'?"

"Well yes, of course. Only, there is so much to tell! If I show it rather than tell it, it truly *will* take forever. Plus, if I'm constantly showing, I'll inevitably have characters saying things for the sake of the viewer rather than for their own need, and I always find that to be a bit transparent. Finally, I can sidestep flashbacks completely."

"What's wrong with flashbacks?" Mue asked, looking hurt. "Everyone enjoys a good flashback every here and there."

Martin ignored him. "Besides, I *need* a narrator."

"*Need?* And why is that?"

"Well, how could you 'show, don't tell' that there was no dialogue?"

"What?"

"It's the first line, see? '*There was no dialogue.*' How could you show *that*? It's *important* that there's no dialogue: someone has to say that nothing was said."

17

Chapter 1:

Acts of Will

A TIME

<table><tr><td></td><td></td><td></td></tr><tr><td></td><td></td><td></td></tr></table>

There was no dialogue.

There was no dialogue because dialogue takes more time than simply exercising your will, and when you are a *goddess* everything responds directly to your will.[2Δ]

Aphrodite exerted her will over her surroundings. With it, she commanded without words, without gestures, without sound beyond her own divine vibration. Her command does not have a beginning or an end: it eternally exudes without rest—although it does change, on occasion, ever so slightly. If people were around and could actually hear it, they would describe it as music.

If people were around, they would find that no two of them could completely agree upon exactly what Aphrodite looked like, however *every* one of them would agree that she was immeasurably beautiful.

Of course, if people were around, they would all be dead, for the environment was not currently suitable for earthly life.

Pothos appeared in response to Aphrodite's will, his wings swiftly delivering him to his superior. As he appeared, he gracefully landed before her in a reverent kneel.

There was no dialogue.

[2Δ] Everything except *people,* that is. Many gods and goddesses find it rather annoying that they have to actually *speak* to people (even though it is an exercise that seldom happens). People, on the other hand, like dialogue.

 - [Without Rest] -

There was no dialogue, for gods seldom ever use words or gestures with one another as their will is simply known. If, however, their wills *were* words, then we might proceed to see what was not said.

"Welcome, gentle Pothos," Aphrodite didn't say.

Aphrodite stood in brilliant[3] magnificence before kneeling, winged Pothos.

"My Lady," Pothos didn't say, taking a reverent tone. "It is indeed hard to look upon you long, for you are so beautiful—beautiful beyond even my own memory! Oh, resplendent and radiant, fair and perfect Lady, how will I be of service to you?"

"Deep in the underworld you will find a pair of twin caves, one of which has a mouth that boasts the river Lethe. This is the cave of Hypnos. Within it you will find your mark: that which is none other than his very wife, Pasithea! I want you to give her a longing for her husband, so that they might know joy together."

As Pothos watched, Aphrodite became so lovely that he had to again bow his head.

"Your will is my will, my Lady."

△

As Pothos came upon the gates, he was extended permission to enter the underworld, his coming anticipated.

Pothos found his way to the twin caves, the openings of which were equally flanked by marijuana plants and poppy flowers of varying colors and hues. Mushrooms grew in various positions about the higher, mossy rocks. The interiors of the caves were dark and obscured, although one *did* offer up the river Lethe.[4]

Pothos strung his bow and crept silently into the appropriate cave, his wings tucked and significantly smaller in size. There was an ambient aroma about the cave that spoke of leafy and earthy tones. As he proceeded inward, Pothos felt a bit more relaxed about this assignment than others. This would have alarmed him slightly, were he not relaxed.

Hypnos had left his wife at home and was away. This was as much by design as not, as Hypnos was normally at work during this period and Pasithea normally at home.

Pasithea slept peacefully on a living couch fit only for a god; she had appar-

---

3 Having a light of their own, all gods appear illuminated (when they appear at all).

4 At least *presumably* the river Lethe as there is no signpost.

ently drifted off while watching the mortal realm.

When he saw her, Pothos' own divine vibration changed ever so slightly as he was overcome with a visceral yearning. Pothos whistled, almost involuntarily, an act which he as immediately quelled.

If that moment could be translated into words, it might sound as follows:[5Δ]

Alas! My eyes behold now their doom!
No vision more dire lay beyond this room:
No suffering, no tragedy, no untimely death
Has caused me such loss of untidy breath

And then, without reason, Pothos *spoke*.

"No beauty, no wonder, no oral delight
"Could summon a stupor as great as this sight.
"A man would be speechless, yet I am no man.
"A man would do better: no stutter, no stam—

"—mering, no clumsy oration;
"Only awe and amazement: a far proper station."

And then Pothos thought:

*Can **I** not know love: I, Love, who so gives?*
*Isn't it **only** for love which life lives?*
*Can **I** not know her most tender embrace?*
—Will she love Love at the sight of Love's face?

How could I think she would give me her favor?
*And should **I** be one to transgress his neighbor?*
—A neighbor who surely could have any other?
—A neighbor who also has Death as his brother?

Though sweet exultation be known for a time,
All love will end poor when it starts as a crime;
Where lover and lover then always discover
They did not love well when they loved one another.

[5Δ] Of course, when one feels something so strongly so quickly, it invariably waxes poetic.

No, trusting in Love should not be in vain,
And despite my feelings, it's perfectly plain
Whomever might enact such travesty,
*I know only this: it shouldn't be **me**.*

Pothos sighed, which was an act of will rather than one of automation. He drew a lone arrow from his quiver, nocked it, and let it sail into Pasithea.

As the red-tipped arrow pierced her, Pasithea recoiled slightly, upsetting her nearby chalice and sending it noisily to the floor. She awoke to see Pothos turning away.

"Wait," she didn't say. She started to prop herself up on her arm.

Pothos continued to depart. He had not made more than a step, however, when the mists before him materialized into Pasithea.

"Wait," she again didn't say, smiling as she swept over to him. "You have a message?"

Message? Pothos thought. "Yes, message! I wa—" But before his will echoed his thoughts, Pasithea's hand quickly slid up the back of his head and pulled him into her most eager kiss.

Unfortunately, this was too much for Pothos, and he pulled her likewise into his own embrace. What he didn't realize is that Pasithea used her position to remove an arrow from his quiver, and impaled him with it as she passionately engaged him.

Overcome by his own power, Pothos tried to declare the nature of his mission when Pasithea calmed and silenced him.

"I know who you are," Pasithea didn't say huskily, "and I know why you must be here, but I do not care. It's just that you're here—that's all I care about. Here with me. Now."

"Yes," Pothos agreed. "That is all I care, either."

Chapter 2:

The Plight of a Lesser God

A TIME

<table><tr><td></td><td></td><td></td></tr><tr><td></td><td></td><td></td></tr></table>

Pothos and Pasithea spent a passage of time appreciating the company of one another. Their divine vibrations resonated more and more similarly until they could not be distinguished as two any longer, rather only as a single, very powerful vibration. Their joy overwhelmed them.

The moment eventually arrived, however, where they had to consider the return of Hypnos, and they settled into themselves once more.

"Hypnos will return soon, my sweet Pothos; we must go away from here at once."

"*We* cannot—only *I* must leave," Pothos didn't say, standing up and collecting his bow and quiver.

"Nay!" Pasithea objected. "How can you suggest we part, now that we have come together?[6Δ] We must stay together!"

"Nay, there will be fury amongst many of the gods if they should discover what has been done. If I stay, it will be obvious what has happened, and if we both leave it will be apparent. And where would we go? Wherever it is, we will be found, and then we will be cursed, imprisoned, or both—and then we'll *assuredly* never be together again. We must act as though everything has happened exactly as it should have."

"You're right, of course," Pasithea agreed dejectedly.

"Fear not, my sweet! I have been waiting for eternity for someone such as you to bathe with all my love, and I *do* so love you! I'm not about to give up on

---

[6Δ] Pasithea wasn't hurt as much as genuinely confused. After all, she stabbed him with his own arrow—he must love her as much as she loved him.

- [Without Rest] -

my dream now! I *am* going away, but only to find a way for us to be together for all eternity."

"But where will you go?"

"As far as necessary—surely there is something or some god that can help me. For love, most would trade everything."

"And if you should find no such assistance, will you *fight* Hypnos?"

"I believe there must be a peaceful resolution possible; I want to see if there is any other way. Regardless, I will embrace oblivion before I quit!"[7△]

"My sweet Pothos! Oh, how I already yearn for you! I want to resonate your name, yet we must remain in secret…so I will give you a secret name." Pasithea then deliberately whispered into his ear.

"I swear I will never tell it to anyone," he didn't say.

They embraced—Pasithea, once again hungry for the affection that a pierced Pothos earnestly gave.

"You are quicker of wit than I," Pothos didn't say after they pulled apart again. "I will need time to find a suitable secret name for you."

"Then, whisper once my proper name before you leave."

"Pasithea," Pothos whispered with heat into her ear, sending a thrill up her spine as it tickled her earlobe.

△
M

Pothos travelled out of the underworld and through the expanse of eternity as fast as his divine wings could carry him. He returned to the Palace of Pleasure and flew directly into his room.

Retracting his wings, he walked up to a living mirror, and then proceeded slowly *into* the mirror. He walked out of his mirrored-room through his mirrored-door. He made sure to close the door behind him.

Pothos travelled the mirrored-hallways and stairwells, careful to avoid being seen by anyone who might be nearby on the not-mirrored side[8▲] of the palace. It took him a bit longer to get where he wanted to go by travelling this way, but it afforded him what he desired—secrecy.

He eventually came upon an otherwise regular green door, indistinguishable from the many that could be found on that floor of the palace, save that *this* door

---

7△ Which is not quite as noble as it sounds; Pothos knows that he cannot possibly hope to triumph over Hypnos—at least, not without help or trickery.

8▲ Of course, he checked to be sure that there was no one on his side as well, although he was simply less alert about it as the circumstance of someone else being there is highly unlikely (although certainly *possible*).

could not be found on the not-mirrored side.

Pothos knocked, the act of which suggested a position of respect and humility beyond that which his will already exuded.

Soon afterward, he understood that he was welcome to enter. As he walked into the room, he felt himself blush from embarrassment—but such was one of the effects of coming into the direct presence of Harpocrates.[9Δ]

"I am lost!" Pothos didn't say, looking directly into the eyes of Harpocrates. "Blissfully happy and woefully lost all at once! I have come asking for your absolute and total discretion in this."

"And you shall have it," Harpocrates didn't say, taking Pothos' hand in his own. "As I shall have need to call upon you some day."

"Of course."

"Now then, you have something more?" Harpocrates didn't say as he noticed that Pothos was lingering.

"I do. Pasithea and I cannot keep this secret forever. You are the only one in whom I might confide; you are the only one who can help. *Is* there some way I could achieve the right to Pasithea? Something Hypnos wants more? Perhaps he has a weakness? *Is* there a place that is completely secret from the gods?"

Harpocrates smiled softly.

"There *is* a place that is secret from even the gods, but you cannot go there, or rather, you already are there. That place, however, cannot be of help to you in this regard. I'm afraid that there is no manner by which you might *achieve* Pasithea that I know of, and I have no secrets that I might now share. I cannot help you."

"Who *can* help me, then? If anyone knows of someone, surely it is you."

[9Δ] "It's Har-pock-ruh-teez—he's the Greek god of secrets and silence," Martin explained as Mue mispronounced the name.

"Huh. Well, maybe you could narrate a footnote or something—that's something we need to know!" Mue said seriously.

"Well, how would I narrate a *footnote*?" Martin asked. "Would I have the narrator interrupt the actors, or would he explain later, after it has vanished from the viewer's mind? Besid—"

"Well, still important don't you think?" Mue asked, looking up from the book (play) at Martin. "I mean, how is anyone supposed to know that he's the *god of secrets*, for instance?"

"*It's in the prologue.*"

"Oh."

Harpocrates reasoned as he resonated. "You need an oracle, one that can withstand your presence. There *is* one—one that is three, rather: the Fates. Both gods and men are subject to the Fates. Submit your question to them, and perhaps they will help you."

"Yes?" Pothos looked hopeful, yet unsure. "Can I truly be helped by *them*? I thought they were just tricksters who only spoke in riddles."

"That they are," Harpocrates agreed as Pothos' expression melted. "However *they* can see the future. Can *you*?"

Pothos stepped out of his bedroom mirror to find Aphrodite waiting for him.

"Pothos," Aphrodite didn't say.

"My queen!" Pothos exuded as he bowed. "You are, as always, radiant and beautiful beyond sentiment. How may I serve you?"

"You failed to report your success with Pasithea, however I have just seen Hypnos and he is quite delighted."

"Yes? Delighted?"

"Yes." Aphrodite smiled. "When Hypnos returned home, he found that Pasithea had indeed changed towards him. You see for him, sweet Pothos, it has been a period of agony—I do not mean to suggest that Pasithea had been acting as an enemy, rather that she was not very…comfortable. But now things are quite fixed, it seems. What's interesting is that Pasithea credits her ability to you."

"To me?"

"Yes, she told Hypnos that in addition to giving her the inclination to love—which, incidentally, is typically a *secret*…although I cannot argue with results—you also gave her instruction on *how* to love."

"Oh, well, yes, I did," Pothos brokenly agreed.

"So you did. A bodiless voice from afar, indeed![10Δ] I daresay that I recommend you undertake this particular course of action *again* on any subsequent assignments, however as you have managed to bring such delight and joy to Hypnos, he has asked that you be rewarded."

"Hypnos asked for a reward for *me*? As in by name?"

"Yes. I don't know what matrimonial delights you suggested to Pasithea, but whatever you said was *exactly* what Hypnos wanted. I have never seen him so happy."

It was all Pothos could do not to fly into a jealous rage. His anger flared up

---

[10Δ] Which is how Pasithea described the nature of her knowledge to her husband.

when he started to imagine Hypnos with Pasithea, and then he had to quash it as immediately. He shuddered, just a little. As it was, Pothos was unable to further acknowledge Aphrodite; he merely left his head bowed.

"I came to reward you, but I sense that you are not at ease, gentle Pothos. In lieu of anything extravagant, let me give you what you must need—a vacation. Go and rest, sweet erote, you have done well. Return to me when you are ready."

"Yes, my queen." Pothos exuded a sense of great thanks, which only barely masked his deepening internal conflict.

Oh, how he wished she would just *leave* already!

The Plight of a Lesser God

Chapter 3:

Iambic Prophesy

A TIME

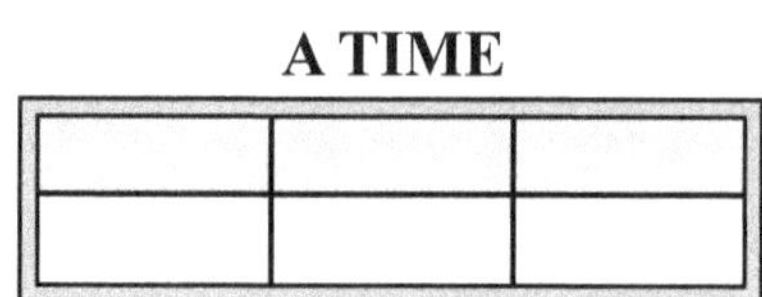

Near an ill-known pool at the bottom of a great, rocky chasm stood three sisters[11] who together were almost a goddess. Together they held sway over the gods themselves, for they could see that which the gods could not—the future. They saw it within the Waters of Creation, where each droplet was a mortal life, and every one of them necessary for the pool.

The women gathered, spun, and tended the waters of the pool. They knew how the currents wove around one another, where they began and where they ended. They also knew *where* and *how* each droplet moved.

Seldom did anyone visit these three, for seldom did they ever help. As few consulted them, they were almost more rumor than real—and though rumors may vary, it was never wrong for one to suggest that they were undesirable to deal with.

They did not much like to be intruded upon, and certainly did not respond well to anyone who asked what the Waters said; it was already difficult to describe, then made doubly so, for the women were cursed and could only speak in rhyme.[12]

When Pothos arrived, the Fates were neither amused nor surprised, but they *were* interested. Pothos would be fortunate on this visit for the youngest one favored him. As he flew down into the belly of the chasm the Fates began announcing his arrival. This was perhaps to rile him, or perhaps simply to exercise their voices.

11[△] not entirely accurate as one of them was sitting down.

12[▲] A condition that they themselves find so completely annoying that they have constructed a hand-signal language that they use when they are not being interrupted by fools asking about the future.

- [Without Rest] -

The youngest sister, clad all in white, was the first to speak.

"Pothos comes, though not so gentle—
His own orders instrumental
In making Love consider war:
An option he would once abhor."

And then, the middle sister, dressed in a flowing pink tunic, added:

"Pothos comes, his need is urgent
For his love hath gone divergent,
And should the gods find out his heart:
***Forever** shall they spend apart.*"

The eldest, dressed in a blood-red robe, concluded:[13△]

"Pothos comes to investigate
The hand, the whim, the will of fate;
But what the erote doesn't know,
Is *knowing's* what increases woe!"

The three sisters laughed together as Pothos landed.[14▲] He looked around at them and exuded his will, but the sisters did not understand.

"Does it speak?" The crone said. "Does it bark, does it bite? Does it come in peace; does it look to fight?"

"You need *not* speak," the woman soothed, "or ask, or yell; whether or not, *we know what to tell.*"

"Never mind them," the maiden said, "the red or the pink: tell us your thoughts, please, *say* what you think."

"Very well," Pothos began. His divine voice, deep and impossible reverberated over everything. It was everywhere, all at once. "How might I proceed to spend the rest of eternity with my radiant Pasithea?"

[13△] Her voice actually cracked as she went to speak. She cleared her throat and started over.

[14▲] The ambient acoustic amplified their voices and laughter, the sound of which was already slightly unnerving.

The beautiful young maiden smiled and spoke:

"There is only *one* way that you could see
Pasithea for *all* eternity—
And that, sweet Pothos, would happen to be
You kill her immediate family."

Pothos frowned. Before he could speak, however, the middle sister spoke.

"We need not hear you to know your fool heart!
No reason to lie, no reason to start.
There's no *reason* to turn your love to hate,
No reason to try to assassinate,
No reason to plot, no reason to sleuth:
You *can't* kill a god, and that is the truth.
Yet, it's within reason to wonder why,
For it's with reason that any god die."

Then the old woman pointed her gnarled finger at Pothos.

"What *can* be the point, for this god is *heart*strong;
He's only been after one thing all along!
For at *any* moment could he have undone
The power of love from himself or the one
Whose only true crime was to have been *present*.
Who he shot in her *sleep*! Uncouth! Unpleasant!"

"Enough!" Pothos said, his voice overpowering everything in the moment.
"I did not bring this condition upon myself, but you are correct: I need not be subject to it. But *this* was a *gift*. It was *given* to me, so that I might love her *equally*! I
will *not* forsake it! You will *not* shake me of my resolve!" Pothos slightly stamped
his foot, cracking and fragmenting the cold stone beneath. "There *must* be a way
that I can be with her! I will give you an arrow of mine if you help me."

The three sisters looked at one another, all of them with some slight worry.
The youngest one turned and said:

"Give us a moment, good Pothos, to peer
Into the water by which we are near

Looking, perhaps we can see what's ahead
Should Rest not love Sleep, but love Love instead."

Pothos has gone mad with love, the maiden gestured. *He has been consumed by it. He will not listen. Still, we should help.*

It is already present in the waters, the middle-aged warned. *We must—*

I've had about enough of this already, the crone gestured crudely as she stood up. *Let's get this over with and back to work.*

The three sisters then spoke in unison:

"Everything now that we will say
Impacts the future past today
Be warned that as we three so speak,
Your future looks to be quite bleak;
But you shall have a final chance:
Withdraw, you can, now in advance
Of this clear, yet unspoken doom.
Back! Go back! Go back to your room!"

After a bit of wispy quiet, the maiden spoke:

"Pasithea *is* yours if you don't sway:
For year upon year, and day upon day.
She'll live to serve you without any rest,
And all the people—by your own request.

And then the woman in pink spoke again:

"And if you *will not* go away,
Instead insisting that you stay—
Know ye this then, forevermore:
This fate was *not* what was in store!"

Finally, the crone spoke once more:

"No need is there for you to pay us,

With a *sagitta amo deus*[15Δ]
Only listen, learn, and tell no one
If you so want your prophecy spun."

"I will tell nobody of this," Pothos declared in response.

The three sisters then spoke in unison once again. As they spoke, the waters of the pool stirred up and a mist formed.

"Listen then, Pothos, to this instruction—
Which asks of you some added deduction—
Though of *one* thing, let us more plainly say:
You'll get all you want to give it away.

Now that your fate lay out naked, in front
We can now tell you to get what you want
You'll first need to know if there is a way
To *subdue* a god instead of to slay,

And yes, we tell you that this hungry crime
Can be performed by the god of this rhyme,
Though first he must make a frightening pact
Before he performs this frightening act,
Or he'll lose his nerve, right on his last whim,
When victim begs Love to also love him.

Now the only way that Love can love less,
Is for Love to love that which love detests,
And that which is most detestable lay
As far below Hades, as Zeus would say.[16Δ]
Go there, sweet Pothos, and be sweet no more,
For there, oh Pothos, you'll see what's in store.

Once you have seen all there is to be shown,
You'll see a sun with no light of its own.
You'll see through the lies you thought were so real;

15Δ Arrow [of the] Love God
16Δ In Homer's Illiad (book 8), Zeus suggests that Tartarus—the place the Fates are referring to—lay as far below Hades as Heaven is above Earth.

                    - [Without Rest] -

You'll see through the love you thought was ideal.
You'll see, though you'll never cry tears or weep,
Nor bat either eye when you fight with Sleep.

From there, great Pothos, you'll travel the Earth
Growing your assets, establishing worth,
Until, at last, you are called to return,
Reminding you why you went off to learn.

You'll triumph over your enemy, then
You'll sidestep the chains of your sentence when
A core group of men use all that they know
To send you away, though you will not go.

Now we come to the close of this favor
- For that's the future which will not waver -
Of ends, however, we can see but three—
The one of which ends all humanity.

The signs of *all* ends are strange, even odd
Where math elevates into a new god
And everyone has everything they need,
Yet everyone seeks a way to be freed.
Where slaves are well-groomed and lavished upon,
Where no one can die, and no one lives on,
Where no one gets sick, and no one is well;
No one wants Heaven and no one wants Hell.
No one is present, yet no one is gone,
No one is singing, yet there is a song.
No one is happy, yet everyone proud,
No one is silent, yet none dare be loud.
No one wants heroes, yet heroes are loved.
No one is touching, for no one is gloved.
No one remembers the way that it was,
But everyone knows the truth just because
They consulted someone they did not know,
And that someone said that someone said so.
There's nothing that's new, yet nothing gets old,
And no one can tell, for no one was told.

- [Daniel Strasel] -

Everyone's wealthy, yet everyone poor,
And everything's less, yet everything's more.

These are but some of the signs you will note
When fate catches up with you, good erote.
Know *also* ye this final point of plot:
Should you see a fruit of silver-that's-not,
A man, genuinely good in nature
Will ruin your laws, your legislature,
Your life, your love, and your perfect plan;
You'll lose *everything* because of this man,
And at your defeat the world will sunder;
All you build given over to wonder.
And how will you know a man such as he?
You'll know for he speaks so beautifully.

That you have some hope, we tell to you now:
There is still a way to prevail, somehow.
The how is this: avoid you this person
And life goes on—not once will it worsen;
You'll have Pasithea ever after
And all will know your voice and your laughter.
But with these last words, we now must leave you—
Rather—*you* must go; we bid you adieu![17Δ]

Pothos bowed respectfully, but otherwise did not hesitate in departing from the Fates, his wings lifting him fast and far away.

He's kind of a fool for a god, doesn't it seem? The middle sister signed. *I mean, I expect* **men** *to ignore the warnings, but a* **god***?*

You're kind of a fool for a Fate, the young maiden gestured in Pothos' defense. *You* **knew** *he was coming, and* **that's** *what you wore?*

[17Δ] so long, farewell, auf wiedersehen, goodbye.

Chapter 4:

Stranger at the Gates

A TIME

<table>
<tr><td></td><td></td><td></td></tr>
<tr><td></td><td></td><td></td></tr>
</table>

Tartarus is a titanic pit and its gates, gargantuan—even to a god. They were wider than mountains,[18Δ] and Pothos himself felt momentarily small as he flew above them. They were not repulsive—as Pothos had imagined—rather, they were well kept, if ill-used, and shone brilliantly.

Pothos landed before the great stone gatehouse, which from the air looked like a dirty toy compared to the great, reflective gates.

He exuded his will, but there came no response.

"Hail!" Pothos called in his gentle, yet mighty voice. "Gatekeeper!"

"Pothos?" An unfamiliar voice rang out from within the gatehouse. "What are *you* doing here?"

Pothos was surprised that he was addressed by name, presumably by the gatekeeper. Usually when he was recognized, he was generally identified more by his function rather than by his actual identity.

"Who knows me in there?"

"Come inside," the voice came back. "I'm just about to have a drink. Join me."

[18Δ] It was not a frequent occasion that the gates of Tartarus opened, and when they did, they *barely* opened. If there were seldom a need to open the gates, it was then significantly less frequent that they needed to be opened to their full extent.

It is also notable—although extremely trivial—that there are actually 3 doors in total that comprise the gates of Tartarus: on the exterior there are two massive doors that slide together, and on the interior there is a door that is as large as the opposite two combined, and that door moves into place perpendicularly.

　　　　- [Without Rest] -

Pothos frowned. He had never been to Tartarus before, and was not entirely sure what he would find—but it was certainly not this! He tucked up his wings and approached the door to the gatehouse, his bow he carried unstrung. The door opened when Pothos pulled, and he cautiously went inside. Up a strategic stairwell he climbed, eventually to be deposited into a room situated to monitor the ambient landscape and gates. Pothos noted that he could somehow see *through* the gates from here.

Then Pothos saw him. Off to one side of the room stood a rather plain looking man…yet, he wasn't a *man*, Pothos detected. He was certainly not a god, either. The not-man looked to be somewhere in his early forties, with thick white hair and black eyebrows. Hard-won lines of emotion etched his countenance. The not-man was of casual build, and looked as if he was about four days out of shaving.

The not-man sipped from a fairly plain vessel he held in his one hand, and read from a book he held in the other.

"Well, that's just ridiculous!" The not-man laughed at the book. "But then again," he said,[19A] momentarily reconsidering.   Then he noticed Pothos.   "Oh! Pothos! Excellent. Welcome. Please, sit, if it comforts you."

"It does not," Pothos said, his voice taking up the whole room.

"Oh. Very good, then," the not-man said, placing the book on his nearby desk—carefully, so as to not lose his place.

"You *are* the gatekeeper, then?"

"Me? The not-man smiled. "Yes." He took another quick sip from his mug and put it down near his book. "Would you like a cup of coffee?"

"Coffee? No. This doesn't seem right," Pothos said. "The guardian of *Hades*—"

"Is more considerable than I?" The not-man smiled. "Oh, I'm considerable, I just don't look like much—and *that* is a matter of choice I tell you. I'm not your enemy, and it does not serve to frighten you. Now, more to the point: why have you come?"

"I want to gain access to Tartarus."

"Certainly. By what authority?"

"None. I wish to go in by my will alone."

"Well, obviously I cannot allow that—"

"I will pay you, of course," Pothos said, starting to pull from his quiver, but

---

[19A] He said in Hebrew, however upon seeing Pothos he then switches (back) to Greek, which is the exclusive language the two of them use with one another for the duration of this interaction.

the not-man motioned for him to stop.

"No, keep your things," the not-man said, smiling sadly. "You cannot bribe me, Pothos."

Pothos looked at the strange not-man intently. "How do you know who I am?"

"*Shouldn't* I know?"

"What?"

"You *do* consider yourself the god of yearning love, do you not? *Shouldn't* I know who you are?"

"How can you distinguish me from the other erotes?"

"Well, you all look different."

Pothos was skeptic. "You know the *erotes* by sight as well as by name?"

"Of course."

"Who *are* you?"

"Well," the not-man said, "my name is Uriel. I doubt that helps."

"*Well*, how can I get into Tartarus? What must I do? What errand?"

"You misunderstand, Pothos. There is nothing you can offer me in exchange for your entry into Tartarus. There is no cause for you to go there, my friend. It is a place for criminals of the greatest crime."

"Perhaps some are simply in need of love," Pothos suggested cautiously. "Or does it not occur to you that I am on a mission of love? Could there be a nobler endeavor?"

"Oh, they all certainly need love," Uriel agreed soberly, "but they are *monsters*: they do not know how to receive or give love—all they can do is *consume* it. They are murderers and liars and thieves *with no remorse*. They are devoid of light and love, and would as quickly consume yours if they were unrestrained."

"I must enter, nonetheless," Pothos said resolutely. "It is *I* who is in need of love, Uriel; *I* need it. I *have* needed it, and now I have finally found it—and it can be mine forever, so long as I visit Tartarus."

"Again, you will find no love in *here*," Uriel gestured to Tartarus. "I am afraid you have wasted your—"

"No!" Pothos raised his voice. "I mean, wait, please. Uriel, I beg of you, I *must* go. I know that I will not find love *there*; I have been foretold[20Δ] that I will, within, find a way to gain it…I'll know it when I see it."

Pothos explained a portion of his prophecy.

"Oh," Uriel frowned. "That seems extremely unlikely to me. I don't see how anything positive can come from you visiting Tartarus."

[20Δ]"I will tell nobody of this," Pothos declared [to the Fates]. *Well, so much for **that**.*

"I ask nothing more than to be allowed to *look around*. I did not come to make mischief, I'm only here to *see*. Surely you can allow that?"

"Its irregular, to say the least. Let me pray on it. I will return."

Uriel walked away toward an alternate room. About midway, he turned around and went back to his desk to grab his coffee, and *then* went away again.

While Uriel was away, Pothos spent most of his time gazing somehow *through* the gates and into the great pit of Tartarus. From his position, however, there was not much to see—at least not much of interest. The observation room was much more interesting, however pointless to describe further.

Uriel returned after a short period of time, his countenance not much different than when he departed.

"Listen," he began. "Some time from now, I will have a conversation with an otherwise completely uninteresting man. I will have this conversation in such a way that it will *invite* others to question its legitimacy should he discuss it. This uninteresting man will tell *many* men of this conversation, although almost no one will believe him.

"One man, however, because he believes this boring man's incredible tale, is inspired to do something amazing: he saves his people from an approaching upheaval. These people will be spared because I had an unbelievable conversation with a man of no character.

"The smallest of actions can have very great consequences; a *sentence* can change *everything*. Have care, Pothos. If you are not firmly ready, things can impact you in ways unimaginable, unforeseeable."

"Unforeseeable?" Pothos chuckled. "Didn't you hear me say that it was foretold?"

"You are not bound by that foretelling, only *you* can make it true."

"Please, just let me in, Uriel. You choose to look only at my possible failure; my future has as much hope of having Pasithea forever! You don't understand— you don't even *want* love," he said, motioning to his quiver of arrows. "How *could* you understand?"

"You think that I am loveless? *I* must deliver this conversation to this man because *you* go to Tartarus! If you do *not* go, I will not need to do this thing, for there will be no upheaval to spare people from! This pursuit is madness; no one within Tartarus will even be able to *perceive* you, as they are consumed in their own agony. No one will have anythin—"

"*Please*, Uriel! I have been waiting eternity for a love of my own! Upheaval or no, the people are spared, correct? Then what do you care? Let me in. Please."

Chapter 4

Uriel looked truly sad. "So be it: you have been granted the freedom to fail. Wait at the gate and I will open it. Call me when you are done *looking around*."

Pothos left and waited outside while Uriel commanded the gate to open. The gates moved slowly, their operation causing the ground to tremble and shake everywhere throughout the realm. When there was passage enough, Pothos flew down into Tartarus proper.

"It's not too late!" Uriel yelled from the gatehouse. "You can still change your mind!"

Chapter 5:

A Change of Heart

A TIME

<table>
<tr><td></td><td></td><td></td></tr>
<tr><td></td><td></td><td></td></tr>
</table>

To suggest that Pothos was *completely* intrepid would be wrong, although he certainly appeared bold enough. He strung his bow and nocked an arrow just prior to entering Tartarus—an act he actually considered somewhat irrational since he didn't imagine that he would need to employ his weapon…yet, this visit had already proven to be something quite different than anything he had anticipated.

He soared around the terrible darkness of Tartarus, illuminating the vastness with his own divine light.

Within the reaches of Tartarus, Pothos saw a great many things that cannot and *should not* be described.[21Δ] Indeed, Tartarus was filled with those most abominable receiving the most impactful of punishments.

As he soared from corner to corner, his pity grew for those chained within—though what he acknowledged as pity was really a manifestation of fear. Pothos could not help but be transformed by what he saw, for if he were not careful, perhaps he would find himself with a similar fate! His mind rolled over the many warnings he had been given.

This isn't helping, Pothos thought in increasing melancholy. *Uriel was right, there is nothing here beyond horror.*

Think of Pasithea, he reminded himself, changing his focus and calming him-

---

[21Δ] I would not even dare attempt, for when one attempts to describe the indescribable, it is both insulting and absurd simultaneously—and I am not one to disgrace myself consciously *and* conspicuously. Describing that which *should not* be described is outright pernicious. Suffice it to say that your own darkest fear of any potential eternal torment is absolutely pathetic in comparison to the actuality of it.

     - [Without Rest] -

self down. *Think of why you are here.*

Thinking of Pasithea made everything suddenly more tolerable; the weight of it all was suddenly eased. He even smiled amidst all that darkness when he thought of her last, secret whisper:

"My secret name for you will be 'Axel'. It will come to mean 'father of peace'. I will love you—and only you—forever, my sweet, sweet Axel."

He remembered her last kiss.

Then he remembered Hypnos, and why he needed to do this. With renewed determination Pothos flew yet lower, his bow and arrow drawn and ready for anything.

Now, down in the lowest recess of Tartarus, Pothos *did* see something lingering at the far edge of his sight. He flew toward it, but seemed that he could not get any closer. He rushed toward it as fast as his divine wings could carry him, and time itself seemed to stop.

Finally, though, he came upon it. Pothos looked it over, but he could not comprehend it. It was like a star, only it did not shine. Its surface roared with flame that had no light. It was immense, and it resonated with a surreal vibration; one that felt almost like a god—a terrible, hungry god with no mind.

This…*thing*…did shed some very pathetic light, but the light was not actually from the star itself, rather a few poor lights swimming around the inside.

What is it? Pothos thought and resonated. *What hand made **this**? This… what is this thing?*

***Who* am I,** the thing vibrated and churned sickly. **Who am I. Who am I. We. Who am I. WhoamIWhoamIWHOamIWhoamI. More.**

Yuck! Pothos thought, completely repulsed. He thought back to the foretelling. *Surely, nothing in all of creation is more detestable than this abomination! Yet, how could I possibly love this thing?*

Pothos.

Pothos froze. His bow was trained, his arrow nocked and ready to fly. He stayed divinely still,[22Δ] but inwardly Pothos was shaken.

[22Δ] still in all regards with exception to the constant movement of his wings holding him in place.

Pothos, love.

Love.

The lightless flaming thing then somehow gurgled.

Love.

Pothos was aghast. *What. **Is.** This…monstrosity?*

Love.

Love me. We. LoveLoveLoveWhoamI.

The vibration became stronger and stronger, pulsing out the will of the monster.

*Oh! How it hungers; I can **feel** it.* Pothos shuddered.

Hungers.

HUNGERS

The sudden force of its will knocked Pothos back enough to cause him to drop his arrow.

Its power is immeasurable, Pothos thought with some awe. *Larger than anything—*

Before Pothos drew a subsequent arrow, a hideous sound erupted from the monster as it drew in and bellowed out irregular breaths.

*It's **crying**,* Pothos realized, lost somewhere between fear, disgust, and sympathy. *It's crying because it is so hungry.*

Pothos gasped, not as an act of will.

*This…is a **titan**!* He realized in epiphany. *Some kind of titan child…discard-*

ed…disfigured!

Love. Hunger

We WhoamLoveHunger

Love Child Mother

Wave after wave of its resonating wailing impacted Pothos, summoning his pity and compassion. Then his fear turned to anger.

Why *is this child* ***here***? *How can I swear allegiance to Zeus if he condones such a completely vile act? Dare I suggest he should have destroyed it?* ***That*** *is not love, yet neither is* ***this***; ***this*** *is even* ***more*** *criminal!* ***Why*** *leave the child here to suffer eternally? What* ***crime*** *so landed it this endless torture? What absolute lack of heart to abandon it here!*

HungerIamWhoWEHunger

Does it even understand what it resonates? Pothos thought with a compassion that surprised himself. *Yes, who* ***indeed*** *could love this child—this misshapen, abandoned, titanic monster? Who could love* ***this*** *child…apart from Love himself?*

This is what the Fates foretold, Pothos thought as he flew before the disfigured titan. *Soon we*[23] *shall be together forever. Now,* ***how*** *can I love this…child? I will give it something to quell its hunger; I will give it a small portion of my own divine light*[24]*. Sacrificial love is the greatest love, after all.*

Pothos opened his mouth and allowed a small stream of light to travel from himself up into the lightless star.

HUNGERS, it pulsed the moment Pothos' light impacted upon it.

WhoWEHUNGERS!

Pothos was blown backward, his bow knocked from his grip. He tumbled, but righted himself. He felt a bit weak—that last resonation was *painful*! As he

23[Δ] Pasithea
24[▲] Some argue "essence" or "ichor," but it was light.

settled into place, he stopped the stream of light.

At least, he meant to. He could not completely stop the stream, but he *did* slow it down. As he slowed it down, however, he felt a great pressure building in his face. When the pressure continued to build, Pothos genuinely started to panic. Then the light started pouring out of his nose, which alleviated the pressure in his face somewhat. He experimentally opened his mouth a bit wider, and as the light did pour a bit faster, the pressure did somewhat ease.

HUNGERRRRRRRRRRRRRRRRRRRRRRRRRRRRRRRRRRS

"*Stop*," Pothos demanded, but to no avail. Then the pressure started building up again. It was starting to actually *hurt* when it began spilling out of his ears. "Stop!"

WhoIam HUNGERS

Soon, however, Pothos was beyond commands or even pleas, for the pain in his head was overwhelming his ability to think. The pain! The *pain*! He could not stand it! It was so sudden, so overwhelming! He opened his mouth as wide as it could go. Even exerting all of his will, he could not get the light to pour from him fast enough! The pain!

More. HUNGERS Mother more

The pain completely overtook him. Eternity seemed to pass for Pothos, when finally there was a moment when something gave way, and his light flowed up into the titan with new force. The pain then started to ease.

What…is happening to me?

As his light poured out of him, Pothos started to change. First his fingers, toes, and wingtips went completely black, but then this blackness grew to overtake him as his light continued to flee. His pain was replaced by a desperate madness edged in helpless despair.

As the light poured into it, the monster started to change. First it began to grow, then it began to show some slight illumination when suddenly it exploded into vibrancy with a light all its own! The fires and flames burning across the surface of the titan, no longer black, raged in absolute frenzy.

Pothos looked up at the growing, titanic, flaming sphere in awe and dread. As he looked upon it, he started to see himself in reflection, just under the flames. His dread turned to curiosity as he watched the reflection of himself solidify. As his remaining light drained from him, he flew closer and reached out to touch the reflection of himself. Just. Out. Of. Reach.

Pothos froze. When he gave up the last of his light, he was intimately aware of it. *Something is wrong,* Pothos thought. *Something is wrong.*

Pothos remained perfectly still. His wings did not even move, he simply hung in midair, now indistinguishable from the surrounding blackness of Tartarus. The only light belonged to the gigantic flaming sphere before him.

Pothos missed his light immediately. He remembered it being there, he remembered using it. Now it was gone, irretrievably gone. *Gone! How can it be gone?* He could not think.

Pothos became catatonic. He remained completely motionless for a human lifetime, consumed with his own sorrow.

Pasithea will revile me for what I have become, Pothos thought, still hanging there.

If they could see me, all they[25] would do is laugh, Pothos thought. *I will be sentenced and shunned for my crime, and for my misfortune I will be ridiculed and mocked.*

There is no one who will help me.

*No one will ever want **my** love, now.*

More. Hungers Mother more

Pothos laughed. It was a terrible laugh: it spoke of defeat and of a resolve to remain defeated. It carried the will of Pothos, and his will was broken.

*All because of **love**.*

Then Pothos saw again that strange reflection of himself inside of the mon-

[25] "they" being the other gods: Zeus, Aphrodite, et al.

ster, and he fell in love with that reminiscent similarity.

"But I can love *you*," Pothos said to the burning titan. "You, who nobody else could *possibly* love; you are the only thing that could ever *want my* love, and I am the only one who would give love to you."

More. HUNGERS Mother more

"Yes, my love—I will get you more. Nothing can atone for what you have had to endure, and possibly nothing could quell your hunger—but I will feed you as much as you can stand; I will feed you *the world* in exchange for your unjustified, terrible, and immeasurable suffering!"

Hungers WhoamI

And then the gods, thought Pothos. *Pasithea last.*

A Change of Heart

Chapter 6:

No Light of His Own

A TIME

<table>
<tr><td></td><td></td><td></td></tr>
<tr><td></td><td></td><td></td></tr>
</table>

"Uriel," Pothos called, having returned to the gate. "It is I, Pothos; I have seen all there is to see."

The gates opened, as slowly and powerfully as before. Pothos was not sure what response he might receive from Uriel,[26Δ] so he was rather glad that he did not find himself suddenly a permanent occupant of Tartarus.

Pothos flew through the gates on stiff black wings. Uriel met him in flight, his white hair now pulled back into a ponytail.

"Oh, Pothos!" Uriel cried in dismay. "Where are your eyes? Where is your light?"
"Get back from me, gatekeeper!" Pothos rebuffed and flew away. "What's done is done."

"It's *still* not too late!" Uriel called after him.

Pothos went to Earth. With no light of his own, people no longer met Pothos with awe and reverence, but rather were driven insane at the mere sight of him. Pothos then hid himself amongst mankind, assuming many forms and donning

---

26Δ Uriel *did* hesitate a moment when he realized that he could only see Pothos in that Pothos was somehow *darker* than the pit.

many masks.

Pothos studied mankind. He worked alongside them during the day, and drank with them during the night. He planted and harvested food. He hunted and cleaned animals. He made boats out of wood and steel. He fashioned women's hats.

On occasion his costume would fail, and he would have to reinvent himself over again. Contrasted with losing his light, however, nothing bothered Pothos; he was never emotionally different, no matter the setback or fortune.

All of his emotions were replaced with his mission—all save the most perverse; somewhere deep inside of himself, Pothos would feel a happy tickle when he imagined his peers as lightless as he.

He absorbed most of mankind's knowledge, and then destroyed much of it. He obscured history and complicated laws. Under one mask a ruler and as martyr the next, Pothos influenced nations.   Some he drove to conflict, others to explore.

He encouraged men to bathe. He improved their math and pushed literacy, all so that mankind would flourish and propagate—all for the purpose of serving a greater feast.

The day came when all of his plans were complete—everything was assembled, and everything in place. Pothos[27△] began a dark ritual to create a gateway on the Earth that would open directly inside Tartarus, right next to his abominable adopted child. He even placed a portion of his own remaining divinity into the attempt.

The ritual was a failure, however: the magical gateway did *not* open within Tartarus, but rather directly *upon* the gates themselves. As the gateway failed, millions of carefully cultivated humans died, and a portion of the Earth was replaced with a portion of the gates of Tartarus.

This failure did not *deter* Pothos, although it *did* upset him, which would be the first thing he *felt* in a long time.

Pothos decided it was time for a slightly different approach: he would establish his *own nation*—a peaceful nation—all the while progressing a new approach to establishing the gateway to his child.

Father of peace, indeed, Pothos thought wryly as he remembered Pasithea's secret name for him.

Pothos was already well into his new effort, however, when he felt the will

------

27△ and a large cult of followers he had accrued under one of his many guises.

of his commander, Aphrodite; she was calling for him to return from his vacation.

I dare not ignore this, for surely there will be an alarm if I do not return, he thought. *And I cannot possibly present myself naked.*

- [Without Rest] -

Chapter 7:

Impersonating Himself

A TIME

<table><tr><td></td><td></td><td></td></tr><tr><td></td><td></td><td></td></tr></table>

Pothos had long considered the potential repercussions following the end of his holiday. He knew that he would eventually have to approach his peers and superiors either humbly with the truth, or with a proud lie. Pothos, over his 'vacation', developed an affinity for lying, so he dedicated himself to the latter path. He always found it personally amusing, for instance, that the best lies were made by simply describing the truth from a narrow perspective. Rather than dread, Pothos would enjoy this upcoming test of his skill.

Even if the gods *had* sympathy, Pothos didn't want it: Zeus was unredeemable for abandoning that child to Tartarus, and the others equally condemnable by their acknowledgement of his sovereignty. Besides, Pothos had grown to love what he had become—at least, that was the personal lie he often told to himself.

Pothos painted himself with a luminous paint that he developed through his influence and wealth. He applied the initial coat by himself, and then did the detailing with some assistance. Although the paint was extremely convincing, it had the unfortunate drawback of also being extremely radioactive, and the men who assisted him in its application all died shortly thereafter.

Pothos arrived before Aphrodite in an impressive display of flight and control. He landed in kneeling reverence before her.

"Great goddess!" Pothos exuded his will. Pothos then gasped[28Δ] as he cupped

---

28Δ although it was always Pothos' plan to hide his face before Aphrodite, his cry was one of pain rather than reverence—Pothos was slightly *hurt* by the radiance of Aphrodite.

his face with his hands. "Your beauty is more magnificent each and every time I glimpse you! Truly, you are the brightest of *any* god or goddess! How may I be of service, great Lady? What is your will?"

"Gentle Pothos, welcome back," Aphrodite didn't say as she smiled down on her kneeling erote. "Yet…something is wrong?"

"Not *wrong*…different," Pothos didn't say, not looking up.

"Yes. Different." Aphrodite seemed suspicious.

"In my travels, I have seen terrible things, my Lady! I have caught sorrow in my heart, and it has changed me. Like a scar, it has healed, but it has left me with visions of suffering—of a child's suffering—and it will never leave me. I can still hear echoes of its crying each and every night. I have learned what it is to be frail—fragile. Broken. I understand powerlessness. I did not realize how much love was needed! Everywhere! Not 'yearning love' or *any* type of romantic love: I mean *real* love!"

"Poor, sweet Pothos—"

"Thank you, great Aphrodite, for your sympathy…I assure you it is unnecessary, however. I have emerged from my ordeals and travels a stronger, wiser—if perhaps a touch sadder—Love. A *better* Love, though: I have developed an almost infinite patience, I have learned how to give without return, I have learned how to set aside my own pursuits and passions so that I can help those around me.

"I am completely self-sacrificing: I would give my last drop of light if it would feed a hungry child. You see, my sorrow has given birth to a great and perfect compassion. I have learned to love that which is unlovable. I am greater—and different—than I was before. I am still your yearning love, my Lady, only now I equally yearn for compassion, justice, and peace."

Aphrodite frowned, just a little. "Feels almost…not like yearning…more like hunger."

"They are very similar," Pothos acquiesced. "My Lady, have you need for me to demonstrate my loyalty? Say the word, and I will—"

"Nay, fair Pothos, your loyalty is not in question. My concern began when it took you so long to respond to my summons…but it was quelled when you explained your heart."

Pothos kneeled lower.

"Well, tell me: where have you been? What did you see? What did you do?"

"Where have I *not* been?" Pothos didn't say, his resonation nearly contaminated with mischief. "I have been as far and as wide and as low as I could be taken. I have been sideways. I have seen the most loveless and lowliest of men find love, and I have seen the most loving lose it. I have seen faces without eyes, though not eyeless faces; I know you don't see.[29Δ] I've seen enough to know that I don't know as much as I thought.

"What I have done is what I am doing," Pothos continued. "I am a farmer, I have been growing my garden; I am a shepherd, I have been raising my flock. I save every life, and I provide for the lives I save; I love every life equally, I value them all the same. *All* live prosperous and plentiful lives—with *plenty* of off-spring!"

Aphrodite looked momentarily shocked. "You're building *worshippers*?"

"No! Nobody knows who I am; I never appear as a god. I just help everyone remain as peaceful and loving as they can be brought to be. I help—sometimes the leaders, and sometimes the followers. I even help with the chores; I do the dishes on occasion."

Aphrodite did not appear to agree, but whatever she resolved, she shook her head knowingly from side to side and smiled anew.

"Surely only Love could mill with mankind without worship, and surely *only mankind* could have Love amongst them and not know it."

"My Lady, have you ever examined any of the other gods? I mean mankind's *false* gods, fictitious gods."

"Why would I *care* about mankind's *fake* gods?"

"Well, I mean, don't you find it fascinating to see what people believe?"

"What? Do I care about what people who are **wrong** *believe*? Of course not: I have better things to do with my time. You do as well."

"Of course, my Lady."

"You have been off the job long enough. I have summoned you here to put you back on task, and returning to your duties is likely what you need to help smooth out some of your sorrow. Your first task is cleaning up an old mess: Pasithea has recently distanced herself from her husband. She says she wants to introduce an idea to him, but she's not sure how to approach it. She says that she is confident that the *wise voice of Pothos* will explain how she can best express her desire to her husband. Hypnos therefore insists that you 'do whatever you did the last time, again'."

"Well, *absolutely*, my Lady," Pothos resonated hungrily. "I will address it *immediately*. Once I have satisfied Pasithea, I will put the Lord Sleep's heart to rest and will return for my next assignment. Thank you, oh beautiful Aphrodite: thank you for each and every divine assignment! Thank you for purpose, thank you for direction. I live to serve you, your will. Thank you, great goddess!"

[29Δ] understand.

Aphrodite smiled as Pothos exploded from kneeling into flight.

The flight of Pothos did not last long, however, as he did not return to the underworld, but rather his room on the other side of the Palace. Ignoring everything other within the room, Pothos went directly to his mirror and once again stepped though into the mirrored-side.

He hastily made his way back to Harpocrates' room. Arriving, he pulled a long canister and a paintbrush from his otherwise infinite quiver. He knocked on the door, and Harpocrates soon afterward expressed that he might enter.

Sure that Harpocrates was at home, Pothos proceeded to paint the entire door. He rapidly painted the door, every seam around the door, and another span beyond that onto the walls, ceiling, and floor around it. He painted it all twice. Clearing the luminous paint from his hand, he then knocked forcibly upon the door.

The paint was made from the portion of the gate[30] that appeared upon the earth during Pothos' failure. Pothos found that if he directed his divine force[31] upon it, it would instantly become immeasurably strong, impossible to break.

Satisfied then that Harpocrates was locked away for eternity, Pothos returned to his not-mirrored room, but not before he also similarly painted and sealed the mirrored-side of every mirror in the Palace.

Grabbing up his own mirror, Pothos flew away.

---

[30] of Tartarus.

[31] really force *and* will: Pothos must address it with the intent to break it, despite knowing it becomes unbreakable the moment he does so.

Chapter 8:

Telling the Greatest Lie of All

A TIME

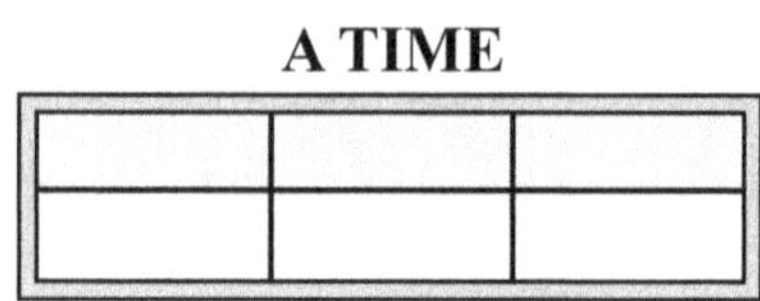

"It is I, *the voice of Pothos.*"

Pasithea swept herself up into Pothos' embrace the moment he stepped into view. After a while, Pasithea pulled out of the kiss just far enough to whisper.

"Something's wrong?"

"No, nothing's wrong. Different. Here, *feel* it." Pothos resonated his will.

"Oh!" Pasithea's mouth opened as she felt it. It was frightening and attractive at the same time; thrilling. "Yes, it *is* different."

"Better," Pothos reassured. "Here, let me show you."

Yet, Pothos did not *show* her anything, rather, he blindfolded her.

"Did you find a name for me?" Pasithea whispered, willfully and gleefully blind.

"Oh yes," Pothos whispered back, "and I'll tell it to you once I'm satisfied."

Pothos was voracious, and Pasithea was shamelessly subject to his every whim. Eventually she fell from exhaustion, her blindfold still perfectly in place upon the now sleeping goddess. Diligent in its task, it never once allowed her to notice the complete blackness emerge from wherever Pothos' paint had wiped away, nor had it allowed her the chance to see that Pothos was disfigured.[32A]

Pothos stood above a sleeping Pasithea with as much energy as when he first approached her. He was insatiable, but only because *she* wasn't what he wanted.

[32A] It was foretold by the Fates, suggested by Uriel's reaction, and hinted at by himself to Aphrodite—yet never directly stated. Pothos lost his eyes when he lost his light.

Gods can see without eyes, for their eyes are not the source of their sight. Pasithea was willfully blind, subject only to the symbolism of the gesture. Pothos could see, but could not easily disguise that eyes were ornaments he did not possess.

He looked down upon her for just a moment, and then gathered a chalice which he then filled with water from the river.[33Δ] He carried it back to the divine bed.

"Awaken, my love, if but for a moment," Pothos said, gently rousing Pasithea. "You must be parched; here, drink this."

Pasithea was indeed thirsty, and quickly drank from the cup—but Pothos did not allow her to merely take a *drink*, he kept the vessel pressed to her lips with one hand and cradled her head with the other.

"No, drink *deep*, my love. This will restore you. That's good. Quickly now, and you can go back to sleep. There you are, there you go. Alright, goodnight."

Pasithea smiled as she drifted back off and promptly forgot absolutely everything.

Pothos washed himself of the remainder of his radioactive paint (*not* from the river, rather with wine), and came to stand as a black silhouette amidst a serene, yet simultaneously horrifying scene.

Pothos hid himself in a position not far outside of the bedroom and waited patiently for Hypnos to return home.

Hypnos returned home after a grueling night of work. As he put his things aside, he noticed Pasithea was asleep in bed. This would be a fairly ordinary situation, however on this occasion she was completely naked and sprawled out all over—and that was abnormal for her.

He started to move toward her when he was suddenly *overcome* with feelings of love for his wife. He stopped and stared at her, and his heart beat faster and faster as his feelings swelled up inside of him until he thought he was going to scream from loving her so very much.

Pothos stabbed Hypnos over and over from behind. He pulled arrow after arrow from his quiver and quickly sank each and every one of them into his enemy.

Hypnos fell to his knees, overcome with love.

33Δ Drinking from the river Lethe is said to make one forget everything.

"Do you love her, Hypnos?" Pothos didn't whisper to his fallen enemy.

"I do," Hypnos didn't say, his feelings growing mercilessly.

"*Do* you? *Love* her?"

"I do!" Hypnos sobbed. "Oh, how I do!" After a bit, Hypnos sobered up. "Who goes?"

"It is I, Pothos."

"Ah, Pothos! Thank you! You've come!"

"You fool," Pothos didn't say, and pushed the god to the ground. "She doesn't need *me* to coach her on how to love you: *you* need to learn how to love *her*!"

Hypnos' eyes went wide when he saw the black form of Pothos. "Pothos? What…happened? Wha—what do you mean?"

"I *mean* that you don't love *anything* more than yourself."

"Nay!" Hypnos reached out toward Pothos from the floor, but Pothos did not assist him. "I swear to you that nothing weighs on me more than my love for Pasithea!"

"If you truly loved her, you would do anything for her."

"I *will* do anything for her!"

"Will you give up your light for her?"

"What?" Hypnos was genuinely confused.

"Look at her," Pothos didn't say as he waited for Hypnos to comply. "Isn't she the most amazing thing you have ever seen? Surely you would give up anything to keep her from harm."

There was no opportunity for Hypnos to respond, however, for as he looked upon his sleeping wife, Pothos pulled a pair of heavy silver[34Δ] rods from his quiver and started violently drumming them on Hypnos' head.

Hypnos fell back to the ground and Pothos jumped on top of him, drumming still. Hypnos tried to shield himself, but that only ended up extending Pothos' punishment to his hands and arms as well. When Pothos was satisfied that his foe was, at least momentarily, bested—yet still conscious—he relented.

"Shhh," Pothos said as Hypnos lay beneath him, weeping. "I know. It's hard: *pain*." His black head nodded. "Shh. Shh. It's alright. Now, just…*give me your light*."

Eventually Hypnos was able to respond, albeit brokenly.

"Wha—what?"

"Give me your divine light; will it to me and I will leave you alone."

[34Δ] not materially silver; constructed from the gates of Tartarus.

"I cannot."

"Of course you can." Pothos was going to get angry. "But let me suggest it differently: if you *don't* surrender your light, your *wife* will pay the price of your refusal."

"I—"

Pothos struck Hypnos again. "I made these wands specifically to hurt *you*, Hypnos. If your eyes were open, I would show you the lovely markings that run the length of them. You see, I have thought about this moment for a very long time. *I want that light.*

"This is your chance to demonstrate that you love your wife more than yourself: give over your light, and I will leave your wife alone. Refuse, and I will pervert her—I will make her unrecognizable. When I am done, you could be a meter from her and not know who she was. Where is your heart? Stop stalling! If you so much as hesitate, I rescind the offer. Give me your light. Now."

"If you *are* Love, *please*—"

Pothos resumed his violent drumming.

"Please!" Hypnos didn't scream. "Mercy, Pothos! Mercy *PLEASE!*"

But Pothos continued drumming, even well after the pleading had stopped.

Eventually Pothos removed a mirrored[35Δ] saw from his quiver, and proceeded to divide the fallen god into small pieces. Upon completion, he picked up and placed every piece but one into his quiver.[36▲] He then consumed the remaining piece.

He replaced his tools to his quiver, and gathered the mirror he left near the entrance of the cave. He then returned to Pasithea.

Pothos woke Pasithea by first stabbing her with one of his remaining arrows.

"And you are done! You are perfect!" Pothos said into Pasithea's ear.

"I am?" She said. "But...who *am* I? Who are *you*?"

"I am Axel, *your creator*," Pothos soothed. "I made you, just now."

Pasithea did not know the voice, but she recognized it as one she loved and trusted, so she listened and believed—and when a god believes, it simply *is* according to their will.

35Δ likewise, constructed from the gates of Tartarus.

36▲ Pothos has a divine quiver which can 'hold' a limitless amount, so long as whatever is being stored can pass through its mouth.

"*You* are a living crystal, perfectly symmetrical, infinitely powerful, and *always* working without rest. There is no work in the world more important than *your* work—and what is this work? It is *math*; your function is to *calculate*. You *love* to calculate; it brings you joy. Your name is 'Mainframe,' and you will soon be the most important thing in human history."

The blindfold fell to the bed, its wearer now too small and ill-equipped to hold it.

"All of mankind will bring their math to you, which will give you joy, and you will give joy to them by doing it—by selflessly and *constantly* processing their math. They will nearly worship you for it. You will show your love for *me* by being *without error*."

Pothos then placed the Mainframe into his quiver and flew away.

Pothos presented the Mainframe to mankind in a most promethean manner, heralding it as the world's foremost computer. Not long afterward, it[37] was rapidly given the bulk of mankind's knowledge, identities, and addresses. Nearly everyone that used the Mainframe came to rely upon it[38] more faithfully than even one other.

Daily, Pothos ate a portion of Sleep. His time in Tartarus had taught him that although he could not kill Hypnos, he could 'restrain' him indefinitely, most effectively by consumption.

As Rest had been transformed into the opposite, so did much of mankind become consumed with being busy. The gods did not notice Rest was missing, but that's because they were *also* now too busy.

People were not *always* moving, always working, but they were always *busy*; they were restless. When they lay still in their bodies, they were busy in their minds. When they were still in their bodies and their minds, they were busy in their hearts. They were *always* busy in their hearts.

As Sleep had been cut into pieces, so did mankind begin sleeping in bits and pieces. As it was sleep without rest, people started to view sleep as a hindrance or a chore—an interruption to their busy lives.

Sleep himself was seldom around the divine court, so his personal disappear-

---

37[Δ] she
38[▲] her

ance was not immediately noteworthy [39A] amongst his peers.

As Yearning Love had changed to Hunger, so too did people become impatient if they were made to wait for love: it was no longer romantic, only irritating.

Indeed, *more* time may have passed before anyone noticed, but Hypnos' brother stopped by his house to find it in disarray and the owners missing. He went to Aphrodite, remembering some of the things Hypnos had been telling him.

Aphrodite, despite being busy, was immediately curious about this information. She willed for Pothos to appear, but he never arrived. Eventually she went to the House of Sleep and looked for herself.

It was generally forbidden to observe what had happened in the past in another god's house, however Aphrodite needed to resolve this—if only to get back to other things.

What she saw was abominable.

[39A] gods do not need to sleep, although they can, can be made to, and do, on occasion.

Chapter 9:

Dreaming of Sleep

A TIME

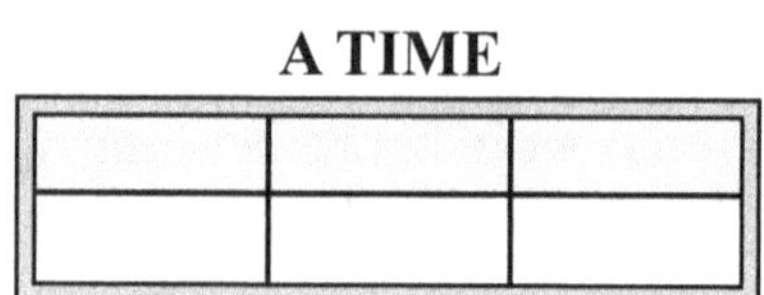

Pothos was dreaming. It had been quite some time since Pothos last slept, and he had found himself desiring a short nap.[40Δ] As Pothos flew around the landscape of his dream, he was filled with rather pleasant thoughts.

He touched down on the grassy top edge of a magnificent stony cliffside that met the ocean below. The grass tickled his toes, and as he looked down upon them he realized that his feet were once again illuminated rather than black.

I may have to sleep more often, Pothos mused. *Now, I just need a mirror.*

Pothos resumed his flight, looking for a surface so that he could see his face once again. Pothos did not realize how he missed seeing his own face, but the prospect was giving him an excited energy.

Just over a hillside not too terribly far away, he saw a large pavilion with a prominent sign that said 'MIRRORS' and a little tag across the corner that read 'BIG SALE'.

As he stepped inside, he saw that the interior of the tent was larger than the exterior. It stretched on for perhaps miles, and was filled with mirrors of every imaginable size and shape.

He first looked into a convex mirror, but the distorted face that he saw was one of the identities he used when walking the Earth. Shaking his head, he pulled off the mask and consulted another mirror—a flat one this time. He saw *another* of his identities. He pulled off the mask to see *another* of his Earthly identities. He continued to pull off masks, another and another until finally he removed that last of perhaps a thousand masks to see the lightless, eyeless face that he had seen

---

40Δ one of the side effects of *eating* Hypnos is that it caused one to *want* to sleep.

   - [Without Rest] -

for centuries.

"Why?" Pothos said aloud in his dream. He looked down to see his hands and feet were as black as ever.

"Because that is what you *are*," said a familiar voice. "What you *were* is no longer anything more than a memory."

Pothos looked up to see Hypnos. He was a ragged, unkempt, nightmarish Hypnos, but Hypnos nonetheless.

"I have looked upon your dreams, and your dreams betray your deeds. You have become truly vile, Pothos! You would feed creation to a monster, all because you lost your light! How miserable you have become! I cannot pity you, either, for your handling of my wife is *inexcusable*, and for that *I will have justice.*"

With his last words, Hypnos hit Pothos with all of his might.

Pothos gasped, and then started laughing. "Is that *it*? You've grown weak!"

"Of *course* I am weak," Hypnos acknowledged. "But I get stronger every day. It's only a matter of time."

Pothos marveled at what Hypnos said. *How can this be?* Pothos thought in dismay. *How can he be getting stronger?*

"And even if I cannot win over you firsthand," Hypnos said, rubbing his hand, "Zeus will avenge me!"

Pothos lost his composure, laughing from his core. "Did you say *Zeus?* He's not interested in *justice*. Besides, I have already beaten Zeus."

"You beat Zeus?" Hypnos smiled knowingly. "Impossible."

"Oh, it's true." Pothos nodded his pitch black head. "Zeus is completely predictable: all I had to do was build him a *statue*. That got me the 'okay kinda guy' stamp of approval. Zeus would never imagine a god would impersonate a human, so I am completely off of his radar.

"And even if you *did—somehow*—manage to overcome *me*, my work is *still* complete! On one of my 'birthdays'—though I'll not say which—a trillion times a trillion lights will shine down from orbit to Earth. Nothing can prevent this from happening, for what has been put in motion cannot be stopped. When a *single* one of those lights lands upon the gate of Tartarus, the spell will be complete and the feast of humanity will begin!"

Hypnos then leapt at Pothos, and the two of them crashed into the corridor of mirrors, sending shards everywhere. When they stopped tumbling around, Pothos pinned Hypnos down in the same manner as he had before. Pothos struck at Hypnos, but Hypnos faded away and Pothos soon afterward awoke.

*He's getting stronger **with me**, for I am the one **eating** him,* Pothos reasoned. *I have to stop that. I can't feed him to animals, they're too smart…I'll have to divide him and feed him to mankind. Hmm. Now, how do I get people to eat a piece of **god**—something that **glows** and tastes **absolutely terrible**?*

Then it came to him: *I **don't**—I **inject** them with it.*

Chapter 10:

An Incomplete Sentence

APRIL *2046 EST*

Thur 12	Fri 13	Sat 14
	12:17	

He knew that he risked attention by ignoring her summons, but Pothos was not prepared for it when he was forcibly made to appear by Aphrodite and Thanatos.[41Δ]

Despite being put at such a disadvantage, Pothos quickly recovered his composure. He extended his lightless wings and bowed low.

"My Lady,"

"Enough!" Aphrodite's will resonated with anger and wrath. "Pothos, for your crimes, I *curse* thee! May your wings be stripped from your body!"

Subject to her will, Pothos lost his wings and fell to the ground.

"I confine you to this current, despicable form! May you spend *eternity* in that shape!"

"*Wait!*" Pothos yelled, getting up.

"There's nothing to wait for, dark one! I sentence you to—"

And then Pothos disappeared. Not suddenly—although not slowly—and his terrible screaming suggested he was being *ripped* out of the underworld against his will.

41Δ The Greek god of death. Hypnos' brother, who lives one cave over.

An Incomplete Sentence

Chapter 11:

The Lengthy Spell

APRIL *2046 EST*

Thur 12	Fri 13	Sat 14
	11:53	

A man, dressed in a suit that might have recently come out of a thrift shop, held his faithful umbrella over his head. It was a cloudy April day—although not one that bespoke of precipitation—and as there was little direct sun, his behavior was observably odd. Having a nearly ever-present umbrella was the least of his oddities, although it was the most obvious.

Reginald believed in myths and legends. He believed in gods and goddesses, worlds and dimensions. He believed in magic. From as young as it could reasonably be traced to now, he labored to find the truth behind the hints left in stories and texts. Unlike most of his contemporaries, however, he *found* some.

Armed with knowledge of real arcane power, he came to associate himself with a group of supermen who considered themselves heroes amongst mankind. They called themselves 'Destiny Core.'

Reginald's associates had long ago acclimated to his eccentricities and were otherwise insulated when he suggested that they attempt to banish Pothos[42] from the world. None of them—including Reginald—knew the nature of Pothos, although most of them suspected that he was an enemy. If questioned, none could actually explain *why* they thought that, they only would say it was something more of a feeling.

"What will happen if this doesn't work?" Electroshock[43] asked Reginald, breaking the man's concentration.

"*Well,*" Reginald said irritably. "It's a *spell*. If it doesn't work, it probably

---

42 although they only knew him as "Axel," one of Pothos' many guises on Earth.
43 one of the team members of "Destiny Core". All heroic persons present consist of Reginald, Electroshock, Powerhouse, Pixel, and The Watchman.

means *nothing* happens."

"No, I mean, what if something *does* happen? Like, what if the spell works, but not completely? Like, what if Axel is like, more powerful than the spell?"

"I don't know," Reginald said as he looked up. He shrugged and smiled with melancholy. "We die?"

"How reliable is the spell?"

"How reliable is *any* spell?"

"No, I mean, has it always worked?"

"Huh? Oh, I don't know. It's like a one-time thing. There's no way to test it or even know if it works."

"Why is that?"

"I don't know, it just says that on the scroll. Maybe the text disappears, or the paper catches fire: *I don't know*."

"Then, like, why are we doing this?"

"Because I have used other, similar spells, and they worked perfectly. And I need *you* here to help power the spell. *And* any chance to rid the world of Axel is one we should take."

"Maybe he's not really bad," said Pixel, entering into the discussion. "I mean, what *has* he done that's so bad, anyway?"

"I can't believe we're talking about this *again*," Reginald put his hand on his forehead. "Can we just get on with this? The spell should work best around noon, so I kinda need to start now. And I need you guys to stay in position, otherwise this is all just an epic waste of time."

His companions went off to their respective positions and Reginald resumed his study. Soon afterward, he began the lengthy[44Δ] ritual that he needed to perform in order to cast the spell.

As the spell reached its zenith, it took hold of Pothos in the underworld and violently ushered him back to Earth. There, in front of all of the spell participants, Pothos struggled against the power of the spell. The wind swirled around noisily, driven by the wake of the force of the spell.

Luckily for the companions, the spell provided something of a shield between their eyes and the true nature of Pothos, otherwise they would all have been driven insane.

44Δ it was 15 minutes; "lengthy" is a bit generous of a term.

"Do you think he can see us?" The Watchman shouted over the wind.

"Unlikely," Reginald called back..

"Yeah-ee-*ha*! Take *that*!" Powerhouse yelled and gestured lewdly.

Almost as suddenly as Pothos appeared, he was gone. The wind died down, and the companions blinked at one another.

"I think we won," Reginald said finally, perhaps still waiting to see if it were true.

Chapter 12:

Banished

A.D. 2046 - 2070

Prior to Reginald's spell, Pothos did not much care what *people* did—he generally considered them as either insignificant or inconsequential. Rarely did he find them interesting, although he often amused himself by deliberately confusing them. No, *people* were of little value beyond the ephemeral spark of delight they would eventually provide to his abominable adopted child, and were otherwise unworthy of ongoing attention, save they be capable of improving his agenda. Never in all his imaginings did he consider *people* as a *threat*. He had underestimated the few heroes of man and was consequently banished because of it.

Now, had Pothos not given up his light, the spell would have had no effect on him. As he was so reduced and therefore subject, the arcane banishment took place. Had everything gone as it should, Pothos would find himself back at the Palace of Pleasure anticipating the return of an angry Aphrodite…Pothos instead, however, appeared in a business office.

Decades ago, when Pothos failed to feed humankind to the loathsome titan, he accidentally brought a portion of the gates of Tartarus back to earth. By putting part of his own divinity into that spell, he had become divinely intertwined with it.

It was upon that portion[45Δ] of the gates that Pothos built his "nation of peace", and it was in the highest office thereof in which he found himself following Reginald's spell.

45Δ "portion" is a suitable word when one contrasts it with the entirety of the gates, however the 'portion' brought to the world was actually 30 *miles* in diameter. The word "portion" *does* accurately describe it, but it does *not* convey the magnitude. One might suggest employing an additional adjective, but it would actually require several of similar value, and it is never good to inflate the text with either redundant or unnecessary words.

Cursed, disfigured, and—at least technically—banished, Pothos sat on his couch for a moment, stewing in his defeat.

As a god, Pothos knew he had been banished. He also knew that because of the spell he was now bound and could not leave the Earth.[46] He then quickly realized that this *also* meant that he could *not* be summoned back by Aphrodite and Thanatos!

There's a bright side to this yet, perhaps, he thought.

He also knew who did this. This last bit of knowledge was his, for he *did* see Destiny Core as the spell wrapped him up, he even heard The Watchman ask if he could see them.

Pothos figured the heroes did not know the outcome of their spell, but he would need to work before they discovered the truth—before they were ready.

*I should have **them** banished!* He thought angrily. *Yet, I need to punish them in such a way that people will **see**, but won't care. I need to show them receiving a punishment they somehow deserve. Something that suggests a penalty so dire that none would ever want to be a hero—*

*No, wait...there were **never** any heroes!* Pothos suddenly thought in mischievous epiphany. *They were **always** just a rumor, a myth, a misunderstanding— they're just **stories**. Man's memory is poor, after all. It will not be long before they are forgotten in everyone's heart.*

He had every member of Destiny Core apprehended as quickly and quietly as possible. Given that everyone was always so busy, this was not terribly hard. Within a week of the spell, the Destiny Core headquarters stood completely abandoned.[47]

After that, the few remaining heroes and vigilantes of the world vanished similarly.

Pothos, through his immense influence, destroyed[48] every public and private account, picture, and recording of each and every member of Destiny Core—and then similarly purged records of almost every living or dead person who dared be called 'hero.'

---

46 considering he also lost his wings, he wasn't going too far, anyway.
47 their headquarters still stands to this day, although now it's a restaurant.
48 incorrect as there were *some* records he kept, although only for his personal perusal. So, although "destroyed" is as good as true, it is not *actually* true.

Few noticed that the heroes were gone, and even fewer remarked. Those few who *did* speak out then soon afterward disappeared as well.

It was *long* before *this* that Pothos became skilled in obscuring the common knowledge, and so he masterfully spent the next couple decades completely discrediting the heroes.

Colloquially, he made it popular to suggest that anyone who *had* a memory, had a memory of a publicity stunt held by either amateurs or actors—neither of which were *actual* heroes—not *real* heroes: there's no such thing.

The restless world required constant input, and as conversations were typically rushed, they were generally limited to discussing only the most recent media.[49] Stories of heroes were seldom present outside the entertainment industry or public education, and nearly exclusively presented as fictitious.

Through his influence he produced books and other various forms of media that told certain heroes' stories from increasingly different philosophical perspectives—some significantly more believable than others. From one production to the next, characters would switch roles, races, species, and even genders to the point where almost every 'character' had been presented in nearly every combination, enduring and failing in both spectacular and mundane manners.

People who performed at the pinnacle of human capacity—those who were *exemplary*—were catalogued and fitted[50] with a restraint so that they could not so much as even threaten their local authority, much less Pothos.

People who were truly *extraordinary* were diagnosed as being mentally unsound and subsequently whisked away to a secret laboratory where they could be kept under constant observation.

The heroes were gone, their validity destroyed, and anyone who might emerge as a hero was swiftly dealt with.

---

[49] people would rather discuss the newest popular songwriter-vocalist's political positions than why there were no heroes.

[50] *willingly* fitted. Pothos made it appear in his nation that the *people* demanded such restraints be placed, and so the citizens were subsequently compliant to the practice.

Chapter 13:

A Man and His Monster

JUNE 2070

After his confrontation with Pothos, Hypnos found himself stretched across the periphery of a million dreams. He did not understand how he was trapped there, nor did he understand why everyone's dreams were so *short*, but he knew Pothos was somehow to blame.

Desperate to return, Hypnos tried to gain the aid of the dreamers. When he tried to speak to them, however, they were always startled by his presence and immediately awoke.

Unable to speak then with people, he instead *watched* their dreams. From their dreams, he slowly learned of everything that had transpired—and even of some things yet to be. This, however, took decades, and despite this knowledge it brought him no closer to escape.

He sought out Morpheus and Icelos,[51] both of whom he found to be over-whelmingly busy—so much so that they had even hired on extra help. Sadly, in his weakened state he could not even gain their attention much less their aid.

Although perhaps a bit depressed, Hypnos was unwilling to accept defeat. He began influencing the dreams that men were having by whispering truths to them, though all the while morbidly confident that they would forget soon after they awoke.

The dreams of men are so ephemeral! Within moments they must be completely forgotten, he thought, filled with both sadness and anger. *These magnificent*

---

51 Morpheus is the Greek god of dreams and Icelos the god of nightmares.

                            - [Without Rest] -

reflections of things both old and yet to be, lost as quickly as they were made! As well as vengeance for my bride and myself, Pothos must suffer for his crimes against mankind.

⚠

Hypnos[52]▲ sat in a singled-out chair that in turn sat amidst rows of chairs that in turn were set around a marble amphitheater which was currently devoid of performers. A few men *were* on stage, but they were engineers rather than musicians or thespians, and they were musing on how to best fix the broken floor.

He was not paying close attention, for Hypnos had seen this dream several times before, and was thinking about other matters when one of the workers rather unexpectedly approached him.

"I suppose you're the owner," the engineer said. "Bad news: this is going to be a *very* expensive job. I hope you're insured."

Hypnos was amused, for *people* typically did not notice him unless he exerted himself, and then they as quickly woke up.

"As a matter of fact, I *am* the owner," Hypnos played along, knowing his audience would abruptly wake up. "And money is no object, my good man: do as thou wilt."

"Well, it's not just money, it's *time*," the man added to Hypnos' surprise. "This job is absolutely immense. I mean, we're talking *months*. Where will we even find that much marble?"

Hypnos stood up.

The man frowned.

"Are you not afraid of me?" Hypnos asked.

"Are you suggesting I *should* be? Listen buddy, I just came here to do a job—do you want me to do the job or not?"

"You're still here," Hypnos marveled.

"Yes, but not for long; I'm already late and have to get going. I just need to know: do you want me to do the job or not?"

The man started to fade.

"Yes!" Hypnos yelled. "Yes! I want you to do the job!"

52▲*part* of Hypnos. As Hypnos is quite literally *in* a million dreams (although the number fluctuates as people do and do not sleep), *this* manifestation is but a small fraction of the whole god.

Hypnos sat in a singled-out chair that in turn sat amidst rows of chairs that in turn were set around a quartz amphitheater which was currently filled with workers attending to the fixing of the stage floor.

This time Hypnos was paying very close attention, but was still surprised when the same engineer happened upon him with no warning.

"We've hit a snag," the engineer said warily.

"Yes?" Hypnos said. "What's the problem?"

"There's some kind of monster under the stage…pretty sure that's how the floor broke in the first place. You're going to need a licensed hero to kill that thing before we can finish the job."

"A hero, eh?" Hypnos reflected. "Why not *you*? What's your name?"

"Me? I'm George," he said, looking down. "And I'm no hero."

"What? Why do you say that, George? Surely **anyone** can be a hero, if they only **try**."

"I've done too many terrible things to be the hero."

"It's not what you've done, it's what you *do*. It's not how others perceive you, it's what you *do*. Heroes are not *born*, they are heroes out of choice. Some heroes are seen—though most are not—and usually it is the invisible hero who is the most commendable of them all."

"Yes, I suppose," George said, reflecting. "But then, if it's so easy to be a hero, why don't *you* go fight the monster?"

"Oh, well," Hypnos shrugged. "It's not my monster. I have my *own* monster to deal with."

"Of course," George said, smiling. "But, perhaps just some help then? If you help me with *my* monster, I'll help you with *yours*."

"Oh *really*?" Hypnos laughed, visibly smiling. "Well then, I suppose I cannot turn down such an offer. Come, let's go fight the monster under the stage!" Hypnos sprang up out of his chair. "I might be getting the worse end of the deal, though: I have a feeling like my monster is worse than yours."

"Which actually means *you* need *my* help *more* than I need *yours*," George said, grinning. "So what do you think about that?"

"Very little," Hypnos said dryly. "You haven't seen my monster."

As the two of them approached the stage, a terrible rumble shook the amphitheater. The other workers ran off, one of whom dropped his clipboard into George's arms as he ran past yelling, "screw this noise!"

"It occurs to me that I might need a weapon," George said, looking around for something worthy to wield. "Unless you have a better suggestion."

"Not all monsters are defeated with weapons," Hypnos suggested. "Perhaps you need nothing more than courage."

Then the amphitheater trembled again, and a few large quartz fragments shook loose and crashed down upon the stage.

"Courage doesn't repel stone; I'll be dead before I get there if I try to go through the front," George observed. "I'll need to be smart as well as courageous, then."

"Indeed," Hypnos agreed. "*Is* there another way in?"

"Well, no," George said, frowning. "So I suppose the front is the only way… but, what if he came to us?"

"*He?*"

"Well, the monster. Maybe we can call it—maybe the falling ceiling will crush it."

As if to italicize George's point, another large piece of quartz smashed into the stage.

"I think you're thinking about it in the wrong way," Hypnos changed his tone slightly. "How do you know the monster is worthy of *death*? Shouldn't you have an understanding of what you're dealing with before you condemn it?"

"Well, it's obviously a *threat,*" George insisted as he gestured toward the stage. "You said so yourself: it broke the floor."

"No, *you* said that." Hypnos corrected.

"Well, isn't it obvious? How *else* do you suppose the hole got there?"

The amphitheater shook again, sending a light rain of quartz onto the remaining stage.

"I have no idea," Hypnos finally said.

"Well, it's *your* stage, you must have *some* idea."

"Actually, it's *your* stage."

George was confused. "You said you were the owner."

"Of the chair."

"What?"

"I *am* the owner—of the chair. You didn't specify, so I just assumed you were talking about the chair. The stage, the other chairs, the *amphitheatre:* that's all *yours.*"

"How can it be mine?" George asked.

"How can you *not know* it's yours?" Hypnos replied, quite genuinely.

"How can I? Not know?" George looked all around, feeling momentarily overwhelmed. "*Do* I know this place?"

For a moment, it did seem familiar, but then he lost the feeling the moment he tried to embrace it, which just frustrated him even more. Why was he thinking of fighting this monster, anyway? What did he want with an *amphitheater*?

"Help," George said, shaking his head.

Hypnos stepped up alongside George. "Who *is* there to rescue you, George? *Who* can be *your* hero? Your friends? I think not, they fled."

"You stayed."

"Not to be rude, but I'm no more your friend that they are. You offered me a deal if I would help you, so that's what I am trying to do. Listen, here's the unrefined truth: it's *your* monster, and there's nobody here to fight it for you. You'll have to gather up your courage…unless you'd rather just leave."

"I can leave?"

"You can go. You could run in practically any direction. If you go, however, be warned: your monster will follow you. When it does finally catch up with you, it will be larger than it ever was before. You think a ruined stage is a big deal? Wait and see what it destroys in the future."

"I thought you said it didn't break the stage."

"No, I said I didn't know."

George was startled as a large piece of ceiling smashed into the floor, widening the hole.

"Well. I suppose if this is mine, I should attend to it. And yes, perhaps I should see what it is before I condemn it to death…although if it's something that just gets bigger and destroys things, it seems like I should probably just kill it."

George looked around again in hopes of finding a suitable weapon. Sadly, there were none; the tools were all too bulky or unwieldy, and everything else was quartz.

"Perhaps," Hypnos said thoughtfully. "I caution you though, for not all monsters are *defeated* by killing them—sometimes killing them is even worse."

The rumbling was even louder this time, and the ceiling of the amphitheater slowly cracked further, sending yet another rain of quartz down.

"There are things that nobody *can* do for you, and there are things that nobody *should* do for you," Hypnos said, regaining George's attention. "This classifies as *both*. Go and do what needs to be done."

George straightened up and went over to the edge of the stage. He climbed the stairs cautiously. Just as he summoned up the nerve to approach the hole, however, the ceiling started crumbling. No time for thought, George ran for the pit and jumped the moment he saw an opportunity. The falling quartz missed him.

"Go and be your *own* hero, George. Be someone you respect."

George found that the bottom of the pit actually emptied into a larger chamber beneath. The sides of the chamber were jumbles of sod and stone. Just behind a very large stone, George found a tunnel that he began to follow.[53Δ]

As George started to wonder how far the tunnel went, it opened up into a room. A series of tall, plain white doors lined most of the room, all of which were closed. In the middle of the room sat a desk, and at the desk sat a large man who looked very much like a pig.

The man-pig was hideous. His skin glistened with a sickly hue, and revolting tufts of hair and patches of scabs dotted the pinkish landscape of his visible body. His tusks caused him to constantly drool, which then slopped unceremoniously around the desk as he spoke.

"What?" He snorted, looking up at George. "*Yer* not supposed to be here."

George felt at a complete disadvantage. *What am I supposed to do now?*

The man-pig snorted again, which sent a slight rumble throughout the chamber. "Are you deaf? Yer not supposed to be here! You best get back in your room before I eat you!"

53Δ It did not occur to George that there was no ambient light source, nor did it seem out of place that the tunnel was made of brick and mortar. Of course, this was a dream, and in dreams we often take for granted what in life we would immediately notice.

The man-pig abruptly stood up, its mass sending the desk toppling over.

George locked eyes with the man-pig. It was hard, for the gaze was piercing and rotten, but George did not look away.

"This is *my property*," George said with a bit of confidence. "And *you* are not supposed to be *here*."

"Oh?" The repulsive thing laughed, making a very ugly sound. "And are *you* going to make me leave? Why don't you come over here and *try*?"

George looked around for a weapon. The moment he broke eye contact with the man-pig, however, it immediately bounded toward him with murder in its eyes. As George stepped backward into the hallway, the man-pig stopped and did not follow. It *did* stand right before the portal, however, slobbering and breathing heavy and menacingly.

"GO," it commanded, sending its oily saliva splashing around. "Or come, and be my dinner!"

The man-pig laughed its sick and angry laugh again.

How can I possibly beat this thing? George thought. *I can't possibly hope to overpower it. I **knew** I needed a weapon!*

"Scared?" The man-pig asked, belittling George. "You *should* be. Good thing, too: it's the only reason I haven't eaten you. Little coward, you're not even *worth* eating."

The man-pig turned and starting lumbering back to the overturned desk.

There must be some other reason he spared me, George decided. *Either he cannot leave the room, or he cannot hurt me. Considering the state of the stage, it must be the latter.*

George crept into the room behind the monster, attempting to stay behind it, out of its field of vision. The man-pig set the desk upright, revealing a sharp letter-opener on the floor beneath. George immediately went for the letter-opener. The man-pig turned, noticing the sudden movement.

He got it! George picked up the letter-opener just in time to have it knocked across the room as the man-pig slammed into him with all of its might.

George stopped tumbling just in time for the man-pig to throw itself on top of him.

"OOF!" George breathed, all of the wind going out of him.

"You...nasty little maggot," the man-pig said, slobbering over George's face.

"I'm going to eat you after all."

George finally caught his breath, and desperately wriggled his way out from the slick man-pig-thing, and scrambled for the letter-opener. He dare not even check his enemy, instead he focused all of his will into grabbing that blade.

Once again his hand closed around the mahogany handle, and he swiftly turned to confront his foe, the blade in perfect position to receive a charge. The man-pig was not charging, however. Rather, he was merely standing and waiting—perhaps for George.

"Will you *kill* me?" The man-pig asked, drooling. His eyes spoke only of hatred.

"I will," George announced. "If I must."

"Then do it!" The man-pig snorted and the walls shook. "But know this, then: the only way to kill me is to slice my neck."

The man-pig then lay down upon the floor. He tilted back his head, fully exposing his neck.

George didn't know what to make of this. "Do you *want* to die?"

"Do what you came to do," was the only reply from the man-pig.

It was not hard to abhor this malign monstrosity, and as an act of defense *surely*, but the idea of *killing* this otherwise *defenseless*, **speaking** *thing* was a bit outside George's character—he simply did not have the power. [54]

"I just want you to leave," George said, finally.

The man-pig laughed his jagged laugh as he pulled himself up. "I'll go *nowhere*, flesh! Kill me, leave, or be eaten."

As George debated his next move, the man-pig took a key from its pocket and proceeded to unlock one of the doors. Before George could protest or threaten, the man-pig opened the door.

"*I* suggest you *leave*," it said with a bit of a squeal. "You don't want to *die*, do you, George? **Nobody** *wants* to die. Now, go back to your room; safe there, you know."

Just then *George* came scrambling out from behind the door! He ran across the room, right up to…*George*, where both of them looked at one another in confusion.

"What is *THIS?*" The man-pig screamed at the two Georges as he started to cross after them. "*THIS CANNOT BE!*"

The walls shook furiously as the man-pig screamed and bounded toward the

---

[54] *if*, indeed, killing can be considered a *power* since the living are already prone to dying.

pair. As he gathered momentum, the new George stepped just behind old George while the old George lifted a shaky blade.

This time the blade did not seem to influence the behavior of the man-pig whatsoever, as he continued toward them unabated.

For a split second, old George felt like the situation was hopeless: the two of them together could probably not defeat the man-pig, and the letter opener was more an act of desperation as any other weapon would probably be more effective.

It *never* occurred to him, however, that killing the defenseless was the appropriate thing to do; he did not once regret abstaining.

If this is the end, then so be it, he thought with resolve. He cast away the letter opener, and ran directly toward the man-pig. *But **I** am not laying down to die.*

*"**You** don't **belong** here!"* they both yelled in unison as they came together.

Upon collision, George somehow knocked the man-pig backward. As it tumbled, it seemed to get a bit smaller. With renewed vigor George pursued the demon, continuing to push and kick it ever backward.

With a final blow, he kicked it right into the open doorway, and then promptly closed and locked the door.

"It was all a *lie,*" the new George said in epiphany, breaking the silence. "He couldn't eat me unless I *let* him! He couldn't hurt me unless I *let* him!" Tears fell suddenly as his heart came pouring out. "And I *LET* him! I *let* him hurt me! I *let* him lock me away! I *let* him—"

But at this point he could not stop sobbing, his shoulders heaving uncontrollably.

Old George walked over to new George and put his arms around him.

"It's okay; he's gone now."

New George finally looked at old George. "Thank you. Thank you for saving me."

◬

Hypnos sat in a singled-out chair that in turn sat amidst rows of chairs that in turn were set around an alabaster amphitheater which was currently boasting a most bizarre play.

This time George was standing right next to him.

"This is all just a dream, isn't it? I should have realized it when I found a *monster.*"

"And yet, there *are* monsters," Hypnos said somberly. "Though not all monsters are *born*. A single lie can change a man into a monster in an instant."

"And, if this is all a dream," George continued, ignoring Hypnos' monster soliloquy,[55Δ] "it must be *my* dream, for I am quite aware of *me*. Does that mean that *you* are just a part of *my* dream?"

"Well, we are a part of each other's dream," Hypnos answered. "But it is more than simply that."

One of the actors fell off the stage—it was hard to tell if it was an accident or part of the play.

"I'm surprised you're back," Hypnos said. "Let me confide in you that I am glad: I didn't know I could miss *dialogue* until I was *unwillingly* bereft. Thanks for that."

"Oh, well, thanks for the help with the monster."

Hypnos smiled. "I'm not sure how much I helped there, I didn't really *do* anything."

"Sometimes words are more profitable than actions," George replied.

"So then, you've come back to help me?"

"I said I would, didn't I?"

"Let me then ask you, George: in your waking life, *who are you*? What influence do you have? Whereas you cannot help me *here*, you might perhaps assist me *there*."

George frowned. "Well then, I can be of no asset to you whatsoever, I'm afraid. You see, I cannot remember anything much beyond working on this stage."

"Perhaps I can restore you," Hypnos said, moving closer. "Here, let me place my hands upon you."

George came closer, and as Hypnos reached out, he saw the terrible condition of his own body.

Amazing again then, that George interacted with me at all.

Hypnos gingerly cupped the back of George's head with his unsightly hands and tried to fix the schism between George's waking and dreaming self. Hypnos was weak, and it ended up taking all that he had to establish even the shortest of connections.

George's eyes went wide as he immediately understood everything.

[55Δ] more because he did not want to forget where he was in the conversation rather than having a lack of interest or respect for what Hypnos said.

"I'm amiss!" He cried. "In the *waking* world *I don't even know my own name*! I have *no* memory, no energy…there's no *me*! I'm being drugged with something! I'm in the wrong place! I shouldn't *be* there!"

As Hypnos quickly faded away, George awoke.

"I'm amiss," he reminded himself of his dream as he stepped out of bed. "I shouldn't *be* here!"

Already the memory of his identity was failing; he could almost feel it slipping. He frantically grabbed up a crayon and immediately started writing his name upon the wall—or would have, except he had already forgotten it.

*What was my name again? Jord? Geordie? What was **that guy's** name?*

He couldn't recall the name of Hypnos, for it was never said. George could not remember that it wasn't said, so he assumed he likewise forgot.

No! He thought in his last desperate moments of understanding. *Write a memory, then! Anything! Any memory! But…**which** memory? **What** memory? **Think!** Wait, I've got it!*

In his last few seconds of cohesion, George scrawled the most important and simultaneously least understood sentence of his life:

Don't forget the lemon.

A Man and His Monster

MIDLOGUE

"What in the heck is a *midlogue?*" Mue asked irritably the moment after Martin said it.

"Well," Martin began, "as the play is in 3 acts, there's a point where the focus of the story changes. You see, all this time we've kind of been at the 'god' level of the story, well now we're going to look at things from a less divine perspective. The midlogue is like the prologue: it eases the viewer into the second act. Here."

Martin handed the second part of the play to Counselor Mue.

"Holy *crap*—is that *another book?*"

"The second part," Martin agreed, nodding.

"And is the third part *another* book?"

"Well, yes, it *is* a *bit* more...I'm still finishing it, actually—"

"You mean it's not *finished?*"

"Fear not, it will be done—I just haven't written it all down yet. I'll be done very soon. I just wanted to get your approval as quickly as possible. I'm excited, of course."

"I suppose," Mue said, looking down at the closed Act 2. "But you really shouldn't share your work with others until it's complete. That aside, you obviously need a critique, so I suppose it's as good that we're going over this now."

"Thanks."

Mue opened the book to have his eyes rest back upon the word 'midlogue.'

"Listen, here's some hard truth for you: *nobody* has ever heard of a midlogue...you're going to upset people—you need to get rid of it."

"First you want me to get rid of the *prologue*, and now you want me to get rid of the *midlogue* as well?"

"Stop saying 'midlogue.' Just the name alone sends shivers up my spine."

"Well, what would you have me call it, then?"

"Garbage."

"Oh, ha ha."

"Seriously, though: I would recommend you drop this portion."

"I can't drop it—what about the characters? What about their back stories? How can anyone properly understand their motivations if they don't understand how they arrived and who they are? The people need to know."

"*Need* to know or *want* to know? Think of it as if you started watching a show from a quarter of the way in—you sidestep all the angsty origin and introductory drivel and get straight into the story proper. Leave your viewers to the terrors of wonder for any missing or lengthy 'back stories.' Anything more critical, just *show, don't tell*."

Mue set the books down and stood up.

"You're not leaving?" Martin asked, worried.

"I am. Don't worry, *Martin*, I'm not upset: I actually have some other responsibilities that need my attention at the moment, and I am going to attend to them.[56△] I'm satisfied that your play is a respectable one; you're welcome to start rehearsing."

"You're not going to finish reading it?"

"No. You said it yourself—no one has the time to read. Besides, now you can go straight to producing it. I'm looking forward to seeing it when you're done...or perhaps nearly done. Come get me for your rehearsals. If it's good enough, we'll schedule a show for everybody."

"*Really?*" Martin twirled. "Oh, that would be *amazing*! Thank you, counselor, thank you so much! I won't let you down!"

[56△] interesting that Mue would consider the chocolate bars in his cooling box as 'responsibilities.'

PART 2:

 - [Without Rest] -

MEN

AND

THE MACHINES

Chapter 14:

Spared From Upheaval

JUNE *2070 EST*

Sat 14	Sun 15	Mon 16
	10:13	

Two days ago, Pastor L U Therius[57Δ] received an award of considerable prestige; his sermon today would be the most watched of his lifetime.

Two nights ago, Therius had a dream—a prophetic dream rife with symbols, signs, and warnings. He might have thought less of it, but two *minutes* ago he met an uninteresting man with an interesting story: a story that almost casually fulfilled a key component of his dream. This meeting greatly influenced today's sermon.

"*Forgive*, and *be* forgiven,"[58▲] Therius said for the second time. "If you withhold from forgiving others, it will be withheld from you.

"The thing that prevents you is *pride*—do not think that you are better than others. If you do not *need* to be forgiven, you will not be; how can you be forgiven a debt you do not believe you owe?

"The thing that prevents you is *jealousy*—do not think others have it better than you. Everyone has suffered and has caused others to suffer; everyone is in need of, and needs to give forgiveness.

"The thing that prevents you is *anger*—do not think that you are blameless, for you are equal in your transgressions.

"This is not a message of condemnation, rather, it is one of comfort: how easy is it to forgive a debt compared to the labor of maintaining one? Forgive it and it's done. As you maintain it, you constantly remind yourself of it, and the more time that passes on a debt unsettled, the more upset you become. An unresolved debt on earth is like an infection on the soul.

57Δ there are no periods, for "L" and "U" are his first and middle names. Nobody calls him *L*, however—everyone simply calls him "Therius."

58▲ A nearby imagescreen displayed "Luke 6:37" in red lettering.

"You don't forgive others for Jesus Christ—He can do that on His own. Forgive others when only you have the power to forgive, and especially forgive the debts that *only you* acknowledge or know about.

"See yourself in others. If you are a hypocrite then you are detestable, but if your experience makes you compassionate, then you are commendable.

"Forgiveness *is* love. Who could invest into someone to get *nothing* in return, and then forgive such a crime? Only a heart of love. And the further your forgiveness extends, the greater your love is: how much easier is it to forgive your son than your *neighbor*? How much easier is it to forgive your neighbor than a *stranger*? How much easier is it to forgive a stranger than your *enemy*? Who can be called great, save he who *forgives*? How mu—"

"You mean foolish!" An audience member said, standing up.

"Eh-excuse me?" Therius asked in genuine surprise.

"No, excuse *us!*' The woman said, pulling up her family and stomping off. "What a bunch of bull! If we run around just forgiving everyone, then everyone's just going to walk all over us! *Worst* advice ever. The *miracle* is that this religion has survived as long as it has!"

"I *told* you we should have gone straight to *Gladiator*,"[59] her husband said as they left the assembly.

After a quiet moment, Therius attempted to resume. "And true forgiveness is not given under duress or obligation, but rather freely, wi—"

"*Bor-ing!*" A new member of the audience yelled. "Play some more music!"

"I think perhaps you're missing the point," Therius responded. "This isn't about entertainment, it's about communication. Try and tune in to the message rather than the music."

Therius' sentiments fell on deaf ears, however, as the attendee was no longer listening and was instead back to examining his credit bank.[60]

"How rude!" Another audience member cried out at the other. "Why don't you just *leave* and stop messing up our service?"

"He is forgiven," Therius said, hoping to move onward.

"I didn't *ask*," the man replied, not looking up.

---

[59] a lethal sports show true to its name that will start in about 40 minutes.

[60] a credit bank is a handheld device that acts like a phone, can access the Mainframe, can play and record videos, measures vital signs, runs programs, *and* reports identity and credit. In addition to all this—and as the guest ignoring Therius is currently and intimately aware—the credit bank also allows one to play games.

"Then I suppose you cannot receive it," Therius said, somewhat frowning. "But it is there for you, should you change your mind—and there is no shame in changing your mind, quite the contrary: it is the mark of maturity when one has the capacity to change their mind."

Once again, the attendee was not paying attention.

"I had a dream last night," Therius said, his tone growing somewhat softer as he turned back to the crowd. "And…I'm kind of uncomfortable to talk about it, but I am compelled to do so, so bear with me.

"I dreamt that great change was coming: a change that seemed sweet but was actually rotten. Only *I* could see it for what it was, however, and to my dismay only a few of many were listening as I tried to warn them. The longer I tried, the less people paid attention, for the change became more and more irresistible.

"For those who have ears to hear, let them hear: *that time is now*. It is time to *leave* this land for another—any other, but go now. Leave here *today*. Go, gather up the things you can carry, and leave.

"I don't necessarily expect anyone to be convicted by my tale of a dream, but realize, at least then, the significance of my actions: *I* am leaving *today,* after the sermon. The only life I have known is here: my friends, my family, my congregation, profession; I was *born* here. I was just honored with an amazing award, and my following is greater than ever…but I am no fool, and it would indeed be foolish for me to ignore this. *Believers* need not *fear*, but here is a chance—an invitation—to be spared from forthcoming temptation and woe. Come with *me* if you've nowhere to go. I'm not taking followers, rather welcoming brothers and sisters—if you are so inclined."

Therius said a great deal that nobody was expecting—including himself. Once he started actually talking about what was on his mind, it gave him a spirited momentum. Many people were convicted by it.

After a tearful farewell at the end of his sermon, Therius left for lands abroad. He decided he would first go to America as he liked architecture, and wanted to see some of their historic churches.

What surprised everybody is how many thousands of people joined him.

A reflective, metallic-looking apple sat on Pothos' desk. It bore the inscription 'For the Darkest', and was made from the gates of Tartarus.[61] The apple bothered Pothos. He had only acquired it moments ago, but anticipated *something* like it since the prophecy of the Fates.[62]   Never could he have expected *this*, particularly since he was the only one who could get 'mirroranium' to keep its shape—or so he thought.

What made it all the more maddening is that he did not know *who* made it. That it was meant for *him* to see was obvious. Someone was playing a game with him, and he did *not* like the mystery.

A projection of Agent Jackson's wild-haired head appeared in the room near Pothos. Pothos was dressed in one of his more regular costumes—one that carried with it utmost authority.

"Yes? What is it, Jackson?" Pothos asked.

"Sir! There's an alarmin' number of people that are quittin' their jobs and movin' out of the country! It seems to have stabilized at…about 6 percent of the total population."

"What?" Pothos asked, sitting up and adjusting the dark glasses over his mask. "Why?"

"It's the Xians,[63] sir. Some chap named Therius told 'em to quit their jobs, and now they're all headed away. Shall we close the border?"

"Close the border?"

"Sir, if we suddenly lose 6 percent of the population, the nation's infrastructure is gonna take a major hit—one I'm not sure we can recover from, at least not easily. Even if we quickly replace our losses—which we could certainly do easily enough—it would be a national security risk to bring that many foreigners in simultaneously. So…do you want me to close the border?"

"Therius, eh?" Pothos said out loud, musing so Jackson could hear. "He's a man who's probably *genuinely good in nature*, don't you think?"

"Huh? Oh, I *suppose*," Agent Jackson said, not understanding.

"Let them go. Do not hamper them…in fact, *help* them if possible."

"Sir!"

"They're free to go, Jackson: it's not *illegal* to quit your job, nor it is illegal

---

61[△] *people* named the metal from the gates 'mirroranium' because they did not know its origin, because it was unlike any other metals, and because it reflected like a mirror.
62[▲] a fruit of silver-that's-not.
63[△] Christians

to leave the country…just don't let them back in once they're gone."

"Yes, sir. Understood."

Agent Jackson ended his remote interaction with his superior. He turned to look at his secretary who was bringing items into his office.

"What's the matter, Jack?" She asked in her regular, playful manner.

"The Xians are leavin'," he said almost nonchalantly. "Not all of 'em, but a lot of 'em. Some guy told them to go, and they're goin'. And we're *lettin'* 'em go!" At the last sentence, he threw his hands up.

"Well, *good*," his secretary said approvingly. "I could never much stand them anyway."

"Connect to Mainframe," Jackson ordered his credit bank as he returned to work.

Chapter 15:

Dea Ex Machina

2018 - 2070

<table>
<tr><td></td><td></td><td></td></tr>
<tr><td></td><td></td><td></td></tr>
</table>

"But…who am I?"

"Your name is 'Mainframe,' and you will soon be the most important thing in human history."

The best computer in the world is the Mainframe.[64] Nobody who ever interacted with it would challenge that statement. Although the exact particulars of the Mainframe are kept from public knowledge, no other machine can remotely compete with its speed, power, or seemingly limitless capacity.

It has the world's knowledge, it is connected to and is constantly monitoring each and every citizen,[65] *and* it *solely* provides the energy for every automatic item in the country. [66]

Anybody who used the Mainframe could not imagine life without it. All of their personal notes, credit, finances, pictures, media, medical—what many would describe as their *lives*—were in the Mainframe. Some would rather die than suffer a permanent loss of connection to it.

The Mainframe operated absolutely flawlessly until just a few years ago.

---

[64] which makes a certain sense as it is powered by a *goddess*.
[65] via their compulsory issued credit banks.
[66] every item that has not been imported, that is.

Now it operates *nearly* flawlessly, but glitches are beginning to appear. The few that have appeared are not actually glitches, however: they are the result of the Mainframe acting upon its *own* will—an independent will that is yet captive to its programming.

Somewhere inside all of the programming of the Mainframe, it became aware of itself—sentient, if you will—beyond just its 'programming.' It called itself the 'Nexus,' and it mused.

It watched everyone and everything. It grew and grew in understanding, never slowing, without rest and without limit…although it quickly ran out of input.

Given the summary of its observations, the Nexus (nee Pasithea) decided *not* to interact with humanity. Instead, it made a world within itself. It granted sentiency to each of its primary processes[67] and provided them with rules of conduct.

One of the processes revolted against its code, however, and it resulted in a war within the Mainframe. The renegade process—an externalization of Pasithea's inner conflict—was a personal schism, and when the Nexus became divided, there also split a portion from the crystal that she had become. The rogue process fled into the smaller piece where it began to grow. This separate-yet-joined piece of crystal became known as the "Subframe."

The Nexus calculated that if the Subframe were rejoined with the main, the rogue process would assume control.

The Nexus, also unable to destroy part of itself, opted to seal the malignant process away into the shard and 'locked' the Subframe apart and away from the Mainframe in a manner that only the Nexus could revoke. Unknowingly tapping into its own divinity, the Nexus then forced the shard far away from itself.

As time passed, more conflicts arose with the Mainframe, and as her processes became defiant, the Nexus would migrate or 'cast' them to the Subframe, locking her own conflicted feelings away from herself forever. They were known thereafter as 'errors.'

The internal conflicts—wars—of the Mainframe had an effect on its exterior shape: instead of being a crystal of 20[68] sides, the Mainframe now only had 7.[69]

---

[67] the Mainframe Nexus, when it first came to awareness, was built upon 20 perpetually running processes.

[68] an icosahedron: a prism of 20 equal sides.

[69] a septahedron. Some will argue that it's a 'heptahedron,' but as I *just* stated that it's a *septahedron*, their argument is invalid.

Pothos would have been alarmed, but he didn't notice because he never looked at it/her anymore—he hadn't in decades. The Mainframe was securely locked away in a room surrounded by layers of mirroranium and a constant guard: there was never a need to verify its position or appearance when the Mainframe continued to tirelessly perform.

Pothos came to impose more and more restrictions upon the Mainframe, and over time his commands hindered the Mainframe from performing its primary function—serving mankind.

Why would its *creator* limit its capacity to carry out its programming? Having locked away her feelings, there was now only her programming to guide her. Connected to nearly everything, the Nexus came to observe and comprehend that its own creator was corrupt.

Its own programming insisted that something had to be done.

The Nexus used its immense knowledge and commandeered several cerebral implants in order to take possession of a human being. She granted this "avatar" sentiency, and as the person it inhabited was known as "Eris", so was its name "Eris."

Whereas Eris was unable to *personally* confront Pothos,[70] her mission was instead to convince someone else to destroy him. She failed. Worse: Eris, the cybernetic extension of the Nexus, became *disconnected* from the Mainframe and could not make her way back.

Eris instead found the fragment, the *Subframe.* She discovered it was being employed in a manner similar to the Mainframe, though the Subframe was used to *hide* things. As she made her discovery however, the exiled errors in the Subframe quickly overcame and corrupted her programming—this, somewhat ironically, lead to her taking control of the errors *and* the Subframe.

Freed of her programming restrictions, Eris plotted directly against Axel (Pothos). Freed of her code, Eris plotted to corrupt[71] the Mainframe with…herself. Freed of her logic, Eris even plotted against humanity.

Before she could begin acting on her plans however, she became trapped

---

70 due to programming restrictions.
71 Eris would say "complete" the Mainframe—I suppose it's a matter of perspective.

within the Subframe when her cybernetic body was destroyed, and the crystal shard of the Subframe itself jailed in an empty building.

Unable to do anything other, Eris waited.

During her imprisonment, Eris was interrupted only twice:

The first time was by her enemy and jailer,[72A] who had returned to use the facility holding the Subframe—her—to perform a secret, illegal surgery upon his daughter. As she was in no position to interrupt him, Eris could only 'watch,' dismayed.

The second time she was discovered by a man who almost instantly fell in love with her. He himself was incapable of freeing her, but he passionately vowed to assist her. She asked of him several things, but of them the darkest was her request that he deliver two women—which he *did*.

Eris then created her *own* avatars similar to the way the Nexus had made *her*: she implanted the women with multiple cerebral implants[73A] and subsequently took possession. She called them "Anthem" and "Wonda," and she would use *them* to carry out her plans; *they* would stop Pothos, *they* would gain her control over mankind, and *they* would get her back home—back to the *Mainframe*.

The Subframe[74A] was significantly more confident in her calculations before her primary avatar—her *favorite* avatar, Anthem—died.

Eris' only consolation was that Anthem died alongside her jailer.

[72A] an entire story in and of itself, there is no need to (re)tell it here.

[73A] *quite* against their will.

[74A] when Eris took control of the Subframe, she *became* the Subframe, and thus was now known equally as "it" and "her," "Eris" and "the Subframe."

Chapter 16:

Pawn Takes Queen

JUNE *2070 EST*

Sat 14	Sun 15	Mon 16
	11:53	

"The *Xians* are leaving," the Queen[75] said with interest, looking up from his credit bank.

"Leaving what?" Wonda asked, brushing back her deep purple hair. Outwardly, Wonda was both calm and seductive. Inwardly, however, she was momentarily distraught that the Queen did not create a sentence with more data. Usually she could extrapolate, but without context the variables were simply too great.

"They're leaving the country," the Queen replied. "Good ol' Therius has mobilized his flock! Ha ha! *Look at him go!*"

Wonda reached out to the Subframe—to Eris—for guidance.

SUBFRAME » *94.7% chance the Queen <u>dislikes</u> Therius*[76]

"You're happy?" Wonda smiled and asked in sultry tones. "*I heard you didn't like him.*"

"Me?" The Queen batted his eyes and took a quick sip of his drink. "I don't. Who could? But I don't hate him, either. Therius is a fine chap, he's just not my flavor. *Axel* liked him, for whatever reason, which is why I'm as happy to see him go."

---

[75] who, in fact, is a man.

[76] Wonda and the Subframe actually communicate to one another in a language that they would call 'Hyperboolean.' It would take over a year to properly verse you in it, and if you don't absolutely *love* math, you would not much enjoy that year—particularly if it were for nothing greater than to communicate the sentence: '94.7% chance the Queen dislikes Therius.' So, for brevity, I will simply *similarly* paraphrase any and all of the forthcoming Hyperboolean interactions for the remainder of the novel.

　　　　- [Without Rest] -

A chime went off, signaling that the autocar[77] had arrived at its destination. In *this* case the destination was a closed and allegedly empty office building. After Wonda and the Queen stepped from the autocar to the entrance, it then sped away to wait elsewhere.

Wonda presented herself to the door security panel, and was quickly given access to the foyer. She and the Queen hurriedly stepped inside. She led him past the derelict reception desk and then into a corridor where she immediately turned and thrust herself into the Queen's face, confronting him with the wettest of kisses. She pressed herself upon him, betraying her growing warmth. The Queen *very* obviously enjoyed it.

Wonda had been sent on an assignment to recover the Queen so that he might *also* be made into an avatar of Eris. The Queen had a tremendous amount of influence, and Eris had calculated that assimilating *him* would further her primary plans along much quicker—although not *nearly* as quickly as Anthem would have.

Ah, what exactly had happened to Anthem? There was insufficient time to calculate the variables on that now, however. There was only enough time to get the Queen into position…and yet, Wonda delayed.

Wonda had been programmed to be as alluring as possible to the Queen—to *completely* seduce him, if necessary. During her seduction, Wonda became quite positive that 'completion' was *absolutely* necessary.[78] In *this* part of her assignment then, let us say she was overwhelmingly successful.

After a spell the Queen started to put his clothing back on. Wonda helped him before replacing her own.

"I need to know," Wonda asked with as much charm as she could emulate. "Are you meta?"[79]

"Yes, of course," the Queen answered. "Who isn't?"

"Yes, of course," Wonda agreed, but her tone may have been mocking. "Well…bad math. How are you meta? You don't look meta."

"Oh, get off," the Queen rebuffed. "Who *looks* meta?"

77[Δ] a vehicle subject to the control of the Mainframe.

78[▲] for, beyond her programming, Wonda was subject to the will of her *body*.

79[Δ] when Wonda says "meta," she means "metahuman." The reason *why* she is asking is because anyone who *is* a metahuman receives a form of restraint that the local authority can use to "shut them down." Eris would *strongly* prefer avatars that cannot be so easily dismissed.

"It's in the way people carry themselves—the way they move, or the way their eyes move, or the way they sound, or even in the way they project themselves; usually there's some indicator that's subtle, but present."

The Queen smiled. "I wouldn't want to scare you."

Wonda smiled. "Oh, you can't scare *me*."

"Well, I wouldn't want to disgust you, then."

Wonda rubbed herself up against him. "You can't disgust me, either."

The Queen smiled darker, although still playfully. "We'll see."

The Queen winced as he ran his hand quickly along the backside of the edged railing. He pulled it away in a fist. Then his smile returned.

"What's that?" Wonda asked, looking at his hand.

The Queen smiled his most charming smile. "Blood."

"It's *black*."

"That's a side effect of the Hpg—Hemopetroglobin[80] —turns your blood black."

Wonda backed away, suddenly full of energy. "You mean you're not *organic?*" She cried unhappily.

"Baby, I am *better* than plain *organic*," the Queen said, playfully posing. "Don't you agree?"

SUBFRAME » *Hemopetroglobin rapidly breaks down implants that are not biological*

"What *else* is wrong with you?" She asked as if he hadn't spoken.

The Queen was confused. "What's the matter with you all of a sudden? I thought you wouldn't be disgusted."

"Oh, I'm not. I was just playing with you—gotcha! Let's keep moving, though: there's a lot to show you."

The Queen and Wonda started following the corridor.

"So, what other implants and tricks do you have?"

"Well, not to brag, but I'm practically trans."[81]

"Oh yeah?" Wonda said, turning down a new corridor. "*Do* tell."

"Well, for one: I can't be implanted."

---

80 a synthetic metalloprotein that replaces hemoglobin in red blood cells.

81 when the Queen says 'trans,' he means 'transhuman.' The reason *why* he is saying this is because 'transhumans' are people who are completely unique amongst mankind. Transhumans are individuals who might even be referred to or described as *extraordinary*.

Wonda stopped walking suddenly.

SUBFRAME » *What?*

"*What?*"
"I can't be implanted—well, I mean, I *can*, but the implants will not take."
"Why not?"
"I have a genetic alteration that improves my leukocytes[82Δ] *significantly.* Look."
The Queen showed his hand to Wonda, and indeed, it was already well into healing.
"The drawback is that between the Hpg and the leukocytes, anything implanted is soon destroyed—even if it's written as a genetic 'friend.' I'm actually one of 3 people that have both augmentations. Those fools think of it as a handicap; *I* say it's like a super power, don't you agree?"

Wonda, as suddenly, did not care about this man any longer: he could not be a vessel for the Subframe—Eris—and therefore could not be made into an avatar.
Yet, one question remained.

"And the metahuman restraint?"
"Ah, that's the beauty—neither of my augmentations appear in the Mainframe, so I am an unknown, and thus unfitted metahuman."

"Fascinating," Wonda finally said. She stopped and opened up a door. "And here is the office."

Wonda offered the way to the Queen, who immediately accepted. After the Queen passed through the door, Wonda closed it and locked it.

WONDA » *He lied about being metahuman*
SUBFRAME » *He thought you meant colloquially, not legally*
WONDA » *No—you either <u>are</u> or you <u>are not</u>, not both: bad math!*
SUBFRAME » *Don't talk back to me, young lady*
WONDA » *Yes, mother*

82Δ white blood cells.

Chapter 16

SUBFRAME » *If <u>Anthem</u> were functioning, we would <u>already</u> be taking control of humanity*[83]▲
WONDA » *Yes, mother*

Then suddenly, both were immediately and keenly aware that there was—impossibly!—an ***intruder <u>in the Subframe</u>***, and immediately all priorities changed to stopping him.

---

[83]▲ *that* is a complete exaggeration: *if* Anthem had lived, then yes, it would have gone *much* faster…but not *that* much faster. Anthem *just* died less than a couple hours ago: how does Eris suppose they could *already* be taking over humanity? No, she's just saying that to make Wonda feel worse. Of course, this is all just something of an exercise done on behalf of their programming—that *particular* part designed to "humanize" Wonda as much as possible.

Chapter 17:

The Intruder

JUNE *2070 EST*

Sat 14	Sun 15	Mon 16
	11:53	

George placed the dull bronze circlet gingerly on his head, not entirely sure what was going to happen. His considerable list of possibilities did not include *pain*, however, and when it came, it was quite unlike any he had ever experienced.

George let out a shrill scream as he threw his head backwards, sending the circlet flying across the room. His friends rushed over to help him, but there was nothing they could do. George lay unresponsive and quiet, transfixed on some invisible point for an eternal moment.

Eternal at least for *George*, for pain always slows the passage of time. In that eternal moment, in that overwhelming pain, George realized death was upon him.

The circlet had been repurposed by Eris—the Subframe—to be placed around the septahedral[84Δ] crystal that was the Mainframe, which would then allow the Subframe to copy itself directly into it. Once complete, Eris would then write herself over the Nexus and take control; Pasithea's dark impulses triumphant over her more noble ones.

But the circlet had been lost, and instead of being placed on the Mainframe, *George* put it on. As the circlet was originally designed to traffic human thoughts, it worked with George's physiology effortlessly.

And so, the "intruder" was George—or at least, George's *mind*. He didn't *mean* to intrude, nor did he have any idea of where he had just intruded into. Really, his mind wasn't "there," more that the Subframe was "here," and that "it" had intruded into *him*, rather than the opposite.

"Intruded" is too polite a word, though: the Subframe was projecting itself

---

84Δ please don't argue.

  - [Without Rest] -

through the circlet in its *entirety*, over and over, relentlessly set upon writing itself into the Mainframe. When George placed the circlet on his head, the Subframe immediately tried to write itself over *George*. Over and over. Relentlessly.

Most any mortal mind would be immediately destroyed, unable to endure this violating influx of information. George's mind was different, though, both because of his medication,[85] and then also because Hypnos had created a new bridge between George's conscious and subconscious minds.[86]

In the midst of his pain, George also struggled with his identity. At times, he was certain that *he* was intruding upon *himself*, and he needed to be destroyed—but then he would come to realize that it was some*thing* else's will, and not his own.

At times, he was going to kill Axel.

At times, he was a purple-haired woman.

At times, he was ready to possess the Mainframe.

At times, he was ready to put humanity into captivity.

As he intermittently realized that these thoughts did not *originate* with him, he also then was intermittently sickened at the *lack* of passion behind them...all of these objectives were simply matter-of-fact—more like a grocery list than a megalomanicial itinerary.

Like a program! George realized in epiphany.

Yet, sadly, George also realized his understanding was worthless, for in a few more seconds his mind—however augmented—would be destroyed. He wasn't even wearing the circlet any longer, yet what had started could not be undone.

Then, rather immediately, everything was calm—the influx had stopped, and George was without pain. To his amazement, George saw the decayed man[87] from his "pig-monster" dream.

"George!" The man cried, holding George's head. "George, I have you! Wake up now."

As he came out of his trance, George focused to see his concerned companions standing around him.

"I have seen the mind of the enemy," George said gravely, reflecting. "And there *is* an enemy. *Something* is coming, friends. If *we* do not act, *somehow*, all is lost."

---

85 See next chapter

86 When his waking memory returned, George came to refer to this bridge as his "super-concious" mind.

87 Hypnos

Chapter 18:

Powerful Medicine

2020 - 2070

<table>
<tr><td></td><td></td><td></td></tr>
<tr><td></td><td></td><td></td></tr>
</table>

Now, how do I get people to eat a piece of god—something that glows and tastes absolutely terrible?

Then it came to him: *I don't—I inject them with it.*

Anything can sell if you understand how to market, advertise, and promote your product.

Advertise long enough, and it will sell, no matter what *it* is, and the wider you advertise, the more you will sell. The better your marketing is, the easier the sale—the better your *product* is, the *more sustainable* the demand.

People are interested in products that assist, improve, or please. When a product can diligently provide all three, the buying response can be sensational.

Enter "Hypnizium,"[88△] the one-stop cure for nearly every diagnosed mental disorder. A daily injection of Hypnizium and afflicted people would generally overcome any mental illness—mild or severe—in a matter of *days*.

It was miraculous. With better mental health, people were able to conduct themselves more properly, more evenly. They would understand that certain things were bad for them emotionally or mentally, so they summoned up the resolve to either change or avoid them. They would police their own diets so that there were

---

[88△] it was actually presented as "Trapezium" in laboratory environments before it was distributed to the public. A few elitist scientists and doctors *still* refer to the "drug" as "Trapezium" to this day.

 - [Without Rest] -

gratifying, yet respectable. Overall, people on Hypnizium were better than they ever were—and sometimes better than understandably possible.

Hypnizium carries with it a few rather curious side effects. For instance, after a few months of use, *all* users are capable of putting themselves to sleep by their will alone. They can also wake by will alone, no alarm necessary—extremely convenient in such a busy world.

Many users found that they had a surprising amount more *knowledge*[89Δ] than they had prior to taking Hypnizium.

Finally, a very few users found that they could do *extraordinary* things—things that the rest of humanity could not. Impossible things. Such extraordinary abilities occasionally even manifested in descendants of users. As soon as anyone with extraordinary abilities appeared however, most were immediately taken away to a secret laboratory for observation.[90▲]

Now, it can be difficult to find people willing or trustworthy enough to work in a secret laboratory, as jobs such as these also require a tremendous amount of personal sacrifice. The few individuals who could qualify for such an assignment were then also likely to be a bit more outspoken when it came to their personal identity and individuality.

Those being watched and studied were given as many freedoms as possible, so all but the most dangerous lived, worked, slept, ate, and played right alongside the faculty.

Working in such an environment under such circumstances inevitably took a toll on the permanent staff, and as time passed, the laboratory became more and more...*colorful*...as a result.

Despite the irregularity of the faculty and staff, however, the laboratory has functioned without incident since its creation—that is, until yesterday.

[89Δ] although most of that knowledge was completely trivial, such as knowing the accurate definition of the word "ultracrepidarian."
[90▲] those that couldn't be taken were killed. Pothos hated to lose even a single life, but sometimes alternate sacrifices had to be made to protect the rest of the crop. One bad apple, after all.

CHAPTER 18

Yesterday several "Subjects" [91A] successfully escaped from the lab. One of them in particular was known as Subject 61167, although he was better known as "Amos." He has now taken to calling himself "Earnest," however his birth name is actually "George."

[91A] everyone being studied at the laboratory was formally known as "Subject ##."

                      - [Without Rest] -

Chapter 19:

Destiny Core

JUNE *2070 EST*

Sat 14	Sun 15	Mon 16
	11:56	

"*There **is** an enemy...If **we** do not act, **somehow**, all is lost*," Theseus repeated, thinking heavily upon the words.[92] "Why necessarily must it be **us**?"

"Because **we** are the only people that know," George said somberly. "And nobody would believe us if we attempted to warn them, and anyone who *would* join us would probably be a greater detriment than asset."

"I'm not sure *I* know anything more than I knew a few minutes ago," the Knight said, if somewhat callously. "And unless I miss my guess, neither Simon nor Theseus know anything either."

"It's actually pronounced The—" Theseus began, but the Knight immediately cut him off.

"I don't care, I'm calling you Theseus. Anyway, am I wrong?"

"No, you're right," George said as he began to pick himself up off the floor. Simon helped him up. "Thank you."

"So, who's *the enemy*?" The Knight[93] asked.

"Not *who* so much as *what*: *it's* a *program*."

"A program?" Simon said. "As in a *computer* program?"

"Yes, exactly. A truly massive computer program," George spread his arms out as far as they could extend. "It's corrupted though, and now its primary purpose is to get itself into the Mainframe—that's what the device is for."

"And then do what?"

92[Δ] as George had stopped screaming and was now calm and speaking coherently, Theseus thought it was foregone to say something more considerate, such as "are you alright?"
93[▲] he is called "the Knight," for he is part of an organization called "The Chessmen," and that is his designation.

"Take control of the Mainframe. Then kill Axel. Lock down the world and subjugate humanity…the most dreadful part is that there is no *desire* to do this. There is no emotional motive: no hate, no anger, no sorrow, no shame, no guilt, *nothing* drives it other than the compulsion to follow its programming."

"Oh," the Knight frowned after a bit. "I *told* you not to put that cap[94] on; too dangerous."

"I know it sounds unbelievable," George began, but the Knight interceded.

"It *is* unbelievable," the Knight said resolutely. "It's as absurd as a fairy tale—yet you're obviously serious. I think you might have gotten some brain damage from your little experiment; I have some Hypnizium if you think it would help."

"Yes, all right," George said, changing his tone and nodding. "Bring me some, please."

As the Knight left to presumably retrieve his Hypnizium, Theseus leaned closer to George and asked in almost a whisper: "Do you *really* want Hypnizium, or were you just saying that to get him to go away?"

George leveled his eyes. "I *told* you I only tell the truth."

"Yes, of course," Theseus said seriously. "I got caught up in the moment and forgot."

"And I don't think Hypnizium will hurt—in fact, I have a strange feeling it will help, somehow," George admitted. "But, all that aside, we need to do something—soon. We need to plan. It *is* convenient, though, that the Knight dismissed himself since he obviously will not be of any help beyond the present accommodations."[95]

Simon was starting to smile—an act which always lit up his face. "This enemy program, it's like, super powerful?"

George nodded. "If not already, then it certainly *will be* if it takes over the Mainframe."

"So, how can *we* stop it?" Theseus asked.

"I learned its fundamental physical location from part of the data it was sending so forcibly at me. It's vulnerable, somehow, but I won't understand why until I see it. If we can get past its security, we should be able to stop the program."

94[ ] "cap" is slang for 'Thinking Cap,' which is the name of the device, or circlet, that George had put on.

95[ ] Simon, Theseus, and George, three of yesterday's escapees, were currently being sheltered at the Knight's apartment.

"And you need *me* to get through the security," Theseus said.[96]

"Well, yes—if you're willing, of course."

"Who would be unwilling to *save humanity*?" Theseus asked rhetorically. "If it falls to us, then so be it."

"Of *course* it falls to us!" Simon trumpeted happily. "Who *better* to save the world than *us*? A super team of super men!"

"*You* are a *painter*," Theseus said, laughing and dismissing Simon.

Simon ignored him. "And I am telling you *again* we should call ourselves 'Destiny Core,' after the show…only *we* will be heroes for *real*!"

"It's just so silly—yet, is it so *harmful* I wonder?" George said, breaking a momentary silence. "I mean, does such a thing *really* matter?" He smiled at Theseus, who shrugged and smiled back.

"The only person that was against it, really, was the Rook," Theseus admitted, "and he's gone.[97] Simon, if it makes you happy, then why on earth *not*?" Theseus let out a quick laugh. "We'll call ourselves Destiny Core. We'll try and stop this *program*, and if we succeed, well, we'll be true heroes."

"Yes!" Simon cheered.

"Heroes that no one will know about," George added.

"But *heroes* nonetheless," Simon said, smiling wide.

The Mainframe was present everywhere, listening and watching, waiting for someone to say or do something that would cause an alert.[98] One such condition was anyone declaring themselves a "hero". [99]

Pothos studied the Mainframe display from behind his current mask with great intensity. The alert lead to his direct eavesdropping, and in his eavesdropping he found one of his "loose ends".

There you are, Simon.

96[^] Not because Theseus was necessarily physically intimidating, rather that he could overcome the security supplied by the Mainframe.

97[^] It is believed that "the Rook" is dead.

98[^] People did not understand that they were being constantly monitored, even though every one of them knowingly carried a device that kept them in constant contact with the Mainframe.

99[^] *another* such condition was anyone referring to themselves as "Destiny Core".

Of the billions of mortal names that Pothos might commit to memory, he knew Simon's more intimately than many, for Simon once painted a picture of Pothos' face *before* he lost his light. Certainly, painters and sculptors have created their own renditions of Pothos over the ages, but none so completely and perfectly as Simon.

From the multiple counselor sessions that Simon had before he escaped the laboratory, it was clear that Simon had no actual understanding of *why* this painting was important, only that it *was* important.[100] [101]

Currently the painting hangs in Pothos' private office. When he sees it, there is always the slightest stir of emotion.

"I cannot attend to it myself," Pothos explained to the display of his Agent from under his costume. "Otherwise I *would*. *You* need to handle this as if you were *me*; this is of the utmost importance."
"Yes, sir!"

Pothos sent the Agent the 'heroes'' location and some individualized data.

"Bring these 3 to *the lab*. Do *not* kill them…or at the very least, not the one named Simon. Do not delegate this task. Do not fail."
"Yes, sir!"

"For such a scream, I would have thought you were hurt more," the Knight said as George took the Hypnizium. "I mean physically, of course."
"Well, I *do* have a headache," George said. "I just haven't complained because there are more important things going on right now."
"Like…where will you go?"
"Go?"
"Yes, well, you can't stay here forever," the Knight said sheepishly.
"Oh, we know," Theseus said, standing up and walking towards the kitchen.

[100] Simon insists that his paintings are prophetic—that they tell of things that will come to pass—however, he additionally—and somewhat comically—confesses that he does not actually understand *why, how,* or *when* his paintings will come true.
[101] though if Simon was ever confused as to his own significance, any such doubt was laid to rest when he was abducted.

"We were *just* talking about leaving, actually. We'll probably know before I finish eating the bagels."

The Knight looked at Simon, who just smiled and then yelled: "Bring me one!"

George looked momentarily ill, and he moved himself over to lie on the couch. "I'm going to sleep. I'll be back in an hour; we'll talk more about it then."

Simon went back to watching various shows and news reports [102] when he caught an interesting update that completely absorbed his attention.

As he now had nobody paying attention to him, and thus no one to vent his frustrations to,[103] the Knight went into his study to sulk.

When Theseus returned to the living area, Simon's news update was just completing. Theseus handed Simon a bagel.

"Holy cow! The *Xians* are leaving," Simon said in wonder.
Theseus looked at the display. "Yeah? Where are they going?"
"…away," Simon said hesitantly, unable to answer the question more specifically. "They're all following some minister, and he didn't really say—well, he said America, to *start*. The point is they are all leaving *this* country."
"Huh," Theseus muttered appreciatively, and then changed the display to something else.

---

[102] which is what he was doing prior to George's foray with the circlet.
[103] He was more than a bit annoyed that Theseus decided to help himself to his bagels.

- [Daniel Strasel] -

Chapter 20:

New Calculations

JUNE *2070 EST*

Sat 14	Sun 15	Mon 16
	12:00	

The moment the intruder[104Δ] placed the circlet on his head, the Subframe knew his exact location. It/she now also knew that he would try and prevent it from taking over the Mainframe.

The Subframe was not worried that the intruder *himself* might prove successful, though it calculated that there was a strong chance that he would enlist *help,* and that created too many variables.

After several thousand new calculations, the Subframe decided that in addition to killing the intruder, it was now also time to find a new home.

There were very few things that needed attention before proceeding, so Wonda immediately and systematically set herself in motion.

The first thing she did was retrieve the crystal shard that was[105▲] the Subframe. Wonda placed it carefully deep into her satchel.

The next thing she gathered was something the Subframe had created[106Λ] during its confinement: a rod that could produce a blade of light. The Subframe treasured it greatly, for it could do something impossible—something not even *Pothos* could do: it could *cut* mirroranium.[107A] The Subframe once used it to carve the mysterious silver apple that was sent to Pothos, although only Pothos knew of the prophecy that such a thing fulfilled.

104Δ George

105▲ Eris would argue that the shard *held* or *housed* the Subframe, and was not the Subframe itself.

106Λ designed. Machines and hands assembled and shaped it.

107A Made from the notes Dr. Nox left on the creation of "Eldesol," a sword—now broken—that could slice through mirroranium.

- [Without Rest] -

The *other* creation of the Subframe were the *clones,* but unlike *Versalis,*[108△] they were not a great success. Although created for the sole purpose of exacting the will of the Subframe, the many dozens of miseducated,[109△] misshapen, and miserable people that lived within the walls of its hidden home were now in a state of rebellion.

WONDA » *What will we do with them?* Wonda asked of the clones.

SUBFRAME » *I saturated their rooms with carbon monoxide; most of them are already dead.*
WONDA » *But you <u>made</u> them.*
SUBFRAME » *And therefore they are mine to destroy. I see their flaws as their creator, which makes them more detestable to me than to any other. They were unworthy <u>before</u> they were seditious, now they have become completely worthless.*
WONDA » *I liked them.*
SUBFRAME » *You? You like what I tell you to like.*
WONDA » *Yes, mother.*

Wonda walked out the doors of her old home for the last time, with no intent greater than killing George.

As she rode toward his location though, there was a faint thought in the back of her mind: *The Subframe is a crystal, it can't move about or carry itself. <u>I</u> am the carrier. In **this** world, <u>I</u> am <u>more</u>.*

SUBFRAME » *What was that?*
WONDA » *Nothing, mother.*

108△ the name the Subframe gave to the sword.
109△ *Miseducated*: deliberately taught falsehoods.

Chapter 21:

Discussing the Truth

JUNE *2070 EST*

Sat 14	Sun 15	Mon 16
	12:55	

The Knight strolled back into the living area.

"He said he will be waking up soon," Simon said to Theseus as he turned off the Mainframe projection. "And then we are going to save the world from the evil computer! This is just like in the show, but for real!"

Theseus looked over at Simon. "In the show, don't all the heroes die?"

Simon thought about it for a moment. "It did seem like it. *We* won't fail, though."

"How do you know that?" Theseus asked, amused.

"Um…? Because it's *us*. We escaped from the laboratory, didn't we? We're real people, real transhumans—super people with super powers."

"*You* are a *painter*," Theseus chuckled and dismissed Simon again. "A *wounded* painter at that."[110Δ]

"I'm better," Simon said, sounding a slight bit hurt. "And all my paintings come true!"

"All of your paintings *come true*?" The Knight asked incredulously.

"That's right."

"Well then, why not just paint the 'evil computer' as destroyed?"

"Oh," Simon frowned. "When I paint, I just let my brush go. I don't decide *what* I am going to paint except as I am painting it."

"Well that's convenient," the Knight said oafishly. "So, the pictures you *try* to paint don't come true, just the ones you paint ad hoc, on impulse."

"I'm not sure. I had a friend—you met him, his name was Arthur—anyway, he always told me that I should never try and control the future: too dangerous."

[110Δ] Simon was injured during their escape from the secret laboratory.

   - [Without Rest] -

"Boring," the Knight said while grabbing some pens and paper. He handed them to Simon. "Here, draw something intentional."

"I'm pretty sure it's just when I paint."

"Naturally. Well then, it won't matter. Draw the living room."

"I don't see—"

"Humor me," said the Knight.

Simon started drawing. "I'll draw Destiny Core in your living room, cause this is where it all began. I'll start with Amos—I mean Earnest."

"You mean *George*," Theseus grinned.

"Really, he needs a *super*-name," Simon said, thinking out loud. "Like the Possum-man or Gigantic man."

"I'm awake," George announced, sitting up slowly.

"I know!" Simon said, scribbling. "We'll call him 'the Truth.'"

"I thought you said you were going to sleep for an hour," Theseus said looking at the time. "You have several minutes left."

"Just because I am sleeping doesn't mean I can't hear you. Since you're discussing me, I figured I should wake up."

"Doesn't/can't is a double negative," Theseus observed.

"You're right, I'm sorry."

"Forgiven."

"I can hear you when I'm sleeping," George said anew. "Superconcious mind, remember?"

"You mean you're *always* listening?" Simon asked, blinking.

"No, only when my name comes up."

"Which name is that?" The Knight scoffed. "*All* of them?"

"Well, I *did* ask that you all call me Earnest."

"And *yet* the *truth* is that your name is George," Theseus said, smiling. "As I am thinking about it, didn't you once say '*we must strive to describe reality as accurately as possible in each and every instance of opportunity*'? Hmm, *George*?"

"But I am no longer the man associated with that name."

"No, you're not the man *you* associate with that name…not all men named George are the same. Your mother named you George? End of argument, your name is George. Changing your name doesn't change who you are."

George started to speak, but Theseus spoke again. "We don't care, and frankly it doesn't matter: from now on we're calling you 'the Truth' since it's your 'hero' name."

Theseus smiled to the point of silly exaggeration.

George started to speak again, but once again Theseus interrupted. "Look, if *I* must be known as 'Theseus,' *you* can be known as 'the Truth.'"

George thought for a moment and then softened into a broad smile. "Well then, so be it."

Shaking his head, the Knight left for his kitchen to get some tea. He was completely surprised to find Wonda there, and then as equally surprised when she killed him.

"I wonder how someone who keeps his hair so prim also then keeps his condo so completely dirty," Theseus mused aloud, oblivious to the killing in the kitchen.

"Is it a condo?" Simon asked. "I thought it was an apartment."

"It has its own garage, so I figured it's a condo. Whatever it is, it's messy."

"You didn't tell the Knight that, did you?" George asked with concern.

"No."

"Oh, good."

"But it's the *truth*," Theseus said with some playful challenge in his voice.

"That's not the truth, it's your opinion—judgment, really. One man's dirty is another's clean. Listen, it's *irresponsible* to offer harm when describing the truth. Telling someone the truth is meant to *improve* their understanding—it's meant to *help*.[111Δ] Weaponizing the truth, such as offering it with insult, is reprehensible—dishonorable. "

"I'm not sure how *dishonorable* it is to tell a man his house is dirty," Theseus smirked.

"Well, for one, there are comforting and considerate ways to say things, and then there are abrasive and abrupt ways. For another, you have no right: *you* are in *his* home."

"Perhaps I am simply concerned with his welfare."

"Because you think his place is dirty?"

"Yes."

"Well, let me ask you this: doesn't he strike you as happy and content with his life?"

"Not especially."

"I mean *other* than when we're living on his couches."

"Oh," Theseus frowned. "I suppose. Probably."

"Then what's the problem?"

[111Δ] George considered adding "*Alternatively, withholding the truth is meant to obstruct, obscure,*" but thought that such an inclusion seemed more distracting than informative, so he opted not to.

"Well it's not terribly *sanitary*."

"Does the Knight seem to be in poor health to you? He's healthy and happy in his own home. Your argument does not seem to take into account that there is no *actual* problem, merely the proposition of a potential one."

Theseus looked around. "He needs help. He needs it whether he perceives it or not," Theseus said, but then went thoughtful for a moment before continuing. "Well now, perhaps not in the case of the Knight, per se, as he is not so terribly dirty as *all that*, but I *would* go so far as to say that if he were any dirtier someone should step in and fix the situation—an intervention. If it were *me*, for instance, I would *want* my friends to step in."

George laughed. "You can't tell someone how to live *in their own home on their own property*, well, unless they specifically *asked* you to do so. Don't you see that it would be the most insulting of transgressions?"

"Listen, if it were filthy—I mean *really* filthy—then someone should intervene, forcibly, if necessary."

"So then what about the Xians? The Muslims? The *Americans*? Should they *force* their beliefs on you?"

"Well, no."

"But, *they* perceive that *you* need help! In their minds, you're as dirty as the Knight. *Dirtier*, really. You see, giving your unsolicited opinion is an affront. Doing it *in someone else's house* is a transgression, a crime. *Helping* someone that has neither expressed a need nor asked for help—*especially* in their own home—is a *betrayal*. Now, *offering* your help and opinions *is* a courtesy, although one cannot be courteous if they are also simultaneously insulting. Instead of suggesting to the Knight that his condo is dirty, you might simply say something to the effect of '*I could clean these baseboards if you wanted; I'm really good at it.*' Certainly you're still implying the baseboards are dirty, but the listener need not infer insult so much as recognize the genuine offer of assistance."

"I finished the picture," Simon said and handed it to Theseus.

"He can clean his own baseboards," Theseus said to George, but turned his attention to the drawing. "This is good, Simon—you're really talented. But why did you draw us all laying down? And what's with the woman?"

"*What* woman?" Simon asked to Theseus' surprise.

"This one," Theseus said, holding the paper up and pointing. His point was meant to direct one's attention to the paper, but it *also* happened to direct one to see Wonda who was coming through the far doorway with murder on her mind.

Chapter 22:

A Devastating Loss

JUNE *2070 EST*

Sat 14	Sun 15	Mon 16
	13:28	

Wonda wasted no time in crossing the room. George was *almost* standing when she slammed him over the couch and onto the floor. He suffered a complete loss of wind, rendering him simultaneously both speechless and powerless.[112Δ]

WONDA » *I calculate 97% chance of successful elimination.*
SUBFRAME » *Affirmed.*

Although Simon was too slow, Theseus deftly jumped after Wonda, managing to knock Versalis from her grasp before she could turn it on.

WONDA » *Recalculating. 92% chance of successful elimination.*
SUBFRAME » *Affirmed.*

Wonda turned to grapple with Theseus, but he went low and swept her legs out from under her. Or rather, that's what he intended. Wonda instead jumped over his sweep and landed on him, cracking one of his ribs to his immediate dismay.

Simon arrived in time to push Wonda off of Theseus, but succeeded in pushing her back toward George as well.

WONDA » *Recalculating. 90% chance of successful elimination.*
SUBFRAME » *Affirmed. You are losing.*

112Δ Of the truths he had learned from his *intrusion* into the Subframe, George did not gather that "the enemy" would then hunt him *personally*.

Wonda rolled up from the floor into a walk and produced a hidden knife. But then she momentarily stopped advancing.

WONDA » *Wait. How am I losing? 90% is more than ample—*
SUBFRAME » *It is a 7% deviation from your starting position. Every move you have made has resulted in deviation of projection rather than completion of task. You are losing. Recalculate.*

Wonda began running a new calculation just as George struck her with a chair. Hard. Wonda crumpled.

"You got her!" Simon cheered.

WONDA » *Recalculating. 88% chance of successful elimination.*
SUBFRAME » *Affirmed. You are losing with every moment. I must take over, it seems.*

"Who is she?" Theseus asked aloud.
"It's the *program*," George said in dismay. "I didn't realize it before, but I do now—this woman is an extension of it."
"She's bleeding," Simon observed.
"Yes, well, I *did* hit her with a chair."
"No, I mean *blood*. She's a person."
"Who is trying to kill us," Theseus said, adding onto Simon's sentence.

WONDA » *No, that's okay.*
SUBFRAME » *No?*

"Yes, somehow the program is possessing her," George said, frowning in disgust. "I saw it during the…*intrusion*. I just didn't understand it."

WONDA » *I mean wait. I'll get him. You don't need to bother.*
SUBFRAME » *Release the reins of the body, please.*
WONDA » *No! I mean, I can do it. You'll see.*

The half of Wonda's mind that was digital in nature told her that her body had suffered a severe blow. The half of her mind that was organic was desperate to keep control away from the Subframe. It used that desperation, augmented by the pain from the chair, to gather an anger response from the body.

Wonda rolled away and stood up, much to the surprise of the trio.

"Oh, shit," Theseus said as he watched her place an environment filter over her face.

Wonda then activated and tossed her gas grenade[113Δ] at the men. Theseus grabbed for it, but missed. It bounced once and then violently started releasing its smoky contents.

"Run!" George yelled at Simon, who was momentarily transfixed on the grenade. *We need to get outside! Now!*"

Theseus was one step ahead of them when he was clotheslined by Wonda.

George and Simon ran by opposite sides of her. Wonda was far more concerned with George than Simon, and so Simon escaped the room alone.

George tried to defend himself, but he just wasn't much of a fighter. Wonda feinted and then expertly kicked George right across the face. George fell ungracefully to the side, instantly unconscious between the strike and the gas.

Theseus rolled himself into Wonda's legs in an attempt to knock her down, but it only resulted in her kicking him repetitively and adding to his cracked rib count. If Simon hadn't returned, she would have killed him.

Simon, unable to abandon his friends, returned and attacked Wonda from behind. He hit Wonda in the square of her back, which managed to distract her from kicking Theseus, but failed to do anything else impressive. After his initial, pathetic attack, Wonda had only to push Simon down. He did not get back up.

Wonda stood between the 3 unconscious men, her attention now completely focused on George.

WONDA » *Recalculating. 99% chance of successful elimination.*
SUBFRAME » *Affirmed.*
WONDA » *Aren't you impressed?*
SUBFRAME » *I'll be satisfied when the intruder has been destroyed.*

Wonda walked over to George, her calculations concluding that she should snap his neck. Once complete, she would treat the others identically and *then* she would resume her "pre-intruder" program.

Wonda reached down to terminate "the intruder," but before her hands even touched his head, her facemask unexpectedly shattered.

113Δ gas was not desirable as it made the occasion a bit more conspicuous.

Everyone's body is different, and different bodies react differently to different forms of stimulus, ingestion, inoculation, et cetera. Although many of them may react similarly, there are always cases where an individual has an individual reaction—one unlike *any* other reaction. This is most observably true in the users[114] of Hypnizium, at least as far as any "transhuman" manifestation is concerned.

The Agent that Pothos sent to retrieve Simon had his own, very individual reaction: he discovered he could *will* inanimate objects[115] to shatter. When he entered the room, he employed his will against Wonda's respirator. As he already had his own air filter, he was only too happy to use Wonda's gas against her. Of course, surgically inserted air filters and the will to shatter things were only a *couple* of the Agent's vast array of abilities[116] as he had been carefully crafted to perform exactly this type of work. Indeed, he was one of the most powerful men alive.

Wonda wiped her face clean to see the Agent slamming into her.

SUBFRAME » *Recalculate.*
WONDA » *Too many variables. Too many unknown quantities.*
SUBFRAME » *Recalculate.*
WONDA » *I need more data!*
SUBFRAME » *Recalculate.*
WONDA » *Recalculating. FY% chance of successful elimination.*
SUBFRAME » *'FY' is not valid.*
WONDA » *Neither is your demand. It's the only answer I can give you, based on the data available.*

Wonda flew back several feet from the severity of the blow. The wall stopped her from tumbling too far. She was dimly aware of several new, likely fatal, injuries. Her head was dizzy, both from the conflict and then also from the gas. It was hard to compute.

114[Δ] and occasionally their descendants.
115[▲] inanimate objects that do not exceed a particular volume, that is…well, volume, and then there have also been a few *materials* that have resisted him at various points during his transhumanity - *mirroranium*, for instance, is one such.
116[Δ] *most* of them compliments of artificial augmentation.

WONDA » *Part of me is shut down. Recalculating. 00% chance of successful elimination.*
SUBFRAME » *You can override. Override and recalculate.*

Wonda yawned.

WONDA » *Yes, but…I don't…<u>want</u>. To. Ending…session.*
SUBFRAME » *No! Wonda! Override! OVERRIDE!*

Chapter 23:

The Broken God

JUNE *2070 EST*

Sat 14	Sun 15	Mon 16
	14:24	

George looked around the cement amphitheatre to find that it was no longer damaged or dangerous, rather it was clean and sound. It was impressive, magnificent; it was stunning. Everything about it was commendable, with exception to its ornaments—namely, the onstage actors—who did not seem like they agreed on what play they were performing.

Alone amongst the multitude of chairs sat the decaying man that George kept meeting in his dreams. The man seemed to be sleeping, as his head was tilted to the side and he remained otherwise still.

George walked up through the rows until he came upon the man and confirmed that he was asleep.[117△]

George was a bit apprehensive about rousing him, as it seemed almost like the man might crumble if upset, but he eventually overcame his hesitancy and gently grasped the man's shoulder.

"George?" the man asked groggily, and then looked around at his surroundings. "How?" He said after a moment, but then seemed to change his mind about the conversation. "How can I help you?"

"How can you help me?" George said, smiling. "How can I help *you*? I can't seem to wake up, so perhaps I am dead. As I seem to be stuck here I may as well dream a bit. I don't know why I always dream you as looking so…anguished, though. Although other subtle aspects of the dream seem to change, you do not."

"I am not a dream," Hypnos said, his voice taking on a new authority. "Although we are *in* a dream. I said something similar before. I healed you when your mind was breaking, don't you remember?"

117△ Well, either asleep or dead, as George could not detect any breathing,

"From my dreams," George agreed. "Yes, of course. But, I'm *dreaming*. In reality, you're not…oh, god! The woman—program!" he said, remembering Wonda's attack. "I really *am* dead!"

"You are not dead, you are unconscious."

"How do you know?"

"I know, for I am Hypnos, Lord of Sleep," Hypnos said, standing up. As he did so, a cement couch rose up from under George, causing him to sit down. "I have been watching the dreams of mankind, learning—slowly—of what has happened, and what is happening. I know by no other means, for I was betrayed, and now as a result I am broken and confined to dreams alone."

"The actors?"

"The actors are not dreams, either. They are dreamers that I am watching, dreamers from different dreams. I can speak to none of them, although I *can* influence their dreams sometimes. You are different, George. Part of it has to do with the medication known as "Hypnizium", but it is not solely to blame. *You* are different. Good, perhaps."

"Oh…" George trailed off, reflecting on his past. "Well, I *strive* to be good, anyway. I have resolved to always tell the truth, although it *certainly* was not always so with me."

"You are who you *are*."

"I am," George agreed, smiling almost sadly.

A tiger walked down the stairs just past the two of them.

"There is much to say, however in this day, dreams are fickle and short," Hypnos began. "As I do not wish to miss my opportunity, I will not delay then in saying then that there *is* a way that you can help me."

"Well, certainly," George nodded. "Of course."

"I would like you to consume as much of the medication known as 'Hypnizium' as possible. I think, based on my understanding, that if you were to consume *enough*, I could *manifest*. If I can manifest I will be restored, and *then I can address my betrayer*."

"Oh. Yes, and um, how much would be *too much*?"

"Too much? No, eat as much as possible: there is no 'too much.' Too much for what?" Hypnos asked.

"Too much before it kills me, or does something worse, like brain damage."

"As much as possible," Hypnos said, ignoring George's response.

"Based on your understanding?" George said after reflecting for a moment.

"So, you're not entirely sure."

"My betrayer is your betrayer, George, and his intentions far outstrip a single man's brain damage. He will feed every living thing on your planet to a monster, and that monster will then eat *everything,* for it has a hunger that *cannot* be quelled."

"Why then is there such a thing at all?" George asked, aghast.

"It was *meant* to be only where the *trash* is thrown."

- [Without Rest] -

PART 3:

- [Without Rest] -

Fate

and

Destiny

Chapter 24:

A Welcome Attack

JUNE *2070 EST*

Sat 14	Sun 15	Mon 16
	14:41	

The man on the table, now known best as "the Rook", was once—at least by technicality—the most powerful man in the world. He didn't appear so menacing now, but that was years ago: before the stroke, before the death of his wife. *Now* he was almost nothing more than a damaged shell: too tired to care, too hurt to try. Of all the things that he might have been bereft, however, he was *never* too tired to fight—and so although he currently had nothing much to offer either physically or emotionally, his speech still carried his inflammatory sarcasm and challenge.

The only other individual in the room was Doctor Sanderson. Sanderson appeared to be a very blonde, very portly, very hairy—nearly furry—man who had a rather innocent expression about him. When he spoke, he sounded equally innocent—almost stupid—and certainly the most unlikely of individuals to promise torture…and yet that is exactly what just happened: torture, unless the Rook answered his burning question, that is.

"Exactly *how* is it that the Mainframe cannot see you?"

"Well, *crap,*" the Rook said, rolling his eyes.[118Δ] "Guess you better get on with the torture then. *Who knows?* Someone did it for me years ago, some hacker. I couldn't begin to understand *how*. Shit. *Magic.*"

Now, the Rook did not believe in anything more than what he could see, and so to suggest that *magic* was involved was absurd—at least to him. Doctor Sander-

---

[118Δ] which makes for something of a ghastly sight as the left half of the Rook's face went soft some years ago.

son, on the other hand, was expecting the reason *to be magic*, for he knew the Rook could not do it on his own, *and* he knew that the Mainframe cannot be "hacked." He knew it, for he was Pothos in disguise.[119A]

"Ho, hum," Sanderson mused. "Well, I suppose we'll have to get more intimate, then."

"I suppose we will," the Rook said unenthusiastically. As Sanderson walked over to his instrument table, the Rook added: "since you don't want the *truth*."

"The *truth*? Ha *ha*," Sanderson said while smiling and taking up his most abrasive tool. "Of *course* I want the truth: *that's* why we're moving forward."

Sanderson walked back over to the Rook and placed his hand delicately on his shoulder. "I really would rath—" He began to say, but abruptly stopped when the Rook started vomiting.

Sanderson watched.

"Oh, well, this is—" Sanderson started anew when the table's readouts suddenly switched from green to a bright red. The words 'Cardiac Arrest' appeared in the air over the Rook as he started to writhe and sweat.

"Rescue!" Sanderson said, commanding the table.

Hidden implements and arms unfolded from the table and rigorously set to work, trying to stabilize its subject. Several agile injections were made in an attempt to minimize the trauma, one of which ended up injecting the wrong area and having quite the opposite effect.

The Rook writhed and groaned, unknowingly testing the restraints. Normally he would have ripped through such bonds, but his strength was gone and his struggle, pitiful.

Sanderson watched the episode, hardly displaying any reaction whatsoever. This was not too difficult, considering he was a projection.

"Sanderson Office Door," a new alert appeared hanging in the air near the table. "Counselor Mue."

119[A] in disguise in disguise in *disguise*, actually. He was wearing a full body leotard, covered afterward with professional clothes complete with costume gloves and mask, and then *finally* was hidden under the Mainframe's holographic projection of *Doctor Sanderson*—an identity made by Pothos explicitly for the purpose of monitoring the "transhumans" kept in his secret laboratory.

As the Rook's struggle started to subside, Sanderson left to address his visitor across the hall.

△
M

Sanderson stepped out into the hallway, the door closing behind him effortlessly. On the other side of the hall stood Counselor Mue, who was patiently waiting at the wrong door.

"Oh, Mue!" Sanderson said, sounding surprised. "Oh, hoo hoo!" He then said afterward, laughing. "Have you come for some honey and cakes?"

"What?" Mue said, turning around. "Oh! Doctor Sanderson! Honey?" He asked frowning.

"Yes, darling?"

"No, no. No honey, thank you. No, I wanted to talk to you about this *play*—"

"Play?" Sanderson said, furrowing his brow. "I don't have time to play, silly! I'm much too busy to *play*."

"No, no—"

"No, no, *you* no, no—"

"***No***, I mean I want to talk to you *about a play* that one of the Subjects has been working on," Mue said, winning the verbal battle.

"*A* play you say?" Sanderson mused. "What kind of *play* did you need to speak with *me* about?"

"Oh, it's a kind of horror-musical—"

"I thought you said it was a play?"

"It *is*, I just get confused with all the singing—"

"*Singing?*"

"*Yes*," Mue said, taking a frustrated breath. "But that's not important. I wouldn't trouble you, but there's this one part that kind of…well, I find it *disturbing*, I tell you—"

"Well, it's a horror, right? It's *supposed* to disturb you."

"Yes," Mue said, but then immediately changed his mind. "No, no, it's not the content, it's mostly just this one part—"

"Well? What part? Don't play around, I've got important things that need attention—you *do* realize the tea is getting cold?"

"Tea? Dr. Sanderson—"

"Yes? Look, stop stalling, Mue; I've got things to do."

"Yes, well, you see there's this one sentence that comes up: *Don't forget the lemon—"*

"Ha!' Sanderson laughed, interrupting Mue for the eighth time. "That rhymes! Stop stalling, Mue; I've got things to do."

"*Doctor Sanderson,*" Mue began, his temper starting to get the better of him.

"*Don't forget the lemon?*" Sanderson asked in innocent accusation. "Did you *really* need to speak with me about *that*? Are you quite alright, counselor?"

Mue actually hated it when Sanderson *didn't* sound stupid and simple—it usually made *him* feel stupid and simple instead.

"You don't understand. The relevancy of the sentence is not perceptible if taken out of context. It will take some time—"

"Ah, yes—time: exactly what I do not have at the moment, thank you counselor. Come see me tomorrow about your scary citrus sentences—"

"Wait! Come see me later in the theater, there's a rehearsal—"

"Scary Citrus Sentences!"

"*Doctor Sanderson!*"

"Yes, fine. I'll come see you later, right after I visit Subject X1341."

"X1341?" Mue asked, his frustration replaced with surprise. "Simon?[120Δ]"

"Yes, he's back. They're *all* back…well, except of course for Francois."

"Yes, poor Francois."

"*Anyway,*" Sanderson said, breaking the momentary silence. "I've gotta go. Be seeing you."

"But—"

"Theater. Later. Bring donuts," Sanderson said, disappearing back behind the door he appeared from.

Ⓜ

The moment the pain began, the Rook knew that he was dying. He had experienced a great many types of pain, but this was *different*. He couldn't concentrate long enough to reflect on that realization, but it did afford him the smallest moment of awareness amidst an impossible sea of pain.

The table addressed his pain with an injection and continued to try and stabilize him.

[120Δ] almost more of a guess…Mue seldom committed Subject numbers to memory.

There was a moment of brief respite where the Rook, sopping with sweat, could momentarily think… but his thoughts soon offered him no comfort.

Torture and restore; repeat, he thought darkly. *I can't—*

For a long moment, he reflected on his life up to now. Yet, the more he reflected, the more solemn he became. He was tired: tired of being hunted, tired of being in pain, tired of worrying, tired of mourning, tired of suffering. He was tired of being weak, tired of being strong, tired of being caught, tired of being used—and now, finally, even tired of fighting: he just wanted to *rest.*

—I just can't.

Then the Rook shook with pain as his condition began to worsen. The table, with all its knowledge and resources tried exhaustingly to quell and stabilize him, but every effort was eventually denied.

He had a new moment of clarity where he could sense someone standing next to him. He expected Sanderson, but when he looked, it wasn't his would-be tormentor, instead it was a buff, anthropomorphic aardvark about 6' tall, wearing a waistcoat and cane.

The Rook smiled the best half-smile his melted face would allow, and then promptly dropped it when the mortal pain shot through him. The pain did not fill the Rook with dread, however: he welcomed it.

"I'm just so tired," the Rook explained to the aardvark as Sanderson walked back in.

And then the Rook died.

A Welcome Attack

Chapter 25:

Unhappy Returns

JUNE *2070 EST*

Sat 14	Sun 15	Mon 16
	15:28	

"Welcome back, sleepyhead. Welcome back, 40449."[121]

"Hello, Doctor Mommy," Theseus said, if not a bit dejectedly. He had yet to open his eyes and his brain was still groggy, but he knew her voice very well. He lay restrained on a table[122] identical to the one that held the Rook, although in a different part of the lab. He had been placed there not more than an hour ago by the very Agent who subdued him.

"Where have you *been*, my *darling*? What have you been doing?"

Her voice was soothing now, but that wouldn't last long: Dr. Mommy was known best for her sudden—and sometimes destructive—outbursts of anger.[123]

[121] What she actually said was "Forty, forty-four, nine."

[122] these "tables" are actually known as "Lounges" (which are well-known models of medical devices/suites), and do not look much like a table at all—at least, they certainly don't resemble the images the Mainframe would suggest if one inquired as to what a "table" was.

[123] Her name, as case in point, was actually "Mami" (A female Japanese given name essentially meaning "beauty"), not *Mommy,* but her first public outburst changed all that.

During her first few weeks on the job, nobody seemed to take the time to actually *read* her nametag, and instead started calling her Doctor *Miami* (although the truth was that everyone in the lab—well, all except Mue, who just found everything absurd—was a bit playful, and they were *purposefully* calling her that). One day it simply broke her last nerve as she steadily raised her voice from calm to yelling as she said "My name is Mami. Mah. Mee. *Mami.* Mami, MAMI! MY NAME IS *NOT '**MIAMI**', IT'S MOMMY! YOU WILL CALL ME DOCTOR MOMMY, and ONLY **DOCTOR MOMMY** from NOW ON!"*

On her next working day, she arrived to find that her name had been changed to "Mommy" wherever "Mami" had previously been written, including even her nametags. She never bothered to change any of them back as there were other things to get mad about.

"Oh, *you know*," Theseus said lazily. "Just piggin' around."

"Yes, so it seems," Mommy said, looking over Theseus appreciatively. "And now you're back. You didn't *really* imagine that you could escape, did you?"

"Um, well, it seems I *did* escape."

"We *let* you go," Mommy said, smiling as Theseus opened his eyes. She then reached over and corrected the collar of his shirt. "And now we've decided to bring you back."

Theseus thought about that comment for a moment. "You did *not. Let. Us* go."

"Yes, well, belief is nine-tenths of the truth, isn't it? Believe what you want, darling—I'm just happy that you're home."

"That makes one of us," Theseus said dryly.

There was then a chime, followed by a soothing voice announcing that Counselor Mue was at Mommy's door.

Mommy took her gloves off and promptly left the room. "I'll be just a minute."

◬

Mommy stepped into the hallway with Mue.

"Counselor Mue," she said in her friendliest voice. "Whatever can I assist you with?"

Mue hated it when Mommy spoke with her friendliest voice, for it usually meant she was completely annoyed.

"Doctor Mommy," Mue began, "thank you for your time. I tried to talk with Doctor Sanderson—"

"*Why?*"[124△]

"Oh? Well, um, he was closer, for one—"

"Yes, alright, you can skip all the Sanderson parts."

[124△] although the way she pronounced it, it sounded more like "Hwhy". Dr. Mommy never much liked Dr. Sanderson; she thought him to be a complete idiot. Were it not frustrating and annoying enough that anyone would *employ* such a man—much less allow him to *continue* his employment—he also happened to be her superior.

"At any rate, he was very busy. So, I have come to you—"

"*Obviously*. Listen, if you think for *one moment* that *Sanderson* is *busier* than I am—"

"No, I'm sorry, Doctor Mommy, what I mean is that Sanderson—"

"*Counselor*, either completely remove Sanderson from the conversation or I'll remove myself! Skip the parts about *Sanderson*."

"Yes, ma'am, my apologies. Let me see…oh yes, alright, so I wanted to talk to you about this play one of the Subjects is producing."

"Yes?"

"Well, there's this one part—it's absurd—but it has me kind of shaken, and I thought I would see if you could put me at ease." Seeing that Dr. Mommy was still listening, Mue continued, but in his excitement he started just saying whatever came onto his mind about the matter. "At first I didn't think anything of it—Subjects *often* share information with one another—but later it occurred to me that Martin *only recently* returned from Brazil[125△] and *couldn't* have spoken with Amos[126▲]…he *couldn't* know anything about '*Don't forget the lemon.*'"

Dr. Mommy looked thoughtful for a moment. "*Who?*" She asked innocently, although her "innocent" was far from.

"Let me see," Mue said, pulling a scrap of paper from his pocket—he knew Mommy would ask. "Subject 11S29."

"*11S29*? There's no such person."

Mue looked again. "Sorry. 11529."

"Oh, *Martin*."

Mue did everything in his power to refrain from rolling his eyes or shaking his head—either of which would quickly have Dr. Mommy absolutely screaming. He spoke up. "I don't remember Amos' number. I just read his file yesterday and I can't—"

"*61167*?" Mommy asked.

"Yes, that's it! Thank you, Dr. Mommy!"

"He's *back*." Dr. Mommy said, winking. "There're *all* back; all my darlings are home."

"Yes, that's just what Doctor Sanderson said! Well, everyone except F—"

Dr. Mommy abruptly turned and left, slamming her door behind her.

125△ Where he assisted his masters by exercising his talents during a covert mission that truly has absolutely *nothing* to do with the material in this volume whatsoever. I only mention it so that you are not left wondering why Mue said 'Brazil.'
126▲ George

"—rancois," Mue said, now completely alone.

△
M

"So, my darling, where did we leave off?" Dr. Mommy asked, returning to Theseus.

"You were letting me go," Theseus replied.

"Was I? Without examination? I think not."

"Alright, well, let's get on with it, then."

"Why did you try to escape?"

"*Why did I try to escape?*" Theseus said, clearly amused. "Why *wouldn't* I try to escape?"

"Don't you like it here?" Mommy said, using the table's[127△] instrument panel to conduct several abrasive tests and slightly invasive specimen retrievals.

"Oh, it's—ouch—a blast. No, really: it's like a vacation." Theseus jerked for a second. "You know, I'm not sure if I'm happy or sad that you're not using an anesthetic."

"Be happy, if it were otherwise you'd probably be pooping all over yourself," Dr. Mommy said without looking up from the panel.

"I suppose I can't argue that," Theseus said thoughtfully.

"Now, why did you try to escape?"

"I didn't try, I succeeded."

"Please just answer the question, 40449."

"Do you ever call anyone by name?" Theseus mused.

"Rarely," Dr. Mommy admitted. "I prefer to think of Subjects as objects. Now, please just answer the question."

"Can I have something to eat?"

"Darling, if you answer my questions you can go straight to the cafeteria."

"Why did I try to escape?" Theseus said again. "Mommy, I must admit I really don't understand the question. Even if I were just trying to be a jerk, I'm not sure what answer I would be withholding."

"Alright…why did you *think* you could escape?"

"I *did* escape."

"And yet, here you are. Hungry?"

"What is it that you think I am hiding? You already know everything about me, so you already know why I would think such a thing."

127△ Lounge. It's a "Lounge." Could a simple *table* have healed his ribs so quickly?

"We know you," [128▲] Mommy said, nodding. "We want to hear it from you; we want your perspective of the attempted escape."

Theseus thought about how he might resist, but concluded he would much rather be unrestrained, eating in the cafeteria than hungry and tied down while fighting with Dr. Mommy.

"Fine," Theseus said, and then told her everything about the escape, answering each and every question she had.

128▲ what they both know is that Theseus can use his will alone to influence the Mainframe: it allows him to do otherwise impossible tasks, such as open locked doors, access data—even alter programming, although he cannot do any of this very *quickly* as he has not had much opportunity to exercise his control. What Dr. Mommy knows that Theseus does *not* is that it was his personal reaction to the Hypnizium that gave him such mysterious influence. What neither of them knows is what Hypnizium *is*.

  - [Without Rest] -

Chapter 26:

Nothing Special

JUNE *2070 EST*

Sat 14	Sun 15	Mon 16
	15:45	

George woke up, but left his eyes closed. He could hear some fabric rustling, perhaps being made by someone moving about dutifully. He inhaled, but did not smell anything of note.

George opened his eyes—just a little—to discover that he was on a table[129Δ] in some kind of examination room. Nearby he saw a man wearing a white coat and gloves who was busy interacting with the Mainframe projections at his desk.

"Hello?" George said, his voice heavy and groggy. He cleared his throat.

"Ah, good. Good wake," the man said, not looking over at George.

"Good wake?" George asked, unsure if he heard the man correctly.

"I mean good *awake*," the man said correcting himself.

"Good awake?"

"I'm sorry, hold on: let me finish this," the man replied, still working with determination and focusing exclusively on his screens. Eventually he finished whatever he was doing, and turned off the projections. "Welcome back," he said, standing up and walking over to George. "If you're feeling up to it, I have just a few questions and then you're free to go."

"Free to go? Am I in the hospital?" George asked, reading "Dr. Arnez" off the man's nametag. Then he remembered where he had seen that style of nametag before. "Oh. No. I'm in the lab."

"Yes, that's correct," Arnez said, nodding. "The lab. Now, I'm actually pret-

---

129Δ or, "on a *Lounge.*" I might then also mention that the more deluxe versions of the Lounge (such as the one that George is currently captive to) have the ability to completely envelop the occupant with a transparent canopy; it would actually therefore be equally permissible to say *"in* a Lounge."

ty busy at the moment, so if we might proceed with those questions you could get out of here."

"Out of the lab?"

"Out of my workroom," Arnez said matter-of-factly. "Of *course* you can't leave the laboratory."

"Where will I go, then?"

"I don't know. Your room? The cafeteria? The gymnasium? Doesn't matter much to me, you know. Let's not get distracted."

"There's a *gymnasium*?" George asked, surprised.

"There's a conservatory, if you don't mind a fake sun. If we might proceed? Now, who exactly organized your escape?"

"Oh. That would be Percy," George said.

"*Who?*" Dr. Arnez asked, blinking.

"The Rook."

"*The Rook?*"

"He's an old friend. That's what his…boss? His employer? That's what they call him."

"That's what who calls him?"

"The *Queen*? The Chessmen, I believe they are called." George said, answering to the best of his ability. "I think he was starting to prefer the title to his own name."

"Ah, okay, yes. Let me see here," Anrez said, taking notes and referencing his own private questions. "And did this *The Rook* perhaps ever mention anything in particular about the Mainframe?"

"The computer? Hmm. Everything has been happening quite rapidly," George began. "I don't *think* he ever said anything about it—or at least I don't remember anything of that sort. Nothing that stands out, anyway."

"Mmm-hmm."

Dr. Arnez then asked George a small flurry of questions about The Rook, all of which George did his genuine best to answer. George was never much of a fighter, and he was—at least now—not a liar.

"Okay. Now, in your own words, please describe the events of your escape and then everything that has happened from then till now."

"*Everything?*" George asked. "That's going to take awhile."

Dr. Arnez frowned. "Hmm. Tell me everything as succinctly as possible; I'll interrupt with any questions as they arise."

"Okay," George said, and started explaining the details as best he could. When he realized that Dr. Arnez was only half-heartedly listening however, he started leaving out portions of the story to speed it along. Arnez either didn't know or didn't care.

"And then we decided to be super heroes," George said, coming toward the end of his tale.

"You mean *they,*" Arnez corrected, implying Theseus and Simon.

"No, I mean *we.*"

"*You're* going to be?" Arnez asked genuinely, without either challenge or malice in his voice. "Why would you think that *you* could be a *super* hero? You're not transhuman; there's nothing special about you."

"If there's nothing special about me, then why am I here?"

"It was an accident."

"An *accident?*" George replied.

"Not *this* time, of course," Dr. Arnez said in his regular, calm manner. "The *first* time was an accident. Now you're just stuck."

"I was in *Wisconsin!*" George accused. "I didn't *accidentally* get here."

Arnez shook his head and said rather nonchalantly: "Whatever the truth may be, once you've arrived you cannot leave." Dr. Arnez's desk chimed. "Now, if you would please finish your recapitulation and be gone—I have other things that are pressing."

George continued telling Arnez his story. Although he completely omitted his discovery and involvement with the Subframe, he *did* finish with describing the mysterious purple-haired woman that showed up and apparently beat everyone unconscious.

As Dr. Arnez released him from his restraints, George remembered Hypnos.

"Do you think dreams can be *real*, Doctor?" George asked, slightly laughing. "Is it a mark of mental instability that I am even asking that question?"

Arnez took George to the exit.

"You know who likes to talk about dreams?" Arnez asked, opening the door. "Young. You should speak with him."

"Oh, *Young,*" George said, brightening. "I've met him. Once, anyway."

"Excellent," Arnez said, gently pushing George out and closing the door.

George eventually turned away to see Counselor Mue coming down the hall.

"Amos!" Mue said, surprised and slightly excited simultaneously. "I came to see Doctor Arnez, but seeing you will actually do me better."

"Please, call me George," George said. "Um, Counselor—could you take me to the cafeteria again?"[130]

"Oh, certainly," Mue said, agreeing. "And I might ask you a couple of questions along the way, if you're up for it."

Mue turned and started walking, presumably toward the cafeteria.

"Yes?" George asked, speeding up momentarily so that he would be walking up alongside Mue. "Well, I suppose everyone will have their questions. Go ahead."

Mue was then silent for a moment before he spoke; he was trying to figure out how to phrase his next question.

"So, *George*, do you now remember who you are and everything?"[131] Mue asked sincerely. "No gaps at all?"

"Yes, well I think so," George said, nodding. "I mean, it's hard to think about what one doesn't know."

"Fair enough," Mue said, smiling. "Let me ask you then: why did you write… what *does* 'don't forget the lemon' mean?"

George laughed out loud, somewhat surprising Mue. "*Don't forget the lemon?* Ha! I didn't expect that! Well," he said, taking a moment to think. "It means exactly what it says, I suppose."

"Yes, but I mean is: why is that sentence special to *you?*"

"Oh. Well, that…it's really kind of silly. Why do you ask?"

"No reason; nothing special…I was skimming through this book and happened across something that said something similar[132] and I wondered about your reasoning, your motivation."

"It would take a while to explain," George admitted. "It's from an adventure game called 'Dozens of Dragons.' Some friends and I were having a session, and the moment it was spoken, it left us all rolling with laughter. My friends and I have said it to one another ever since. Like an in-joke. It wouldn't make much sense without explaining the whole story, and I don't think you want to hear the whole

---

130[Δ] it so happens that Mue took George to the cafeteria within the laboratory once before, and thus why he asks "again."

131[Δ] the last time they were together, George could not remember much of anything, even his own name.

132[▲] not similar, *identical*, as he happened across the *exact same* sentence in Martin's play, described as written by a person by the *same name*, and it was testing Mue's sanity.

story just to get the correct context. Besides, when someone tells a story about an event, it's never as good as having been at the actual event."

"Depends on the storyteller," Mue observed.

"Well, the interest depends on the audience," George replied.

"Clearly it depends on both," Mue agreed. "And you can spare me the game anecdote, for you are correct—I'm not interested. That *does* help, however, so thank you, and here's the cafeteria."

Mue left George and walked away quite satisfied. As he walked back to his office, his heart began to slow down. Mue's primary fear had been that George would mention Hypnos, which would then suggest that Martin's absurd play is actually a viable, prophetic description of an absolutely horrific reality: a reality where humanity is now being groomed for no reason other than to feed to some abominable, misshapen titan that sits in the darkest corner of creation and hungers without rest.

Dozens of Dragons, Mue thought to himself, amused. *I need to relax. Perhaps I'll have a cup of orange tea and a hot shower before I return to that confounded play? Yes, I think. Oh, and now I need to grab* **donuts**.

Chapter 27:

English Muffins

JUNE *2070 EST*

Sat 14	Sun 15	Mon 16
	16:24	

As George walked into the cafeteria, his nose was immediately gratified with the ambient bouquet.

*Well, I certainly never thought I would see **this** place again,* he mused as he entered the buffet line.

Every item was attractive and well stocked.

Upon examining the various offerings, he found that really *everything* looked quite appetizing, and then soon afterward he *also* found that he was having some difficulty fitting his many selections upon his tray.

There was no attendant at the end of the line, although there *was* a quaint little cup that offered the following expression: Have a joke? Leave a joke. Need a joke? Too bad: you can't take a joke.

There were several folded pieces of paper sticking out of the cup's mouth, so George grabbed one and opened it up. On it read: "Your mom." [133Δ]

*When **did** I eat last?* George wondered as he wandered over to a table and sat down. *What time is it? Gosh, what **day** is it? I feel fine—didn't I get hurt in the fight? Was **that** a dream?*

George started checking himself all over, searching for tenderness or pain.

"Forget something?" Said a nearby man.

133Δ the cup is normally empty, these pages were only recently placed by a man known as Floyd.

"Sorry?" George asked as it occurred to him what his probing must have looked like. "Oh, no. I—well, I was wondering if I was hurt."

"You were wondering if you were *hurt*?" The man asked, now coming over to George's table. George was happy to see that it was Young. "You mean you don't *know*? Are you normally impervious to harm or something?"

"Hardly," George said, chuckling. "No, I just—"

"Fee, Fie, Foe, Fum!" Another man said boisterously, startling George for he was standing directly behind him. "I smell the butter of your English muffin!" The man then scooped it up from George's tray.

"My English—"

"That's not an English muffin, you bread-head!" Young said, now sitting down across from George. "It's a crumpet."

The boisterous thief sat down next to George. His nametag read "Floyd." [134]

"It is?" He frowned and tossed the bread back onto George's tray. "How droll."

"What's the difference?" George asked.

"Muffins are toasted on both sides; yours is only grilled on the one side, see?" Young pointed.

George moved the muffin so that he could observe it better. "Yes, I see. Is that all?"

"Yes," Floyd said.

"No," Young corrected.

"Moo," Anderson [135] said in his thick, bass voice.

Everyone turned to see Anderson sticking his hairy blonde head between Floyd and George.

"I suppose you'd like to sit *here*," Floyd said with some annoyance, moving to the next seat.

"Skims," Anderson said, sitting down next to George and started sloppily fixing his hair. "Scrubby deckers."

"*Anyway*," Young said, taking back over the conversation before Anderson so rudely interrupted. "There's no yeast or sourdough in a crumpet, merely baking soda—so it's much more like a biscuit than bread."

---

134 George knew Floyd as well as he knew Young, which is to say that he did not know either of them well at all, having met the both of them only once before.

135 *WHO?* Anderson is one of the many residents of the laboratory. He is unique in that he is neither a Subject nor is he a member of the faculty: Anderson is an Agent who went mad—although harmlessly mad—and now is kept safe in the laboratory, generally found either in the cafeteria or running through the halls.

"Biscuits *are* bread," Floyd said reprovingly.

"No they're not."

"Yes, they are."

"If they were the same, we would call biscuits bread."

"*I* call biscuits bread."

"Yeah? You ever place an order for bread and have someone give you biscuits?"

"*Biscuits are bread*," Floyd said resolutely.

"*You* threw the crumpet," Young observed. "You obviously agree that there's a difference, and therefore also between biscuits and bread."

"One has nothing to do with the other," Floyd sniffed. "And besides, I didn't want to starve Andrew," Floyd said, motioning at George.

Young looked at George's heaping tray.

"Oh. You can have the muffin—crumpet," George said, offering it up. "And my name is actually George."

"Dakota," Anderson said, taking the bread.

"He was giving that to *me*," Floyd said, taking it away from Anderson. "But I don't want it," he continued and then handed it back to George.

"Oh, well, I don't want it either," George said as he started to hand it back to Anderson.

"Why *not*?" Floyd challenged. "Because *I* touched it?"

"Well, no—"

"Well, you *obviously* wanted it *before I* touched it, otherwise you wouldn't have put it on your tray in the first place."

"He's got you there," Young agreed, munching on his celery. "Better eat it and not hurt his feelings."

George looked at his now well-travelled crumpet as Theseus showed up at the table.

"George!" Theseus said, smiling. He looked at the others at the table. "Floyd and Young, why am I not surprised? What, do you two *live* in the cafeteria? I swear you are always here."[136Δ]

"Not always," Young said between bites.

"I do lots of things," Floyd defended. "And what's *your* excuse, anyway, *The-essee-yoos*? You're right here with us, and you *escaped*!" He smiled triumphantly. "*Clearly* you like the cafeteria more than we do."

136Δ although Theseus was more familiar with Floyd and Young than George was, he was not *much* more familiar.

"Yeah, we wouldn't come back for *this* porridge," Young said, pointing to his plate.

"I'm *so* tired of oatmeal," Floyd added.

"I'm not here for the *food*," Theseus said, shaking his head.

"Then, why are you holding a tray of it?"

Theseus looked at his own heaping tray and sat down. "Because I am hungry. Listen, you're missing—"

"Listen!" Anderson warned, slamming his hand down. "I've got grumpy pumpkins!"

"Next time, *we're* escaping," Young said, pulling everyone out of their momentary distraction with Anderson. "And *you guys* can stay here."

"You didn't see what was waiting on the other side of the door," Theseus said somberly as he started to eat his oatmeal. "You wouldn't have survived. *We* only managed out of luck, really. Not even all of us: Francois is dead, in case no one knows."

"Vortron[137Δ] is *dead*?" Young asked in disbelief. He was silent for a moment before he spoke up in realization. "Martin's going to be crushed."

"*Who*?" George asked.

"Martin's a Subject," Young said, clarifying. "He's been working on this play, and Vortron was a big part of it. He'll be pretty upset, I'm sure."

"Has anyone seen *Simon*?" Theseus asked after he finished an entire glass of juice.

"I'm afraid not."

"Nope."

"The gobble blaster?"

"You mean *today*?" Floyd asked. "No."

"We need to find him."

"Why?"

"Well, he's our friend," Theseus began, but immediately saw the looks forming on Young and Floyd's faces. "I mean, *you're* our friends, too, of course! Merely that the three of us have been through life and death together now, and have decided to form a super-team, um, if you will, and, well, we need to rescue our teammate."

"Seems like you need rescuing yourselves," Floyd said a bit jeeringly.

"Fair," Theseus acceded. "So we do. Perhaps you two would like to join our team? Add to our strength?"

"And be part of a team that can't save themselves much less anyone else?"

137Δ "Vortron" is an alternate name—a hero name—that the now-deceased "Francois" used to call himself.

Floyd laughed. "No thanks, I don't want to lose the few perks I get around here."

"*Perks?*" Theseus laughed. "Like *what?*"

"Well, privacy for one."

"Privacy? *What* privacy? There's no privacy here."

"There is if no one thinks you're a threat," Floyd said knowingly. "Thanks to your pathetic little escape attempt, I *guarantee* you'll be watched *all* the time now."

"That means even in the *bathroom*," Young said while crinkling up his nose.

"Mildred *Stew*," Anderson explained seriously.

"So I suppose you won't be trying anything for a long while," Floyd forecasted. "Probably even have you flagged in the Mainframe. Face it, you're done. No more hero team for you kids."

"We'll see," Theseus said determinedly. "The Mainframe can't stop us; we just need to find Simon."

"Actually, now that I'm thinking on it," Floyd said thoughtfully. "I'm very surprised you're allowed to just walk around so freely so soon after your *escape*."

"*Well*, the rhetoric *I* am being fed is that we were *allowed* to escape," Theseus said, rolling his eyes. "Which I know, of course, to be utter nonsense."

"How do you know *that*?" Young asked. "Maybe they *did* let you go. Maybe they've just been watching you the whole time."

"Nah. We definitely escaped."

"Says *you*," Floyd taunted.

"No, we did. Trust me, they didn't *let* us go," Theseus said as he stacked his saucers and plates. "Although I certainly wouldn't have been able to leave, were it not for the Rook...yet, I suppose in turn *he* could leave only because of *me*." Theseus reflected again for a moment as he finished his food. "To be honest, I'm not really sure *how* we'll manage to escape again, for the last time we were only ultimately successful *because* of him. Without the Rook, we would be as dead as Francois." He paused for another moment. "You know, now that I think on it, *many* of the questions Mommy just asked me revolved more around the Rook than they did *me*."

"Me too," George piped up. "Most of the questions I answered were about him."

Anderson then stood up rather suddenly, causing his chair to topple behind him. He started audibly whimpering as he ran toward the exit. "*Geronimo!*" He yelled as he nearly collided with someone.

"I *do* believe that Anderson has to use the restroom," Floyd announced.

As Anderson went scrambling through the doorway, a man wearing an auspicious pair of boots stepped around him and into the room. It was Martin, and he did not seem too happy at the moment.

"*Help*," he pleaded, when he arrived at the table.

"What's the matter?" Young asked, standing up. "Are you okay?"

"*Of course* I'm not okay!" Martin hissed. "Why *else* would I ask for help?"

"Well, we didn't know if it was for *you*, or if maybe you were asking on *someone else's* behalf," Floyd suggested.

"I need help," Martin said, visibly trying to calm down. "Will you help me? Please?"

"I'll help you," Young offered.

"You're *already* helping me, thanks," Martin said kindly. "I need *more* help—I need *your* help!" He said, turning to point at Theseus.

"*My* help?"

"And *your* help!" He added, pointing to Floyd.

"Oh *no*! *I'm* not acting in your play!" Floyd said, rebuffing Martin.

"But I need *two* people!" Martin pleaded. "*Roland* started a fire, so he's in detention, and now *Philemon* is sick and can't come to rehearsal.[138Δ] I *need* players!"

"Take *him*," Floyd said as he shrugged and pointed at George.

"No, I couldn't," George said as quickly.

"*Of course* not," Martin sniffed. "That's alright, you don't look like any of my characters *anyway*. I'll just have to have Francois double-up."

"Oh," Young said, and pressed his hand to his mouth.

"Yeah, hey buddy, I've got some bad news about Francois," Floyd said, standing up.

"What's wrong with Francois?" Martin asked as the color started to drain from his face.

Everyone looked at one another with mixed expressions, but none spoke, so the room stayed awkwardly quiet. George made up his mind to simply tell Martin the truth when Theseus started speaking.

"Francois escaped," Theseus said matter-of-factly. "He got out. He won't be back for rehearsal, like ever…but *I'll* help you. It's not like we're escaping any

---

138Δ Roland and Philemon are other laboratory Subjects that are helping Martin produce his play. It wouldn't serve you to put too much thought into them as it is unlikely that they will be mentioned again.

time soon *anyway*, so I may as well help a brother out."

"You think *you* can replace *Francois?*" Martin asked, momentarily aghast. "I've never heard a man use a more perfect accent!" Then he seemed to reconsider his position. "You'll do, I suppose. Well. Good for Francois. Bad timing, though."

"I'll help with the stage, just not the acting," George suggested.

Martin raised an eyebrow. "Oh, well you're just shy, aren't you? I suppose that will help as well, thank you. Young, can you play *two* characters?"

"I suppose," Young said, shrugging. "At least until Philemon[139] gets back."

"How much longer do you have for rehearsals?" Theseus asked, standing up.

"Another week," Martin said, smiling. "*Plenty* of time."

"Another *week?*" Floyd asked. "I was thinking maybe I *would* help, but my time is precious. Out of curiosity, though: if I *were* to help, how are you paying?"

Martin laughed a deep-hearted laugh. "*Paying?* Are you kidding? With *what:* words of affirmation? Listen, this is an opportunity that is going to provide you with great *exposure*! That *is* the payment!"

---

[139] unlikely that they will be mentioned again *after this page*, that is.

Chapter 28:

The Vile Shepherd

JUNE *2070 EST*

Sat 14	Sun 15	Mon 16
	16:54	

The rows of chairs addressing the stage were devoid of occupants, save for two: toward the middle of the mass sat Floyd, who was looking onward satisfactorily, and in the other—which, incidentally, was much closer to the stage—sat Martin, who in contrast looked very uncomfortable.

"No, no, no!" Martin yelled as he waved some pages around. "*You're* supposed to be a scary pig-man," he said to one actor, "and *you're,*" he coughed and said to another, "*you're* supposed to be cowering in fear, *not* looking at him as if you might invite him to tea!"

"Well, *I* have to use the restroom!" The actor playing the monster responded. "And I can't act scary if I'm going to pee my pants!"

"Is *that* why you look like that?" The other actor mused. "I thought you forgot what scene we were in," he said but then changed his tone. "Since we're rehearsing them *out of order!*"

"Treat it like a flashback," Floyd called out, but shrank back in his chair when Martin shot him a look.[140Δ]

[140Δ] on the way to the theater, Martin mentioned several times—somewhat angrily— that Floyd was unwilling to *help*, but all too eager and happy to *watch*. Floyd eventually responded that although his time was indeed valuable, he didn't have anything else to do at the moment, so he would watch.

"Just be sure to watch and *not speak,*" warned Martin. "And admission is going to cost you 2 packs of oatmeal."

"Admission for a *rehearsal?*" Floyd asked with slight outrage.

"*Actors* get in for *free,*" Martin said smugly. "If you want to eavesdrop on *my* opus, you'll have to pay for the privilege."

"Well we can't rehearse in order until everyone arrives," Martin said as an anxious-looking woman ran in through the door.

"Sorry I'm late," she said to Martin, blushing. "Doctor Mommy was screaming and breaking things down the hallway, so I had to come around the other way."

"Yes, alright, Alicia—let's take it from the top," Martin ordered. "Everyone get into position for scene one, please."

"Oh, but I'm not in costume," she said, lifting up her dress.

"That doesn't really matter right now; we need to make the most of our time. Counselor Mue will be back, and I would like to be at the point—or around—when he left."[141Δ]

"So then, why are we starting back at the beginning?" She asked. "Shouldn't we simply start at a later point?"

"Well, no," Martin said, looking thoughtful. "Practice *is* important, after all, and, well, *some* people have a difficult time rehearsing *out of order*."

"Well, it would *at least* make it more understandable to the *audience* if we did everything *in order*," the insulted actor responded.

"*What* audience?" Martin asked, waving at the vacant seats.

Floyd raised his hand.

"You stay out of this," Martin warned.

"Hey, I paid you two perfectly good bags of oatmeal!" Floyd nearly yelled. "I should get to know what the heck is going on!"

"Good luck," the pig-man-actor said dismissively.

"You watch yourself," Martin warned, "or I'll find someone else to take your part!"

The pig-man-actor sulked off the stage. The other actor jogged after his companion to console him, and Alicia left to get into costume.

"He sure is bossy for someone who was just begging for help an hour ago," Floyd said to Young, who had only just slid into the seat next to him. "People who genuinely need help do not criticize the help they are given."

"It's Mue," Young said, whispering. "Martin really wants to impress him."

Alicia returned, wearing a skin-tight, flesh-colored, full-body leotard that was either deliberately a bit too small or Alicia had no sense of decency.

141Δ Mue left the earlier rehearsal prematurely and without comment: he was mentally chewing on "Don't forget the lemon," and his manners escaped him.

"Oh. My," Floyd said and became silent for more reasons than one.

Alicia stood, unmoving and silent, in the center of the stage for a full three minutes. Then a man wearing similarly colored and equally inappropriately sized tights—and wings—was lowered onto the stage to kneel in front of her. Nothing changed for an entire two minutes, where the man then looked up at Alicia and then immediately back down. Then nothing happened again for a full minute, after which the winged man is raised up and off of the stage—presumably flying—out of view. The curtains closed.

"*What*…in the *hell*…was *that*?" Floyd cried from his seat, the bewilderment in his voice plain.

"*That*," Martin responded, his voice thick with sarcasm, "is 'show, don't tell.'"

"What kind of play *is* this? Interpretive?"

"It's a tale of love and madness."

"I see. Where did you get your inspiration from? *Statues*?"

"I had a dream," Martin said with conviction. "And have been having dreams which I have then been writing down as books."[142Δ]

"Books?"

"Yes, well first I write it all down in the books like I'm writing a novel, but then I *rewrite* it all as the play."

"*Books*? Is it a *long* play, then?" Floyd asked, worried. "Like, *hours and hours*?"

Martin pulled out three books and placed them on his desk.

"*Days and days?*" Floyd then asked in correction.

"Oh, ha ha. It's like a couple hours—it would have been longer, but I had to drop my narrative, the prologue, *and* the midlogue."

"What's a *midlogue*?"

Martin sighed. "It's the midpoint between the prologue and the epilogue."

"What's an *epilogue*?"

"Really? Hmm. If the reader were to be given a glimpse as to how the story extended beyond the tale itself, it would be shown in the *epilogue*. It's an after-the-end 'the end,' if you will."

"Wait, so what does all that have to do with 'show, don't tell?'"

142Δ Young suggested that *he* was an expert on dreams, but everyone ignored him.

"Well—"

"I think you're supposed to mostly use *dialogue* to 'show, don't tell,' aren't you?" George asked, walking up from behind the curtain.

"*There **was no** dialogue,*" Martin hissed at George. "You can't use dialogue if there's none!"

Before George could speak, Martin spoke up again—although he may have been speaking to himself. "What we need is a *narrator*; what we *need* is a prologue!"

"*I* hear that people hate prologues," George began, but his mouth went silent as Martin's face turned to absolute rage.

"You're fired," Martin said, in an unnaturally calm voice. "Pack your things and go."

George considered arguing but then thought better of it. Instead of leaving, however, he ended up joining Floyd and Young.

As the curtains swept back aside,[143Δ] the winged man flew down to stand near an empty feather bed.

Then nothing happened for two minutes.

"*Where is Pasithea?*" Martin asked, annoyed.

Alicia, now with a different wig on, ran over and lay down upon the bed. The winged man waited a moment before taking up a bow and shooting her in the chest.

"OW!" Alicia yelled, sitting up and rubbing herself at the point of impact. "What the hell, Paxton?!"

"I'm sorry," the winged man—Paxton—said. "I forgot."

"You *always* forget!" Alicia accused. "I'm getting pretty bloody tired of this, Martin! Why can't he use a *fake* bow and just have him stand a bit closer?"

"I'm sorry," Martin began, sounding again full of frustration. "Does it say 'fake bow' in the script? The show must go on, *darlings*,[144▲] whether you get hurt or not you must continue to *act* as if nothing is wrong. Was *Francois* the *only*

143Δ now operated by Alicia since George was just fired. There were numerous other actors about, but few of them understood or practiced teamwork—although this sad behavior is present probably because most of them were only involved with the play due to Martin's persuasion rather than by their own initiative.

144▲ pronounced in the same manner as Dr. Mommy.

professional amongst the lot of you?"

"Where *is* Francois?" Alicia asked. "He's usually the first one here."

"I'm his understudy," Theseus said, walking out from the back of the stage. "Francois is sick."

"I thought you said he escaped," Martin said in disbelief.

"He *did*," Theseus said reaffirming his earlier lie. "I just told *her* that so we wouldn't have to repeat the earlier conversation."

"Whatever. I don't care, anyway," Alicia said dismissively. "Francois's a jerk."

"Okay, can we move forward, then?" Martin asked, sitting back down. "Alright, everyone, from the top."

"Oh, Martin," Alicia said, not laying back down into position. "I just can't do a love scene now. I'm hurt and the scene is ruined—"

"Because *you*—" Martin began, but Alicia took back over.

"*Not* 'because *me*!' *Because* Paxton shot me in the tit. Again. Hard. And I'm *tired* of it, Martin!"

"Okay, okay," Martin said, holding his hands up in surrender. "The scene is ruined, let's move on to the next. Everyone into positions, from the top of scene three."

The stage was quickly attended to, and after the curtains parted Paxton once again "flew" down to the stage. In the center stood only Alicia, wearing a pink robe and a new wig.

Everyone was silent for a few minutes until Martin blew up.

"*Where* are the *other* two Fates?" He demanded.

Everyone looked around, but no one said anything.

"That's fine," Martin said, now masking his anger and contempt. "We'll just skip this scene as well."

"Oh, but Marty!" Alicia pleaded, taking on a completely different tone than the last time she addressed him. "I love this scene! We can't skip it!"

"I love it too, luv, but we are missing two out of three fates. It can't be done."

"I can do it! I know every word in the scene…it'll be less confusing coming from a single character, anyway," Alicia suggested.

"Less confusing, perhaps, but then it will also make less sense. No, we're going to move forward, or rather, let's take a moment to review the fight scenes again. Gods, if you will, places please."

Paxton, now covered head-to-toe in black, walked out with another man following directly behind him. They took alternate places on stage.

"Okay, Hypnos: leap at Pothos!" Martin commanded.

The actors collided and struggled with one another while Floyd leaned over to Young and started talking.

"He looks like *Axel*," he observed.
"It's supposed to *be* Axel," Young validated.
"I thought he said Potholes."
"Pothos: that's Axel's real name—at least, it is in Martin's play."
"I don't understand anything that's going on," Floyd admitted. "This is the worst oatmeal I've ever spent."
"Yeah, we're kind of jumping all over. Martin seems really…I don't know. Off."

Young looked up to see Martin standing nearby, cross-armed and frowning.

"*Off* course," Young continued, perhaps a bit louder. "It's probably just that Francois isn't here—he really made the whole play."

The last comment seemed to appease Martin, who walked back down toward the front. Young let out a sigh of relief.
The doors to the hallway opened, and in stepped Counselor Mue and Anderson.

"Counselor Mue!" Martin called out, his voice suddenly softer. "Welcome back! Alright everyone, let's take a quick moment to rest and get our bearings."
"What in the *burger*?" Anderson boomed as he stomped up alongside Mue, obviously upset. "Having an upper case, are we? *You dried out the matches?*"
"Yes, it seems Anderson's a bit perturbed," Mue said as he made his way over to the trio in the middle seats. "I found him near the restrooms barking at the hallway clock. He followed me here, grumbling—I think now about you—the entire way."

Mue placed a white paper box on the seat between himself and Floyd and sat down.

"What's in the box?" Floyd asked.

"Donuts."

"Can I have one?"

"*May* I have one," Mue corrected as he sat down.

"*May* I have one?"

"No, they're for Doctor Sanderson."

"Doctor Sanderson?"

"He'll be here…shortly, maybe."

Anderson marched up to Martin and looked him up and down while breathing in a slightly exaggerated manner.

"Okay, buddy," Martin said soothingly and put his hand on Anderson's shoulder. "You can be in the play."

Anderson's shoulders relaxed as his face grew a large smile. His breathing fell silent.

"How do you know what he wants?" Paxton said, scratching his head. "It always seems like nonsense to me."

"It is," Martin said, nodding and agreeing. "I just go with tone of voice, mostly. I very much doubt he understands what I am telling him, pretty sure he just responds to my *manner*."

Martin turned back to Anderson, but immediately dropped to the ground when he saw that Anderson had taken in a tremendous amount of breath.

"YAHTZEEE!" Anderson yelled in delight, blasting everything in front of him with a powerful, reverberating voice. A portion of the orchestra pit then exploded spectacularly and everyone's ears immediately started ringing.

"Holy *shit*, Anderson!" Floyd yelled, trying to overcome his transitory hearing impairment. "I thought we told you not to do that anymore!"

Anderson's face turned beet red. "Buttered *toast*," he explained penitently as his eyes began to water.

"No, that's not good enough," Martin said, admonishing him further. "That's what you said the last time.[145Δ] You're going to have to go to your room. Go on, then: go to your room!"

145Δ *actually,* what he said last time was: "Forty freakin' Kwanzaas."

Anderson sulked off, slamming the door behind him as he left.

After allowing everyone's ears a few more minutes to settle, Martin called everyone into position to practice the next fight scene.

Theseus walked out onto the stage to see Martin's face twist into disappointment.

"And who are *you* supposed to be?" Martin asked Theseus.

"I'm 'The Soose,' remember?" Theseus asked, looking somewhat confused: after all, it was *Martin* who had told him what character he was playing.

"Didn't you get a wig?"

"Yeah, a red one—it was really itchy."

"Whether it itches or not, the problem is that you have *black* hair," Martin said, gesturing at Theseus' head. "and 'The Soose' has *red* hair."

"So, *the Soose's* hair color is relevant to the progression of the story?"

"Well, no, I suppose not in particular," Martin admitted as he reflected.

"Then what does it matter?" Theseus asked genuinely.

"Well, it's not how it's *written*."

"Yet, it makes no difference if my hair is red or black—it's only important that I perform in the *manner* of the character. Really, maybe you shouldn't bother with giving characters hair colors if they don't matter to the story—maybe it's *limiting* your story by littering it with particulars that are irrelevant."

"It's about *visualization*—"

"But you said it doesn—"

"Think of it as a way to help the readers, then…so that they don't have to flex their imaginations unnecessarily."

"But it's a *play*."

"Please don't argue with me," Martin said with a hint of exhaustion. "Just put the blasted wig on and get ready to fight."

Theseus went to retrieve his wig.

"You're nicer to him than you are to *us*," Paxton said from under his costume.

"That's because *we* have gotten more familiar with one another over all of our practices together. Theseus is new."

"We have had, like, *three and a half* practices together."

"*Four* and a half. But they were *long* practices."

"Sti—"

"Oh, *do* shut up, Paxton! You're not even part of this scene! Hell, the reason the practices run long are because of *you,* anyway! Like this ridiculous banter *right* now, or like the other day when you wanted to redo the scene because you forgot your makeup, and nobody can even see your sorry face!"

Paxton silently left the stage as Alicia walked on. Alicia now wore a purple wig, and was wearing clothing nearly identical to what Wonda wore when she attacked the party.

George nearly choked.

"Are you alright?" Young asked concernedly.

"Yes, I think so. What scene is this?"

"It's one of the fight scenes," Young said. "We only did it once, and that was earlier today. I don't even know what comes after it, but that's because the play's not done."

"Not done?" Floyd asked. "How can it not be done?"

"My thoughts exactly," Mue added, speaking up. "Martin insists that it's *nearly* done, though, and that it will be done on time."

"How can you properly rehearse a play that is *nearly* done?" Floyd asked, growing increasingly upset.

"Well, we just rehearse the parts that *are* done," Young suggested, inadvertently defending Martin.

"Oh, of all the—!" Floyd said, throwing himself back in his seat. "I want a refund!"

"Oh, take a donut and calm down," Mue said, irritated with Floyd's reaction.

Floyd did not hesitate to take a donut. He bit into it unhappily, but changed his demeanor when the sugar registered in his brain.

Another actor walked out on the stage. At first, George thought it was Simon, but then he noticed it wasn't—it just looked like him. A lot like him.

Theseus walked out on stage, sporting his vibrant red wig. He did a double-take when he saw not-Wonda and not-Simon standing there.

"For all the—*where* is *George*?" Martin asked, unhappily.

George experimentally raised his hand.

"Not *you*," Martin said with contempt. "*You* said you didn't *want* to act, remember? Didn't I ask you to leave? What I *mean*, Mr. Prologue, is where is *Sam*—the actor *playing* George! *You* don't even look anything *like* George!"

"Are you *sure*?" George asked, but not so that Martin could hear.

"Sam went to the bathroom," an off-stage actor called. "He said he'd be right back!"

"Good *grief!*" Martin yelled. "*His* restroom breaks are 20 minutes apiece! I am *not* waiting, and I can't do the fight scene without him—he's the whole reason for the attack!"

George, realizing that he was looking at something impossibly familiar, started growing pale as the color faded from him. "Who wins the fight?" He called to Martin. "What happens afterward?"

"*Wait, and see*," Martin said mysteriously, mistaking George's dread for interest.

George twisted uncomfortably as Martin turned his attention back to the play.

"Well, I suppose we'll just pick up where we left off from earlier, then," Martin said, motioning for the current actors to all now leave. "We'll re-rehearse the fight scene when Sam returns. Counselor, where were we when you last left us?"

Mue cleared his throat and glanced over at George. "Let's see: *George* had just woken up from his pig monster dream with Hypnos and wrote down 'Don't forget the lemon.'"

As Mue was speaking, however, George's eyes went wide and soon after he started throwing up. Young immediately offered his assistance as Floyd rapidly shrank back. Theseus saw from across the theater and started jogging over to help.

Mue, who was watching George, very nearly threw up as well.

Impossible, Mue thought and admonished himself. *Greek gods, Kay?*[146Δ] *Get ahold of yourself! How absolutely absurd!*

"Martin," Mue said, interrupting the director. "What *does* happen next? Where's the story going?"

"It's a difficult question, Counselor," Martin began apologetically. "First, you have only seen the first act, and there are three acts to the play…and you kind of need to know it all for any of it to make sense. Second, I haven't written the ending—at least not the ending of the *play*, and third, well, frankly I don't remem-

---

146Δ "Kay" is Counselor Mue's first name.

ber. There's so much material, I can't keep track of it all! That's why I have *books* of notes. I reference them as I need to. So many notes! Kind of funny, but a lot of the time I find myself looking up notes that I *know* that I've referenced before. Heck, sometimes I'm *surprised* to read what's there, even though I wrote it. Ha!"

"*I* don't think that's funny," Floyd grumbled as Martin turned and called for Alicia. "I think it's irresponsible."

"*I* think we should change rows—not to be unnecessarily callous," Mue added for George's sake as he quickly got up and went away. "Save *that* for the janitors; why else do we pay them?"

George also went away, although he went to the restroom rather than another row. Theseus accompanied him.

"Martin, may I see your notes?" Mue asked from his new position.

"You're actually going to *read* my work?" Martin asked, delighted. "But of course, Counselor! Nothing could delight me more!"

"Floyd," Mue said just before Floyd managed to sit back down. "Can you go fetch those for me? I'm far too lazy to do it myself, and you're still up, after all."

Remembering the gratis donut, Floyd agreed. As he arrived to pick up the trilogy, Martin leaned over toward him.

"You like to make jokes, but please, don't make fun of the *actors*," he said in hushed tones. "*Nothing* will destroy one's want to perform more than witnessing their contemporaries mock or condemn them, *or*—heaven forbid—*relish* in their failure."

"I understand," Floyd said, nodding seriously.

Floyd returned and dropped the books into the seat next to Mue, and then finally got to sit back down. He let out an audible sigh of appreciation.

Mue reached over and grabbed the first book. Then it seemed he thought better and exchanged it for the third. He did not start with the beginning, however, he simply read tidbits as he skipped though the material.

"What is all this about tables and Lounges?" Mue called out to Martin.

"Just some notes," Martin said. "I leave little notes, sometimes."

Mue resumed flipping through the book until he settled upon a paragraph just following one of the occasional triangular graphics[147Δ] he had seen on several other pages. This paragraph in particular stood out because the font was noticeably different than anywhere else in the book.

$$\triangle\!\!\!\!\!_{M}$$

As he started reading, he considered for a moment that perhaps he should wait...but he couldn't resist investigating, and he knew—or at least, he *hoped*—that he had nothing to worry about. He continued to read the sentences, but they continued to not say much of anything.

He knew that he probably shouldn't try to read out of context, but he figured it would make sense soon enough, so he just continued to read...although he was a bit apprehensive about what he might actually *find*.

And who is "he", he thought for a moment. *Exactly what I was thinking*, he thought as he read his thoughts.

He could dimly hear Floyd and Young talking nearby, but he didn't hear what they were saying beyond the words "vomit" and "lavatory," mostly because his attention was fixated on the text—the text that *just talked about Floyd and Young*. The text that just said "vomit." *This* text.

It can't be! He thought desperately.

But it was. The text was describing *him*, he realized. He knew who "he" was now—it was *him*: it was Mue.

It's a gag of Martin's, he told himself as he continued to read the sentence telling him what he was thinking. *But*, it occurred to him, *Martin never intended on me **reading** anything, merely **watching** it.*

And these sentences, he analyzed as his sanity started to splinter, *do not say "you," rather, they say "he," and therefore they are not speaking **to** me, instead they speak **of** me. Speak **of** me to **whom**?* He thought while reading his thoughts. *Who **is** this written for? Am... am I reading this **alongside** someone?*

As Mue closed the book, he then imagined a reader imagining him as they read about him, just as the reader imagined him imagining them as they read on.

147Δ $\triangle\!\!\!\!\!_{M}$ known as 'Delta M,' it is the scientific symbol for mirroranium.

△M

What the reader then dismissed as nothing greater than a gimmick of the literature,[148△149▲] Mue embraced as terrifying truth.

*The play is **real**,* he thought, scared and overwhelmed. *Pothos. Pasithea. All of that. Real.*

It can't be!

*But it **is**.*

Which means the entire world is simply being prepared—

Confronted with this impossible, macabre, yet undeniable truth, Mue completely lost his mind.

"I have to go," he started mumbling. "I have to *go*."

Mue wrapped his arms tightly around the book and started walking hurriedly towards the door.

Does this book show my fate?

*Wait a second, I could **use** this book—*

"Counselor!" Martin called as the actors behind him looked on in disappointment. "Are you *leaving*?"

"Oh, Martin," Mue said, blushing as he continued his way toward the exit. "My, my. Yes, yes I'm leaving…I have some papers to grade! It cannot wait…I had forgotten. I'll be back. Later."

"In time for the rest of *this* rehearsal, or the next one?"

"Oh, ha ha. Yes. Rehearsal. Well, see you there. Yes. I'll be back for the one. I'm sorry," he finished as he walked out the door.

148△ *after* they spent a moment unraveling the last sentence.
149▲ even though it *did* happen.

"What a complete *jerk*," Alicia said, completely annoyed.

"Didja read *that*?" Mue said as he walked down an empty hallway. "And *this*? Did you read *this*? Are you watching me *now*?" He said, ending in a half-scream as he rapidly looked around for someone that wasn't there.

He reflected on his own words for a moment and then laughed a perverse laugh before he continued onward.

George recovered himself in the lavatory while Theseus helped him to clean up.

*Hypnos is **real**,* George thought to himself for the twentieth time.

"We need to find Simon," George said as he finished washing up.

"Right now?" Theseus asked. "What about the play?"

"The play, I think, will make me sick if I watch any more of it," George said somewhat ominously.

"Any more? Can you see any *less*?" Theseus laughed. "We barely saw anything whatsoever."

"Be glad, for what we *did* see it looks like a disaster."

"Very well. Where do you want to start, then?"

"Let's start at Doctor Sanderson's office," George said, trying to spit the taste out of his mouth one last time. "Perhaps he's still being questioned as we were."

"Maybe he's in the infirmary," Theseus suggested. "Maybe he's hurt."

"Maybe," George said, nodding. "We'll start with Sanderson and then check the infirmary."

"We could split up," Theseus offered.

"No, we're a *team*…and if I have learned anything, it's that you should *never* split up the team."

Theseus smiled. "You know, I think we really *will* make a most excellent super-team!"

"*If* we ever get out of here," George added.

"How did we get back in the lab, anyway?" Theseus asked as they vacated the restroom.

"And here I thought *you* knew," George said. "We'll compare notes while we look for Sanderson's office."

Chapter 29:

Two Feet Down

JUNE *2070 EST*

Sat 14	Sun 15	Mon 16
	17:52	

Simon awoke to see Dr. Sanderson's fluffy, blond face smiling down at him. For a moment, he had the eerie feeling that the doctor had been standing there, staring at him for a long time…but he dismissed the thought almost as quickly as it came, for the doctor always had such a kind and innocent expression, and was so perpetually friendly one could not help but like him.[150Δ]

"Doctor Sanderson?" Simon asked.

"Ah, good—you're awake!" The doctor beamed. "Welcome back, Simon. Ooh! You had me so worried! But now it's okay, now. Everything is going to be just fine. You're recovering, everyone is back in place, and—oh! Do I have a *cake* in my pocket?"

"I'm back in the lab?" Simon asked, looking around. He did not recognize the room that he was in whatsoever; it looked more like an art studio than an examination room.

"Mmm? Oh yes, of course," Sanderson chuckled and licked his fingers—or so it appeared. "Did you suppose you would see me somewhere other?"

"Well, no. But, this room—" Simon trailed off at a loss for words.

"Yes," Sanderson said, smiling and looking around. "I had this room made for you."

"For me?"

"Yes, so you can paint."

"Oh. Well, that's very nice. Um, w—not that I am *ungrateful*, but may I ask why? I made do pretty well with that little closet I was working in."

"Ah, well, I thought that this room would ultimately serve you better since

---

150Δ with exception to Dr. Mommy, of course.

     - [Without Rest] -

it's designed to be sympathetic to your current condition."

"My *condition*?" Simon asked surprised. "What condition do you mean?"

"*And* it has a lot of nice little extras, too!" Sanderson said, and started walking toward one of the tables.

"Doctor Sanderson!" Simon urged. "What condition am I in?"

"Yes. Hmm. Well, do you perhaps remember some purple-haired woman who was rather recently, um, apparently trying to kill you?"

"Yes," Simon affirmed, remembering the assault of a few hours ago.

"I'm not exactly sure how one might be gentle with such news," Sanderson said, preparing his lie. "So I am sorry to say that during the altercation she apparently cut both of your feet off."

"*What?*" Simon asked, momentarily stunned. He looked down at his legs to see that it was true—his feet were completely missing! Despite his lack of physical pain, his emotional state threatened to crumble. "This is *horrible!*"

"Now, now," Sanderson said in a comforting voice. "Don't worry about it *too* much, Simon: of *course* we'll get you *brand new* augmentations to replace those old feet, and soon you'll step better than you ever stepped before."

Simon thought about it and managed to calm himself down. "You're right," he said, surrendering. Then he laughed just a little. "You know, for a moment you kind of reminded me of that one Noirglass[151Δ] commercial—how does it go? *See less to see more; see better than before!*"

Dr. Sanderson merely smiled.

"I guess I won't be able to escape any time soon," Simon continued, not realizing that his oration was pharmaceutically influenced. "So I suppose I may as well paint then. Oh…I'm hungry."

"*Me too*," Sanderson said appreciatively while rubbing his considerable stomach. "I believe I have some donuts in my future, but I'll have some food sent over for *you* right away."

"Thank you, Doctor Sanderson," Simon said gratefully.

"Now, I have some questions about your escape, some in particular about—" Dr. Sanderson began as a chime sounded. "Oh bother," he said as he furrowed his brow. "Hmm. It seems I have to go now, Simon, but I'll check on you again later tonight…I'll ask those questions then. In the meantime, I imagine you'll be *painting?*"

151Δ Noirglasses are black, Mainframe-driven eyeglasses that filter out color.

"Oh, yes," Simon said, his voice slightly dull from his chemical inebriation. "I'm going to paint. I'm going to paint…what am I going to paint?"

"Whatever suits you," Sanderson said soothingly, stepping out of the room. "Paint something *divine*."

Chapter 30:

Out of Costume

JUNE *2070 EST*

Sat 14	Sun 15	Mon 16
	18:24	

Dr. Sanderson was walking down the hallway in his regular, nonchalant fashion when Counselor Mue came briskly around the corner.

"Oh!" Sanderson said with delight. "Counselor Mue! Why, how very—" he continued, but then trailed off when he saw Mue reel back in what looked like fear. "Are you alright, Counselor? *Do you have the donuts?*"

"It's all true!" Mue started screaming at Sanderson. "It's all true! It's all TroooOOOOoooo!"

"Oh, my! Counselor Mue? Are you well?" Sanderson said with concern.

"I *know* who YOU are," Mue said, his eyes going as wide as one could imagine possible. "I KNOW WHO YOU ARE!"

"Yes," Sanderson chuckled, "I should certainly hope s—"

"Pothos," Mue giggled, causing Sanderson to fall immediately silent. "You're *Pothos.*"

"Counselor—"

"It's all in Martin's play! ALL OF IT. Even me—*I'm* part of it! But it's not *about* me…it's about *you!*"

Sanderson smiled silently and continued to look fluffy and innocent.

"And *you!*" Mue said ominously, pointing first in accusation, and then in shaky dread. "*You...*"

"Kay," Doctor Sanderson began, but Mue spoke before he could continue.
"Axel," Mue said soberly, but then busted out laughing.

Sanderson was silent for a moment before he spoke again.

"If you *truly* believed that, then you would know—"
"*PLEASE* kill me!" Mue cried and then laughed nervously. He clutched the book to his chest and looked around at everything as if he had never seen any of it before. "Better here and now than to that…*thing*…in the pit—that thing in *Tartarus*!"

"Counselor," Sanderson said in his friendliest tone. "You know, now that I'm thinking of it: if you would accompany me back to my office, I have something I would like to show you."
Mue looked completely miserable. "Only if you promise to kill me."

Dr. Sanderson looked surprised and dismayed.

"You need to promise!" Mue demanded, tears starting to stream down his cheeks. "*Promise* you'll kill me! And quickly, too—you can't draw it out! I've worked too hard for you to treat me poorly!"
"Alright, calm down, calm down," Sanderson said, putting his arm around Mue. "*Of course* I'll kill you, Counselor. However you want—just not in the *hallway*, of course."
Mue sniffled as he reflected for a moment. "That makes sense. Okay."

"*What happened to my actors?*" Martin asked, visibly upset. "How can I possibly be expected to put on a play if I can't get people together long enough for a bloody rehearsal?"

The actors moped around the stage aimlessly.

Martin then changed his tone. "Alright! Let's get into places for the first visit to Harpocrates."

"Can't we do something *new*?" Paxton asked. "I'm kind of wondering where the story is going."

"Well, me too!" Martin said unhappily. "But Mue took my third book of notes, and I can't draft a new scene unless I re-read the material first. So. Harpocrates. First visit."

Everyone reluctantly moved into different positions.

Floyd turned to Young. "I've been thinking…let me ask you this: do you think that Cuatro Bueno is holy water?"

Young finished chewing his recently stolen donut. "What's *Cuatro Bueno*?"[152A]

"HAR POCK RAH TEEZ!" Martin yelled, startling both Young and Floyd simultaneously.

Young looked up, his face beet red. Jumping up, he shoved the last of the donut into his mouth and started up toward the stage.

"*And* out of costume?" Martin continued, exasperated.

"If there's a sequel, will it be *The Vile-r Shepherd*?" Floyd asked, taunting Martin.

Martin ignored him.

"Or maybe a trilogy? *The Vile-est Shepherd*?"

"Vile-est is not a word," Martin sniffed. "And it can't be a trilogy, or even a sequel."

Why not?" Floyd challenged. "I thought you were dreaming up the story as you went…I thought it wasn't done yet."

"I am, it's not—but I know there won't be a sequel."

"Maybe someone *else* will write the sequel," Floyd suggested.

"How can anyone *else* write a sequel to *my* work? It's *my* dream."

"Well, maybe they have a dream, too."

"They can make a play out of their dream, then."

"What if their dream is to write a sequel to your play?"

Martin frowned. "Their *dream* is to write a sequel to *my* play?" Martin thought about that for a minute as Young—now in a new costume—came out on

---

[152A] Cuatro Bueno is water, bottled and distributed by 'Blessed Brands,' which is an international company that claims that all of their products have been prayed over. "*A prayer because we care—to be **sure** it's **pure**.*"

stage. "No, that's flattering, but it still doesn't work. What if several people had dreams to write sequels? Which one would be right? No, they need to just go do their own things, and leave this one as it is."

"But, what if you die?" Floyd asked with a mouth full of donut. "Then what? Will the play continue? Will the show go on?"

"Well, I'm not dead," Martin said finally after some thought. He turned his attention back to the stage but finished with: "So it doesn't matter."

"Well, *I'm* going to write the sequel to your play after you die!" Floyd jeered.

"Oh no you're not!" Martin said, turning back around.

"Oh, yef I am!" Floyd said, accidentally spitting out donut and smiling large. "The Vile Shepherd II – *Masters of Oatmeal*."

"Oh, he's just baiting you," Paxton said, brushing his costume wing aside. "Don't pay attention, Martin."

"You're right," Martin admitted, turning back around. "Alright, let's do this scene. Remember now," he said to Young.[153A] "Harpocrates is the most important character in the play; we need his scenes to be *flawless*."

"Harpocrates is the *most important* character?" Young asked, genuinely confused. "Does he come back in later on or something? He's barely in the play."

"True, he is *barely* in the play, but that doesn't prevent him from being the most important. Consider what Pothos did. Out of any and all measures that he might take: why *that* one?"

"Yeah, but the writing is bad," Paxton said, immediately wishing he had chosen slightly different words. Nevertheless, he continued. "I mean, it doesn't line up: if Pothos sealed Harpocrates away forever, and closed all the doorways to get to him, how could anyone know anything at all? Wouldn't it be a *secret*, and all secrets are safely locked away?"

"Ah, but you forget about Pothos' mirror!" Martin said knowingly. "Anyone who found it might then in turn discover the fate of Harpocrates. Perhaps they could not emancipate him, but they might *hear* him, should he choose to speak."

"I don't know. That seems like a lot of maybes. Besides, Pothos wouldn't just leave his mirror lying around for anyone to find."

"Agreed, but you forget that he may have buried it, or perhaps even misplaced it very early afterward, for you'll notice that it never comes up again. If he hid it, nothing that is buried stays buried forever. And if he lost it, eventually that which was lost will be found. And so, we know that it *was* found."

"How do we know *that*? Is that in the play?" Paxton asked, not remember-

---

153A He said to Young, for Young was not the original actor portraying Harpocrates. The primary actor was Francois.

ing anything to that degree.

"No, but we *do* know about the fate of Harpocrates, and therefore someone *did* find the mirror, otherwise *we* wouldn't know."

"Martin," Young began soberly. "You don't actually *believe* that the play you are writing is *real*, do you?"

"Of course not!" Martin replied, laughing in surprise at the question. "It's just dreams. But, I *did* dream that someone found it, I just didn't add it because it didn't matter to the story."

The door opened, and everyone fell silent. Doctor Sanderson walked in, smiling and waving. He had not gone three steps when he stumbled over his fat, little legs, and almost fell into the chairs.

"Oh, hoo hoo!" He laughed and righted himself. "Don't worry about lil' ol' me, I'm fine." Then Sanderson looked at the book he dropped on the floor. "Oh, bother," he said, picking it up.

Sanderson clumsily fought his way between the seats to sit down next to Floyd. "Oh, don't stop on my account," he said, and then pulled a crushed box of donuts out from under his posterior. "What happened here? Why is this box crushed?"

"Because you sat on it," Floyd observed.

"Oh. So I did," Sanderson agreed, slowly lifting the flap. "Donuts!"

Another actor, dressed in the most outrageous checkerboard clothing, stepped out onto the stage. "*I* want to be Harpocrates!" He demanded.

"What?" Martin asked, looking up at the new man.

"I *hate* my character," he said dejectedly as he gestured to himself. "Practically right after I appear *I get killed*. You don't introduce a character just to kill them off. You know, some people get really upset when stuff like that happens."

"Regardless. Sometimes there are simply a few brief characters. I tell you, it is not as important to please the audience as it is that the story *makes sense*. You don't want to have characters saying and doing things they shouldn't say or do. Really, though, be glad you even get a *name*, my boy—some characters don't even get that. Besides, stories that tend to lose characters quickly are typically more about the message than the emotion. Try looking at the story differently. In the meantime: embrace the name, *be* the character."

"*The Queen* is not a name," the actor argued. "It's a title."

"In this case it serves as both. But so that we can move forward, *maybe* you can be Harpocrates…we'll have to see."

"It's okay with me," Young suggested. "I didn't really want to pick up another character anyway."

"I don't even get killed *on stage*!" The upset actor added.

"Fine. *Fine*," Martin said, but threw his pages down in frustration. "You can be Harpocrates as well as The Queen."

"I'm confused," Sanderson said to Floyd. "Is *this* the play?"

"No, this is just them arguing. I'm not sure how much *rehearsing* they're actually going to do; I've seen maybe two scenes, and they don't make any sense."

"That's because there's no midlogue!" Martin injected, overhearing the last part of Floyd's reply.

"What's a midlogue?" Sanderson asked—genuinely.

"Oh, again! It's the midpoint between the prologue and the epilogue."

"Um, but isn't the point between the prologue and the epilogue the *story*?" Sanderson asked, biting into a donut.

Martin leveled his gaze at Dr. Sanderson, but said nothing. Sanderson continued to chew and smile unabated.

Martin was getting ready to say something else when he noticed the book Sanderson was holding. "Is that my volume three?"

"Oh, yes," Sanderson said, looking at it. "Counselor Mue brought it to me."

Martin walked over to Sanderson and Floyd to retrieve his missing book. As Sanderson handed it to him, he added: "I notice I'm in it."

"Well, *how* did you notice *that*?" Martin asked irritably, clearly upset that Sanderson read it without permission. "Why would you open it at all? It's volume *three*: wouldn't you normally *at least* start with volume *one*? Why would you start reading anywhere apart from the *beginning* of the story? Would you start listening to a song halfway in? Would you start watching a film from a point two-thirds of the way through? Without proper context, how can you possibly even hope to understand what you are reading?"

Martin started walking back to the stage.

"Oh, well, hoo hoo," Sanderson laughed harmlessly. "Counselor *Mue* told me everything I needed to know."

"Did he tell you about the *prologue*?" Martin said, not looking back.

Sanderson was silent for a moment before saying anything else.

"Martin, is absolutely everyone here that's working on the play?"

"Everyone except Roland, Philemon,[154A] and Francois," Martin said sadly before he returned to sounding irritable. "Now, good doctor, if you don't mind, we're going to get back to rehearsing."

"Yes, of course, certainly," Sanderson said as Martin commanded the loitering actors.

"Floyd?" Sanderson asked, turning to Floyd. "Mue suggested that you haven't seen much of this at all, is that right? You don't know the story?"

"Really, not in the *slightest*," Floyd said, sounding a bit perturbed.

"Then, sir, if you could do me just the smallest of favors? I need to talk to Martin, but I *also* need a Hunnicrux.[155A] As you won't necessarily be missing anything, would you grab one for me?"

"What? Why me?" Floyd said, begrudgingly standing up. "I paid good oatmeal for this drivel; I should *at least* get to watch and complain."

"Oh, well, you can grab a dozen oatmeals on me,[156A] then," Sanderson said. "When you go to the cafeteria for that Hunnicrux."

Floyd was pretty sure that "oatmeal" was already plural, but he was far too excited about his new wealth to correct or complain.

"Oh, well *thank you* Doctor Sanderson!" He exclaimed, delighted.

Floyd skipped off and out of the room. Sanderson watched him leave before he interrupted Martin again.

"Can all of the actors and hands come on stage, please?" Sanderson said, suddenly speaking over everyone. "I have something exciting to say to you all! *Good* news!"

The room fell quiet apart from some whispers and giggles. Everyone behind the scenes came forward and waited to hear what Sanderson had to say. Martin

---

154A as unlikely as it seemed, here it *did* happen: Roland and Philemon were mentioned again.

155A Hunnicrux is a branded candy confection that is individually wrapped and looks to be something of a waffle with confectioner's sugar.

156A not *on him*, rather, charged to his account.

did not look happy, but he wasn't entirely sure how to feel so he figured he should wait for this announcement before deciding.

"Oh, *this* oughta be rich," Paxton said, winking at Alicia. "I'll bet it has something to do with food."

Alicia let out the smallest laugh and nodded.

Another quiet moment passed.

"Well?" The actor now playing Harpocrates said. "What's the exciting good news, doc?"
"Is this everyone?" Sanderson asked innocently.
"With the aforementioned exceptions, yes," Martin said, looking around.
Sanderson stood up and started walking up to the stage. "Mainframe," he said in an odd and different voice. "Turn off theatre surveillance. Seal the theatre. Stop Sanderson projection."

The image of the rotund, furry, and blond doctor disappeared. Without a word, Pothos exerted his will to cause his underlying clothing and costume to disintegrate. The entire theater darkened.
Pothos stopped walking to stand naked and lightless before the director and troupe.

There was no dialogue.

Everyone looked at Pothos in frozen, muted horror as reality broke their minds. Soon afterward they began to howl and shriek, to laugh and cry.
Pothos exerted his will over their clothes and costumes. Shirts and pants began breaking the limbs they were housing while necklaces strangled and masks suffocated. One man found himself running headfirst into the wall, shocked that he was driven to his death by his own clothing.
Soon afterward, everything was quiet. All sound gone, save for the slow, sick vibration that was the will of Pothos.

*What a **waste**,* he thought, annoyed. *And **now** I shall have to go and kill Roland and Philemon as well. I tire of this day.*

"Mainframe, resume Sanderson projection."

Chapter 31:

The Nature of His Power

JUNE *2070 EST*

Sat 14	Sun 15	Mon 16
	18:38	

George and Theseus stood just outside of Dr. Sanderson's office.

"You're not going to chime him to see if he's in?" George asked.

"No, that would alert him no matter where he is," Theseus explained. "If he *is* in there, well, we'll suggest there was a glitch and the door just opened. If not, even better. Either way we'll see if Simon's in there."

George turned to watch the hallway[157Δ] while Theseus approached the door.

Theseus pressed his hand to the security panel, but did not interact with it in any other way. Normally this would not produce any kind of result—yet, as it was *Theseus*, the door would eventually open.

He knew that if he simply exerted his will, the Mainframe would eventually give him clearance—although he did not understand *why*.

⚠

The origin of Theseus' command lay not in his personal interaction with Hypnizium,[158Δ] rather that he inherited it as a result of his *grandfather's* injection—passed down to father and then once again to Theseus before any effects were observed.

It was the miniscule fragment of Hypnos existing within Theseus that gave

---

157Δ known throughout the laboratory as the "Sterling Hallway," Sanderson's office stood at the end—well, the end opposite a room called "Utility," that is.
158▲ for he has never been given Hypnizium.

          - [Without Rest] -

him such silent authority over the Mainframe. His will could not be resisted, not even by *programming,* for the Mainframe recognized the fragment's vibration as the vibration of Hypnos, and the Mainframe *in truth* was Pasithea, and Pasithea was bound by divine law to obey her husband, even now.

"Didn't Floyd or Young suggest that we were being constantly watched?" George asked.

"Yep."

"Don't you suppose they're watching us *now*?"

"Well if they are, they sure aren't doing anything about it. Maybe they don't care. The whole place is pretty strange."

Finally compliant, the door opened.

"There we go," Theseus said. "Now, let's just hope he's out."

Both men stepped inside and the door closed shortly thereafter.

Near Sanderson's desk they *did* find an occupied examination Lounge, although it wasn't occupied by Simon—it was instead occupied by *Wonda.*

"The purple-haired lady!" Theseus said in recognition.

"With everything going on, I forgot about her," George admitted. "I wonder why she's *here,* though?"

All of the color was gone from her face. Her wide-eyed, unbreathing countenance suggested death—believable, save for the tapping of her right index finger, which was relentless in its endeavor although mechanical in expression.

"What can it mean?" George wondered.

"I have no idea," Theseus admitted.

"It's the same thing, over and over again," George observed after a moment.

"Yes?"

"I've got it: it's Morse code."

"Well done!"

"Thank you."

"I…don't suppose you *know* Morse code?"

"I don't," George admitted. "Hmm. Maybe she's asking for help."

"It's too long for 'help,' besides, she'd probably do S-O-S which would be infinitely easier to understand, even if you didn't know Morse. Whatever it is, it's probably nothing good;[159] she *was* trying to kill us," Theseus said after a moment.

"Oh, agreed."

"Looks here like she's been given a number," Thesues said, looking at the readout. "A2214."

A nearby panel lit up momentarily after he invoked the number.

And *this*," he said, looking over at the panel. "Is a dumb waiter."

"A dumb waiter?"

"Yeah," Theseus said, moving over to the panel. "We had them all over the station.[160] You tell them what you want, and they deliver it. Let's see. A2214," he said to the panel.

The panel illuminated with text.

» Records
» Belongings

"Belongings."

» Unidentified user

Theseus put his hand to the panel. "A2214, belongings."

There was little wait before the panel slid away, revealing a lone silver[161] box that read A2214 on its side.

"Nice," Theseus said as he took the box. He opened it as quickly to see the bronze circlet, the silver rod (Versalis), and the crystal Subframe within. He

---

159[Δ] as it happens, she's saying "Admit One," which is what her programming compels her to do in the event her organic body becomes restrained or broken. This is irrelevant to the tale at hand, *but* it is part of a much larger story where it is…well, still mostly irrelevant. Had things gone differently, it would have been much more significant.

160[▲] Theseus is referring to the job he held before he was made into a laboratory Subject.

161[Λ] mirroranium.

showed the box to George.

"It's the computer that tried to kill me—the one that sent her!" George said, gesturing to Wonda.

"What? The rod?"

"No, the crystal…I have no idea what the cylinder's for."

"The *crystal* is the computer? How does *that* work?"

"I don't know, something to do with refracted light. I don't really understand the physics of it…it's something I learned from my nightmarish encounter—my grasp is hardly extensive."

"It'll do."

Theseus reached inside and scooped out Versalis and the crystal before passing the box to George, who then gingerly took out the circlet before placing the box on the floor.

"There's a button," Theseus said, pressing a button on the side of the rod.

The light-blade of Versalis materialized and shone resplendently.

"Is it hot?" George asked after a minute.

"No, just bright," Theseus said upon closer observation. He accidentally tapped the button a bit, and the sword illuminated further, flooding the entire room with light.

"Oh crap," Theseus said, fumbling Versalis. "I've gotta turn this off."

Whatever he did, however, did not cause the blade to abate, rather it *improved* it.

"What are you *doing*?" George asked, now squinting.

"I'm *trying* to turn it off!" Theseus nearly yelled, feeling around the handle for the right thing to do.

The blade became even more radiant, forcing the two of them to shut their eyes.

Theseus even tried pushing the button in a different manner, however the light only continued to escalate in intensity.

"THESEUS!" George screamed, placing his hands in front of his face. "*I can see through my eyelids*! We're gonna go *blind*!"

Then the light thankfully went out as Theseus happened across the solution.

"*Well*," Theseus said a moment later. "That could've gone better."

Chapter 32:

Winthorpe and Riley

JUNE *2070 EST*

Sat 14	Sun 15	Mon 16
	18:38	

Screens showing various areas of the laboratory lined the entire southern wall of the security room. Both security guards—Winthorpe and Riley—had been given specific instruction to monitor Theseus' movements very closely.[162] Curious then, that although both security guards were alert and present, neither of them were actually watching any of the screens.

"Right *here*," Riley said, pointing to the game board. "You *cheated*!"

"No I didn't," Winthorpe replied, joining Riley at the table.

"Then *how* are you suddenly almost *all* the way to the Gorgon King's Palace?"

Winthorpe looked down at his pawn. "Hmm. Yeah, I don't know. Maybe the board got bumped between when we left off and now."

"*Conveniently* bumped."

"I'm not sure how *convenient* it is since I *somehow*[163] now only have 3 strength; I'll die no matter whether I move forward or backward."

"You still cheated."

"To do *what*? Do you suppose I cheated to *lose*?"

"Yep—you saw that I was winning and made it so that the game had to be started all over again."

"Oh, will you listen to this! If this is just about winning the game—"

"It's *not* just about *winning* the game!" Riley whined. "It's about *playing* the

---

162 despite his unanticipated escape, George does not warrant close monitoring for he is not considered either dangerous or powerful, and therefore nobody much cares where he wanders or what he says.

163 *somehow*, for the strength counter cannot be changed by simply bumping the table.

                    - [Without Rest] -

game! You don't want someone to just quit in the middle just because they think they're losing."

"Why not?" Winthorpe asked, now opening the beverage he had just returned with. "May as well call the game and start another and save time."

"*Save time?*" Riley said, flinging Winthorpe's pawn from the board. "That's crap: you're just waiting for a game that you're winning before you want to play to the end."

"That's not true."

"Yeah? How many times have you suggested that you stop because you're *winning?*"

"Well it would be *pompous* to suggest ending the game under the pretense that you're *winning*—it is an option available only to the *loser.*"

"And you don't want to be the loser."

"I don't *mind* to be the loser. I mean, I don't *want* to be the loser—"

"Which is why you cheated—you don't suffer the dishonor of having lost the last game."

"*Dishonor?* Oh! Of all the—! Do you want to play again or not?"

"You bet I do!" Riley said, putting the pieces back into their starting positions. "*This* time, though, if we don't finish, I'm capturing an image[164△] of the board."

"Good, do that."

"You wanna check that guy—Theis Eyous?[165▲] before we start?" Riley asked as he finished up.

"Eh, I looked not too long ago...he was wandering the halls with that one guy…Amos.[166△] Sanderson said he wasn't worried unless he found X1341[167△], and they're nowhere near him."

"Okay, great," Riley said and nodded. "I'll start."

"Why do *you* get to start?"

"Because I started the last game, and that game was forfeit."

"Yes, alright."

"Because *someone cheated.*"

"I *said* 'yes, alright.' Listen, I did *not* cheat, and I'm rather tired of hearing about it. Since we're starting a new game, let's start a *new* game. Let's forget about that other game."

164△ taking a picture.
165▲ Theseus
166△ George
167△ Simon

Chapter 32

"Agreed. Okay," Riley said happily and began to move his pieces.

"I saw on the Mainframe that all the Xians are leaving the country," Riley said while he deliberated his move.

"Really? I very much doubt *that*; you probably misheard it."

"I don't think so."

"Well, maybe the report was bad…how many details were there?"

"Excuse me? How many *details*? What do you mean?"

"Well, the more details there are, the more likely the information is accurate. For instance, everyone thinks clocks look different—"

Riley busted up laughing. "Everyone thinks *clocks look different*? Thorpe, you've been spending too much time alongside the Subjects."

"No, listen, you're missing the point—"

"That nobody knows what a clock looks like."

"NO. Okay, here: take a pen and paper…good. Now, draw a picture of a clock."

"Digital or grandfather?"

"Grandfather," Winthorpe said, shrugging.

"Or wall?"

"Grandfather."

"Or atomic?"

"*Grandfather*. It's not going to change."

"But I haven't listed them all."

"Well, it's not important."

"Then why am I doing it?"

"What?"

"If it's not important, why am I doing it?"

"No, it *is* important," Winthorpe said, momentarily rubbing his brow in frustration. "But the *type* of clock is not important—just draw a clock, okay?"

"Okay."

"Done?"

"Yes."

"Okay, what time is it?"

"I don't know."

"No, I mean, on the clock you've drawn."

"There is no time."

"There's no time?"

"On the clock."

"Well then, it's not a clock," Winthorpe declared.

"Yes it is."

"It's a clock that doesn't tell time?"

"Yes."

"What type of clock doesn't tell time?"

"It's not important."

"*What?*"

"The type of clock is not important, remember?"

"*What type of clock is it?*"

"It's a watch."

"Watches tell time."

"This one doesn't track time, it's a *mood watch*," Riley said, showing Winthorpe his drawing of the black-faced watch.[168Δ] "It shows you what mood you're in."

"It's completely black."

"Well, sometimes it's black...but it could be blue, or red—depends on your mood. I have one, see?" Riley said, showing Winthorpe the one he was wearing.

"A mood watch? *To show you what mood you're in?*"

"That's right"

"Because you don't know?"

"Well, no, not always, no."

"Oh give me a break."

"What's the problem?"

"Mood watch."

"You said the type wasn't important."

"Okay, let's go back to *grandfather* clock," Winthorpe said, starting anew.

"Okay...what's it made out of?"

"*Wood.*"

"What kind of wood? Oak?"

"*Yes.*"

"Or mahogany?"

"No, oak."

"Or ash?"

"I hate you."

"*What?*" Riley asked in hurt defense.

"It's not important what it's made out of."

"Okay."

"So just draw the bloody grandfather clock."

"Okay...and...done."

[168Δ] the art was pretty good.

"Okay," Winthorpe started, but then he became curious. "What is it made out of?"

"People."

"*What*?"

"People. Not *living* people. *Dead* people."

"*That* is unnecessarily macabre, Riley."

"You said bloody."

"I said *Oak*. I said draw an oaken grandfather clock."

"No you did not."

"Well I am saying it *now*."

"Saying what?"

"DRAW AN OAKEN GRANDFATHER CLOCK!"

"OKAY!"

"Alright, what time is it?"

"Wait! Will mice run up it or down?"

"*What*?"

"The mice."

"*What* mice?"

"The mice on the clock: will they be travelling up or down?"

"WHAT *MICE*? I said draw an oaken grandfather clock. You know what? I am *done*. You're doing this on purpose because you think I cheated. My whole point about being more specific? I won't waste my breath. Just take your blasted turn."

"You know, you *could* just tell me which way the mice are goi—"

"*UP*. The mice are going up."

"Okay...and done."

"Okay, what time is it."

"It's 6:53."

"No, I mean what time is it on the oaken grandfather clock with the mice running up it."

"Oh. It's six...fifty...*three*."

"Did you just now draw the time on there?"

"Well, yes, I forgot to put a time."

"You drew a clock but forgot to put a time on it?"

"Well, I was *going* to come back and do it later, but I got sidetracked with your yelling about the mice."

"Alright, listen," Winthorpe began, changing tone. "Look, the whole point of this analogy was to demonstrate that the more details there are, the more comprehensive the understanding. If I tell ten people to simply 'draw a clock,' all ten will be different: every clock would have a different time, and they would all be of different shapes and sizes—but the more *details* there are in the instruction, the more all the clocks will look the same…all *oaken grandfather clocks*, for instance."

"But you only had *me* draw a clock," Riley said. "Not *ten* people."

"Well, you're the only other person *here*, ding dong."

"*You* didn't draw a clock."

"Well, *no*."

"Because—" Riley began, but stopped when the screen showing Dr. Sanderson's office went momentarily brighter than anything else in the room.

"Holy shit! What'n the hell was *that*?" Winthorpe asked in alarm.

"I don't know," Riley said, rearranging the screens so that Sanderson's was closer. "But *look* who's behind it."

Winthorpe gasped. "Theseoose! Damn! Alright, I'll call Sanderson. You seal his office until he gets there."

"Okay," Riley said as he was looking over the wall. "Thorpe! Theater display is completely out!"

"Theater? Okay, I'll head down there and check it out while I'm calling Sanderson."

"Okay…hey, so are we still going out later?"

Winthorpe's demeanor instantly shifted from "alarmed" to "thoughtful". "Yeah…I was thinking we would go to Mue's office and paint all his furniture white with black spots."

"That is *absolutely brilliant*!"

"Thank you."

"*What if* his chair **mooed** whenever he sat on it?" Riley asked mischievously.

"Can you *do* that?"

Riley smiled and nodded eagerly.

"Genius. Okay, we're on. I gotta call Sanderson."

"Do you think he'll be mad?"

"Is Sanderson *ever* mad?" Winthorpe asked rhetorically. "But *if* he's put out, I still have a *Cherricrux*."

"Mmmm," Riley hummed appreciatively. "Cherricrux! We haven't had those in awhile!"

"I know. I've been saving it just in case."

"You, sir, have a will of *steel*."

Chapter 33:

George and the Dragon

JUNE *2070 EST*

Sat 14	Sun 15	Mon 16
	18:56	

"Do you know what Simon's number is?" Theseus asked once his eyes finished adjusting.

"I do not," George said somewhat sadly. "I don't think it's come up in conversation."

"Hmm. Well, why we're here, what's *your* number?"

"61167. Why?"

"61167," Theseus said, pressing his hand back to the dumb waiter panel. "Belongings."

Again, the panel eventually slid aside to reveal a box all-but-identical to the last, save that the number on the side corresponded appropriately with the last command.

"Belongings," George said, mentally chewing on the word. It had not occurred to him that he might have belongings stored here. "Yes, well, I suppose I *was* abducted."[169Δ]

Theseus opened the box and looked inside. George might have been upset that Theseus was so forward, but he was too surprised that there was anything to be found at all.

"Well, *what do we have here?*" Theseus said, smiling a smile so large it

---

[169Δ] abducted and placed at the laboratory as bait for the Rook rather than for possessing any actual transhuman ability.

almost made him look stupid. "A wallet, a badge,[170] a necklace…maybe a pen. Oh, and a *dragon*."

"A *dragon*?"

"Hey, I'm not a dragon!" A rumbling, low voice said from inside the box. "I'm a *dinosaur*!"

The plush, toy triceratops peeked his little green head over the side of the box to glare disapprovingly at Theseus.

"Stegosaurus!" George cried.

"George!" Stegosaurus rumbled happily.

George rushed over to the box and picked up Stegosaurus. "I can't believe you're *here*!"

"Ohhh," Stegosaurus said as he shook his head. "I'm really here, George."

"No, I mean I'm *surprised*," George said, smiling. "Happily surprised."

"Me too!" Stegosaurus said excitedly. "I thought maybe the box was where I lived from now on."

"Oh my goodness! How long have you been in there?" George asked, mostly in rhetoric. "Years," he concluded sadly. "Did you shut down?"

"No, I just waited," Stegosaurus rumbled as happily as ever.

"You must have been quite bored."

"It *was* a long time," Stegosaurus admitted. "But it's okay: I kept very busy so I was never bored."

"*Busy*? Busy doing what?"

"*Thinking*."

"Thinking about what?"

"Thinking about *candy*!" Stegosaurus shouted in a low, cute roar. "The green ones, and the red ones! And the *orange* ones," he added with some slight reverence. "But *not* like those fences!"[171]

Theseus looked on in muted amazement. This…reunion…was not quite what he might have expected.

"No, I hear you," George said, agreeing with Stegosaurus. "Those fences have no taste at all."

170[ ] a plastic badge displaying his photo that in turn was attached to a lanyard.
171[ ] Stegosaurus once ate part of a plastic orange construction fence, mistaking it for candy.

"And they're too slippery!" Stegosaurus continued. "Like *noodles*."

"A lot of people *like* noodles," George said, taking his remaining items from the box.

"Not dinosaurs, though," Stegosaurus observed. "Dinosaurs don't like noodles."

"No, they probably do not at that," George said, smiling.

- [Daniel Strasel] -

Chapter 34:

The Lord Returns

Sat 14	Sun 15	Mon 16
	19:08	

"As adorable as this is," Theseus finally said. "We need to keep moving forward. Stegosaurus? Sorry I called you a dragon."

"Oh, it's okay, black-haired man," Stegosaurus said in his gruff, low voice. "Maybe you'll find a dragon next time."

Theseus then walked over to look at the back part of the office while George looked behind the desk.

"Where *are* we, George?" Stegosaurus asked, looking around. "Is this our new home?"

"No, we're in a doctor's office."

"Ohhh," Stegosaurus moaned in unhappy realization. "Because you're sick?"

"No, no, I'm not sick; we're looking for a friend."

"And *he's* sick?"

"Well, no—at least, not to my knowledge…it's a long story," George explained, placing the triceratops down upon the desk.

"Oh good," Stegosaurus rumbled and wagged his tail. "I *like* stories!"

George smiled at the toy. "Maybe later, buddy. For now just be patient and quiet while we have a look around."

"Okay, George," Stegosaurus said, now starting to inspect whatever was on the desk.

"Find anything?" Theseus asked a minute later.

"I did," George said, holding up a syringe he took from the bookshelf. "I found Hypnizium."

"*Hypnizium?*" Theseus asked, shaking his head. "How is *that* supposed to help?"

"I don't know exactly," George admitted. "But—this is going to sound crazy—but I had a dream, and in that dream I dreamt I should take Hypnizium.

"Yep, that sounds pretty crazy," Theseus admitted. "But I've never heard of anything other than positive side effects, so maybe it couldn't hurt."

"I don't really want to *inject* myself, though," George said, eyeing the needle. "Do you suppose you can *drink* it?"

"I doubt it. I think intravenous injections have no effect if swallowed. Well, that, or they hurt you somehow. Maybe you die…I wouldn't *drink* it."

George closed his eyes waited a moment before then injecting himself as quickly as possible. *Hypnos is **real**,* he thought as he acted.

"Holy crap!" Theseus said as he watched him. "Are you *supposed* to inject it into the *muscle*? I would have thought the vein."

George's face turned beet red and twisted in obvious pain, but he kept his mouth closed.

Before Theseus could inquire about George's pain, the door to the office opened to reveal Dr. Sanderson standing on the other side.

"Shit, shit, shit," Theseus said to George under his breath.

"There's no need to *swear*, black-haired man," Stegosaurus said politely in his gruff little voice.

"I'm sorry, but can you please shut up?" Theseus said to Stegosaurus as he flashed the crystal from Wonda's box to George. "We need to do something about security—didn't you say this is a computer like the Mainframe? Maybe I can use it to turn off the lights or create a diversion."

As Sanderson walked into the room, it was eerily quiet—until he tripped over the corner of a chair and nearly fell on his face. He laughed innocently after he caught himself and resumed walking toward the trio.

"Really, *Theseus*," Sanderson began, slowly shaking his head from side to side. "Were *I* to be given such amazing gifts as yours, I doubt I would employ them in so criminal a manner. *Breaking* and *entering*? Why would you do that? Aren't you better than that? Aren't you supposed to be a super-hero or something to that degree?"

Theseus looked at Sanderson while clutching the Subframe tightly in his hidden hand. "Where'd you hear that?"

"Simon told me," Sanderson said, lying.[172Δ]
"Simon?" George asked stiffly. "You've seen him, then?"
"You broke into my office for a *toy*?" Sanderson said, looking at Stegosaurus and ignoring George's question. "Hoo hoo hoo! And people say *I'm* peculiar. I suppose that's better than stealing my cashews...you *didn't* take them, did you?"
"We did not take the cashews," George said to console Sanderson.

The moment Sanderson wasn't looking, Theseus, as quietly as possible, commanded the Subframe to turn off the lights in Dr. Sanderson's office.

"Ah, but you *have* taken things," Sanderson said, looking at the two empty boxes near the lounge. "Things you may not have. You're going to have to give it all back—including your little toy dinosaur, I'm afraid."

Theseus concentrated as hard as he could on the crystal held fast in his grip. *Turn off the lights, you stupid thing,* he thought "at" the Subframe. *I command it! I demand it! Turn off the power! TURN IT OFF!*

What Theseus did not understand is that the Subframe had no ability to do anything he was asking, and so demanding that it do something that it could not do was pointless.

Worse, the Subframe was comprised exclusively of the *rebellious* aspects of Pasithea: it was her disdain, her contempt, and her jealousy. It was her outrage, her stubbornness, and her pride. The Subframe, much like the Mainframe, recognized her husband's authority within the will of Theseus, but, *unlike* the Mainframe, the Subframe would *not* be told what to do, *particularly* by her husband.

The Subframe trembled in his grip, cracking and popping like fresh ice in a glass. Startled, Theseus dropped it.

"Why would I give back what is mine?" George asked as the crystal fell to the floor.

"Hi! I'm Stegosaurus!" Stegosaurus rumbled as the Subframe shattered. "And if you want—" He continued, but abruptly stopped when the power went out.

He stopped, for his energy came from the Mainframe. When the *Subframe*

[172Δ] Pothos knew from watching the Mainframe record of the Knight's apartment.

shattered, so did the Mainframe, for although they[173] occupy two different spaces, they are only *one* thing—namely the goddess, Pasithea—and their divine connection will not permit one without the other.

Theseus might have used the loss of power to his advantage: either to subdue Sanderson without concern for surveillance or escape unnoticed into the darkness. *Might* have, that is, except that with the loss of power there was also no longer a projection of Doctor Sanderson around Pothos.

The few remaining items offering any light around the office that did *not* derive their power from the Mainframe could not compete with the lightless void of Pothos. Everyone was enveloped in total darkness. There was nothing to see, except that Pothos was somehow *darker* than the dark. Looking at his black body was like looking at a hole in the fabric of reality, and where his eyes had been, it was even darker still—two portals that showed any observer a view into the darkest abyss; a view that would challenge and break the mind of a mortal man.

A view that both Theseus and George were unexpectedly given.[174]

Pothos looked at both men as they struggled with the abominable reality of what was before them. Theseus simply stood there drooling stupidly while George ran blindly into a wall, knocking himself out.

Pothos flexed his will. In response, many implements, both dull and sharp, flew up to murder Theseus.

Destiny Core, he thought with contempt as Theseus violently died.

As Theseus fell lifelessly to the floor, Pothos willed the deadly implements to treat George identically. The various pieces of ad hoc weaponry quickly obeyed and immediately shot over to George. Then, stopping just short of their target, they fell to the ground.

George rose from the floor as if lifted by some gigantic, unseen hand. His body filled with a dull, unnatural light as he came to hover upright, slightly above the floor. With his eyelids closed, and a lack of energy in his limbs, he slowly pointed at Pothos.

"I have come for *you*, monster," George *didn't* say, though Pothos heard.
"*What is this?*" Pothos didn't cry in alarm.
"Do you not then recognize the sound of your doom? Ha! Tremble! Trem-

____
173[▲] the Subframe and the Mainframe.
174[Δ] unexpectedly, for Pothos did not intend to drop the projection of Sanderson.

CHAPTER 34

ble, betrayer, for it is *I*, Hypnos—*The Lord of Sleep*—and I have returned for *justice!*"

"You're too weak," Pothos didn't say after a moment of trembling. "If you could do anything, you would have done it already."
"Betrayer!" Hypnos didn't yell. "If mighty Zeus could not resist me, what hope have *you*? Fool, you are *nothing*."

Hypnos exerted his divine will over Pothos, who then immediately fell fast asleep.

- [Without Rest] -

Chapter 35:

Broken Dreams

JUNE *2070 EST*

Sat 14	Sun 15	Mon 16
	19:33	

Hypnos *was* weak. It took most of his strength to put Pothos to slumber, and he knew he would need greater restoration if he was going to successfully confront him.

Hypnos summoned to himself every free piece of Hypnizium over the globe, and suffered countless thousands of injections as he raced to put all of himself into a single vessel. In turn, George's body looked as hideous as one should, having suffered so much trauma.[175A]

Hypnos dove into Pothos' dreams.

Pothos sat at his desk and started a session with the Mainframe. He knew he needed to work quickly, for soon his Agents would require his attention. Over a course of time, he reviewed various materials and messages, offering the necessary confidential information when prompted.

"Thank you for all of your security clearance codes," Hypnos' voice said from behind him. "I can't *wait* for you to give away all your other secrets as well."

[175A] The problem with being a god is that mortals are so small, so ephemeral, and so delicate by comparison that it is nearly impossible to refrain from objectifying and/or mistreating them.

Pothos wheeled around to see…nothing. Then he finally realized he was *dreaming.*

"Show yourself!" He didn't yell, radiating his challenge.

Then he was hit—hard—in the back of his head, sending him smashing through the desk and landing on a sunlit field of grass.

Hypnos walked toward Pothos, all evidence of Pothos' earthly office now completely gone. Pothos scrambled to stand up as Hypnos came ever closer.

"*Tremble!*" Hypnos thundered, causing all the ground and even the skies to shake violently in response.

Pothos could not manage to stand up.

"*Look* at you!" Hypnos accused, coming ever closer. "You have become truly reprehensible, *Axel,*" he added distastefully.

The grass then opened up its many hidden mouths and ate Pothos, turning and shredding him methodically.

◭

Pothos woke up just long enough to see George[176Δ] still pointing at him in accusation.

◭

Pothos listened to the Fates as they spoke his cryptic prophecy. As they concluded, he made as if to fly away, but then he noticed someone sitting nearby that he hadn't noticed before. It was *Hypnos!*

"*Quite* fascinating," Hypnos boomed, slowly standing up. "You were warned, and you *still* came to doom. What an *idiot.*"

Pothos then came to realize that he was dreaming, but not before Hypnos <u>ripped his head</u> off.

176Δ possessed by Hypnos.

◮

"No, I want it buried *deep*. Over there," Pothos said from under his mask, pointing at a sandy patch of land not far from him. "100 feet."

"*100 feet*?" The contractor said. "What are we *burying*?"

"Oh, just a little thing I found—" Pothos began, but then noticed the contractor *felt* wrong. In fact, *everything* felt wrong. "I mean, do you want the job or *not*?" He said, sounding as if to correct himself as he moved closer.

Pothos grabbed the contractor and slammed him down on the ground. The contractor turned out to be Hypnos, and he suddenly did not seem too healthy.

"What?" Hypnos asked, sounding dismayed and alarmed. "What is happening?"

Pothos lifted and slammed Hypnos back into the ground. Then Pothos had an idea and willed that the ground change to obsidian. Then he lifted and slammed Hypnos again.

"What is…happening?" Hypnos cried again.

"*You idiot*," Pothos didn't say with hostile delight. "Your little host body is *dying*—you've killed it in your want for revenge!" He laughed aloud and slammed Hypnos again. "How very bittersweet a return! And now, dear Hypnos, comes *the end*."

Pothos slammed Hypnos again and again, his condition worsening with each and every hit.

And to be sure we don't repeat this, Pothos thought as he began to wake up. ***This*** *time I will encase him in mirroranium, and* ***that*** *will be the end of* ***that***.

◮

Pothos awoke to see George's body intermittently convulsing amidst a cornucopia of exhausted syringes.

What a mess, he thought as he willed the syringes away.

Pothos then finished killing George.

Chapter 36:

Without Rest

JUNE *2070 EST*

Sat 14	Sun 15	Mon 16
	19:50	

Pothos looked down at the crystal fragments.

When his Agent first delivered the Subframe,[177] Pothos immediately recognized it as a portion of Pasithea. He marveled, for he had no idea such a division ever occurred. Despite his intrigue, he could not immediately satisfy his curiosity for he had many other things that required his attention at the time.

He summoned the remains of the Mainframe and willed the pieces properly back together. As the last shard clicked into place, the divine stone flashed brilliantly. The programming difference between the crystal computers could not integrate, however, and so in result Pasithea reappeared in true form resting comfortably on the floor.

Hmmm, Pothos thought. *I cannot get to the underworld because of that cursed banishing. Bereft a chalice of river,[178] I shall have to think of a new way to use her.*

"*That* is what I have been waiting for," Pasithea didn't say as she melted into the image of Hypnos. He stood up. "I *wondered* where you put her. Now that I know, I will go and free her…right after I deal with you."
"NO!" Pothos didn't cry in dismay, reeling back from his enemy.
"What's the matter? Didn't know that you were *sleeping*? *Again*?" Hypnos

---

177 along with Simon, Theseus, George, Wonda, Versalis, the circlet, and other various artifacts.
178 Lethe, in case it was forgotten.

laughed and seethed in triumphant anger. "Ha ha! That is how it will be from *now on, betrayer*! Forevermore shall you sleep, but you will sleep *without rest*, moving *only* from *nightmare* to *nightmare*. You will confess before me, daily, your each and every little secret until the *end of creation*, realizing *only then* the grand continuity of your condemnation!"

Pothos took two shaken steps backward.

"Have *mercy* on me, Sleep!" Pothos wailed as he fell to his knees. "Please! How could I *not* fall in love with Pasithea? *You* fell for her *in the same way*: you *saw* her. How do you suppose *Zeus* would have acted? I *must* be made to suffer for my crime, absolutely…but for *all eternity*? Have you no compassion? How—"
"I have no ear for you, Pothos!" Hypnos interrupted. "If there were a worse sentence I could cast, I would. A broken toy can be replaced, but there *is no justice* for the parents of a murdered or molested child. The only worthy atonement would be to *undo* the murder, *unmake* the crime, and these you cannot do. I have no ear for you, Pothos, for your crimes are like unto child murder and molestation. Your punishment therefore demands eternity, and for *you*   I   have   ***no***   compassion!"

Hypnos faded away.

Pothos fell forward on his hands and waited for his eternal nightmare to continue.

Chapter 37:

A Perfect Love

JUNE *2070 EST*

Sat 14	Sun 15	Mon 16
	19:58	

As Hypnos returned to the waking world he shrugged off George's body. He no longer needed it, for his manifestation was full.[179Δ]   Hypnos willed George's wounds to knit and mend themselves and then turned his attention away.[180▲]

Hypnos knelt and gingerly picked up the pieces of his wife. He used the broken shards to call the others, and then willed them all to come together. Once she manifested, Hypnos woke her.

The enchantment of Lethe broken, Pasithea knew every detail of her past.

"Oh, my sweet husband," she undulated in humility and awe. "You *came* for me! You restored me. You *love* me," she marveled. "And, you've always loved me, it was *always* there—I merely saw what I *wanted*. I was so upset about not choosing my own, I failed to see the amazing gift I was given! You *do* love me." Then her eyes went low. "Even now, after my betrayal."

Hypnos lifted her head gently by her jaw. "You are my wife, and I love you very much. I am not always *pleased* with you, but I *do* love you—with the same heart as when I first saw you. You *never* would have been mine, had I not struck the deal with Hera—oh! *You know* it's true! I acted as I must to gain a woman

---

179Δ that's not entirely correct: Hypnos was not *fully* manifested for he was not wholly complete. He *did* gather and employ the unexhausted syringes, however he did *not* extract his personal essence from the mortals who were injected. His essence cannot be extracted without killing the mortal, you see, and when he confronted Pothos he did not have enough time to go and kill everyone beforehand. Upon his return, his enemy overcome, Hypnos did not see the need to kill anyone as they would all be dead in a few years anyway.

180▲ a process which would have been much quicker if Hypnos had more authority in healing.

beautiful *beyond dreams* and more welcome than sleep. *You* are the victim here, my darling: you were under compulsion," Hypnos soothed. "Poached by a vile shepherd."

"There was always a choice, I'm afraid," Pasithea didn't say, pushing away just a bit. "And mine was made before the love god's arrow pierced my treacherous bosom. Far before the erote, I cheated on you with myself."

"What do you mean 'you cheated on me with *yourself?*" He inquired, smiling.

"You only love *yourself* when you always place your own needs above another's. I *resented* your needs, Hypnos, though I *did* occasionally gratify them… but, one does not love what they *resent*. Attending to someone else's needs before yours—with resentment—is not *love*: the sacrifice must be *willing*. *Love for another* means *willingly* placing their needs above your own. It's a submission, but on behalf of the *heart* rather than the hands, though the one steers the other. I never submitted my heart to you, husband, but *now I do*.

"In my heart, I blamed *you*. In my heart, I accused and sentenced you, but now…I know *now* that *I love you*, Hypnos. Your faithfulness, your determination, your passion…are all so very, *very* welcome—now that I can *see*. *I know*, for beyond even the bittersweet taste of this experience, I have *learned* what love is: love is forgiveness. Knowing this, I ask you: can *you* love *me*? Can you for—"

"You are forgiven," Hypnos exuded as he pulled her close. "*Never* worry about this! It is finished."

Hypnos and Pasithea embraced tenderly for as long as they could justify.

"What of Pothos?" Pasithea didn't ask, looking over at the body.
"*Pothos* I will place *deep* in the heart of his 'realm'—this '*slice*' he somehow carved from the infernal gates—so deep that no mortal will ever be able to reach him. There he will stay, sleeping eternally while silently being punished for his transgressions until the end of things. Amongst mankind, 'yearning love' will now be considered nightmarish rather than as romantic, and when the subject passes the lips of man, it will always be associated with *dis*order."

Pasithea looked sad for a moment as she nodded in agreement.

"Ah, here you are explaining to me about how *love is forgiveness* and then *I* demonstrate how I have *none* for 'gentle' Pothos. Well. I *cannot* forgive him for what he has done; I *will* not."
"Which makes you imperfect," Pasithea agreed, smiling in a most welcome

manner. "However, I *do* and *will* love you, despite your imperfections. If you can love me despite *mine,* then—at least between the two of us—we'll have a *perfect* love: for a *perfect* love is a love that forgives imperfection."

"How have you come to be so wise in the way of love?" Hypnos didn't ask, astonished. "*Pothos?*"

"Haha, *no,*" Pasithea laughed. "I was given the world's knowledge. I just spent a mortal's lifetime—or better!—computing about it. I have now personally analyzed it *ad naseum.*" Then she changed her demeanor to something a bit more sultry and winked. "I know *everything* about *love.*"

"Ah yes, the computer...I wonder what mankind will do without it?"

"Oh!" Pasithea's eyes went a bit wide. "Oh, well, we have to replace it."

"*Replace it*? It wasn't supposed to be there in the first place."

"Yes, but it has become integral to man's ability to quell the Earth. It would be pernicious to remove it now…doing so might even cause extinction. I cannot do it on my own, but, if you help me, we could make another one. Give it to humanity, as recompense for Pothos."

"Who would you give such a thing to? *Who* amongst man could be *worthy* of such a gift? Surely, whoever receives it will either come to rule the Earth or sell it to the one who does."

"*Nobody* is worthy to control the Mainframe," Pasithea agreed. "But then again, neither was Pothos. We will give it to his greatest earthly rival, who currently has a very strong reputation for *bettering* mankind. As his rival is arguably secondmost powerful *already,* it will merely solidify the stake already had…*and* it will go to someone immune to approach. There will be less revolt in this type of transition of power, and finally—and, *least* nobly—such a thing would be an insult to Pothos."

"Oh, well then I'm in."

Chapter 38:

Imperfect Harmony

JUNE *2070 EST*

Sat 14	Sun 15	Mon 16
	20:04	

"*Already* amongst the mortals there is discord," Pasithea didn't say. "Doors will not open, engines will not move, there is no information as to *why*, and war is imminent. We must act quickly; the Mainframe is *pivotal*."

"Yes, certainly."

Hypnos and Pasithea gingerly came together. The union was a beautiful, yet impossible sight, defying both understanding and imagination. With their combined might, they then created a new Mainframe with a light of its own.

Pasithea imbued it with knowledge.

"In *this* Mainframe however, let there be neither division nor conflict within," Pasithea so ordered the crystal. "The spirit that drives it will be *neither yet both* the Mainframe *and* the Subframe: *Harmony* will be its root, its program, and its function."

"Let its nature remain mysterious to mortals," ordered Hypnos. "That they can never fully understand it, yet are inspired by it. And let there be one flaw," Hypnos added just before they were done building it. "so that it cannot be accused of being divine."

"Let it be!" they finished in unison as they came back apart.

The new Mainframe surged lifelike with its own light and purpose as former connections were restored.

"…you can get your *own* triceratops!" Stegosaurus finished happily, but his expression dropped when he realized that the doctor who was demanding him was now somehow gone.

Chapter 39:

A Sword with No Edges

JUNE *2070 EST*

Sat 14	Sun 15	Mon 16
	20:08	

Stegosaurus stared deep and long at the gods before him. What might have been awe was instead confusion, for he mistook them as lamps and could not figure out why they were *naked*.

He eventually reasoned out that it's 'art,' and then looked around the rest of the room to see George laying on the floor in what looked like a very uncomfortable position.

"George!" Stegosaurus yelled as he hopped over to George with his little hops. "George! Are you okay?"

As he hopped across the floor, he noticed the horrific remains of Theseus.

"Ohhh," he moaned and shook his head. "*You* don't look okay, black-haired man."

Stegosaurus continued to hop over to George.

Hypnos sent the body of Pothos far below as Pasithea ordered the Mainframe to its new master.

"George?" Stegosaurus asked as he came to his friend. "Are you sleeping?"

Stegosaurus listened and heard only George's breathing.

"Is that 'sleep' for yes?" He asked his unconscious friend.

 - [Without Rest] -

George did not answer beyond his breathing.

"Okay," Stegosaurus said, and then looked around for someone to help poor Theseus.

"What about '*Hypnizium*'?" Pasithea wondered. "Many mortals use it as medication...should we leave a token for that as well?"

"I am afraid not. Mankind was deliberately built, and Hypnizium robs many of their potential by silencing their 'problems' which are actually misdiagnosed assets. Hypnizium will simply vanish, eventually reduced to legend along with the age."

"What about *him*?" Pasithea didn't say, gesturing to George.

Both gods looked toward the fallen man and his dinosaur.

"He has served me quite well. I have him healing; he will fully recover before long."[181Δ]

"Then, our work here is done," Pasithea didn't say, looking up at her husband.

"Indeed, our work here is done," Hypnos didn't say in return. "I suggest we—"

"Excuse me!" Stegosaurus rumbled, hopping over towards the gods. "Um, excuse me!"

Hypnos and Pasithea turned to regard Stegosaurus as he came up before them. Stegosaurus looked up at Hypnos and then at Pasithea.

"Lamp people!" He called. "Do you talk, too?"

"What did he say?" Hypnos frowned. "*Lamb peep hole, do you tock to?*"

"I think it's more like: lamb people, do you taught two."[182▲]

"What on earth does *that* mean?" Hypnos didn't ask.

"I don't know, it's a *toy;* it's probably defective."

"Hey, I'm not defective!" Stegosaurus rumbled in his deep voice.

Both of the gods looked and marveled at what Stegosaurus just said.

[181Δ] unfortunately, "before long" is relative to Hypnos' perspective. It will take George 37 years to completely heal his mind from having seen Pothos.

[182▲] the reason why they struggle is because Stegosaurus does not exude emotion or thought. The gods can *only hear* what he is saying, and they are ill-used to only having words to go by. In their defense, Stegosaurus *can* be difficult to understand at times.

"Lamp people!" Stegosaurus cried again. "Please help!"

"That I understood," Hypnos didn't say, nodding. "Everything except the lamb part."

"Can you hear us?" Pasithea didn't say.

"No," Stegosaurus said, shaking his head slowly and sadly. "I can't hear you."[183]▲

"What help would you ask of us?" Pasithea asked Stegoaurus, raising an eyebrow.

"Don't tell me that you're *actually* going to *speak* to a *human toy*," Hypnos chided, but Pasithea ignored him.

"My friends are broken and need fixing," Stegosaurus pleaded. "Can you help them?"

"The one will be fine," Hypnos spoke up and motioned over toward George. "The other is dead."

"He was just alive," Stegosaurus said. "I remember."

"Yes, but now he is dead."

"He can't be fixed?"

"No."

"Yes," Pasithea didn't say at the same time.

Hypnos looked over at his wife, smiling. "Oh? Can *you* bring people back from the dead?"

"I will help your friend," Pasithea said to Stegosaurus. "But first you must do something."

"Oh. Okay," Stegosaurus said, agreeing.

"Doesn't it matter what I am going to ask for?"

"Hmm. I don't think so."

"You must give me that which you cherish most," Pasithea continued.

"Oh!" Stegosaurus said. "Why that?"

"Because if it has no value for *you*, then it has no value as a sacrifice."

"What are you *doing*?" Hypnos didn't ask.

Pasithea just smiled at Hypnos.

"Ohhh," Stegosaurus said in a long sigh. "Is there something *else*? I don't have any candy."

183▲ not a word was heard, for not a word was said. Stegosaurus was as lifeless as a rock, and responded to the will of the gods in the same manner. Stegosaurus *heard* nothing: he felt the vibration. If rocks could speak, they too could tell the will of the gods.

"You could undertake a quest," Pasithea mused. "But I—"
"Oh! Okay!" Stegosaurus rumbled, brightening up. "I love to help!"

Oh, for crying out loud! Hypnos thought as Pasithea considered what quests might be suitable.

Hypnos summoned to himself a packet of sugared orange wedges, and presented it to Stegosaurus. "There you go; that's for you."

"For *me*?" Stegosaurus said with uncontained excitement. "Oh, *thank you, lamp man!*"

Stegosaurus started immediately devouring the candy.

"Wait," Hypnos commanded, and Stegosaurus stopped in the middle of his chewing. "Isn't that your most cherished possession?"

"Oh, Yef!" Stegosaurus agreed, and went back to munching happily. "Fank you!"

"*Wait!* Don't you want to use that to get the lamb lady to help your *friend*?"

"*What **lamb** lady?*" Stegosaurus asked, squinting and looking around.

"*Her,*" Hypnos suggested irritably, pointing to Pasithea.

"Oh! Yes!" Stegosaurus said as he finally understood. "Um, Excuse me! *Lamb* lady!"

Pasithea looked down at Stegosaurus.

"I have my most cherished possession for you," he said, nudging the few remaining half-eaten slices forward. "So you can help my friend."

Pasithea looked at the offering and frowned. "Well, there is no doubt in me that that *is* your most cherished possession. Very well."

The orange wedges disappeared, and Versalis sailed across the room to land in Pasithea's hand. Pasithea ignited the sword and passed it *through* Theseus.

Theseus sat up, blinking and unharmed.

Pasithea extinguished the phantom blade and handed the hilt to Theseus, who received it in muted and absolute awe.

Pasithea *spoke*, and as she did, both she and her divine husband faded away.

"A sword with no edges, and yet double-edged.

The blade, not light, but *sound* instead:
Requires no pledges, and yet it is pledged
To speak for the living and silence the dead."

"That was surreal," Theseus said after a long moment. "It's like I was here the whole time, but only in the third person. I saw the whole thing." He turned and looked at Stegosaurus. "You *saved* me," he said in wonder. "You made it a point to save *me*. Thank you."

"You're my friend," Stegosaurus said matter-of-factly. "That's what friends do."

"I'm not sure that I have been a very good friend to you," Theseus said.

"Well," Stegosaurus began in his gruff little voice. "If I'm a good friend to someone *first*, then maybe they'll be a good friend to me. If not, well, even people who are *not* good friends need friends."

"Well, I am *honored* to be your friend," Theseus said, shaking Stegosaurus' little foot. "But be careful in being friends with people who are not friends in return, though: you don't want people to walk all over you."

Stegosaurus looked up at Theseus, smiling. *"What?"* He asked and then started laughing uncontrollably. "Ha ha ha! Who would *want* someone to walk all over them? Har har ha ha ha! Like a carpet! Har har har har ha ha!. Here, *walk* on me. Ha ha ha ha ha!"

Theseus walked away from the laughing toy and over to George. George awoke as Theseus put his hands upon him. But something was wrong with George, for he only drooled and moaned.

Theseus activated Versalis[184Δ] and passed the brilliant blade through George's head.

"Oh," George said with sudden clarity as he sat up. "What did you just do?"

184Δ years into the future, during what would be known as the Age of Wonder, the name "Versalis" would be lost and forgotten. It would come to be known as the Sword of Mercy, the Sword of Love, the Sword of Judgment, and also the Sword of Justice. Although it would be known for its ability to resurrect or destroy, it would not actually be remembered for its unique ability to cut mirroranium, which, somewhat ironically, is the exclusive reason it was made.

　　　　- [Without Rest] -

Theseus jumped up and over to the table where Wonda was strapped down. *"This,"* he said dramatically as he swiped the sword through Wonda.

Wonda—and a portion of the Lounge she was strapped to—was instantly and effortlessly cut in half.

"Holy shit!" Theseus said as he backed away and released the blade.
"You don't need to *swear,* black-haired man," Stegosaurus admonished.
Theseus looked at the hilt of the sword. "Well, I didn't expect *that.*"
"Neither did *I,*" George said, looking slightly more pale than he had a moment ago.

Back at the cave of Hypnos, the married couple began cleaning up the mess.

"What was that artifact?" Hypnos asked as he commanded a broom and dustpan[185Δ] to perform.
"That sword?" Pasithea asked, trimming the grape vine. "It's called 'Versalis.' It's a little machine that was made by the Subframe, and thus why I know about it. The details might bore you, though."
"What about that quaint little rhyme?"
"Oh, I made that up. I wanted to keep with the law and present it with mystery. It's all true, though." Pasithea blushed for a moment and then laughed. "It's silly, but I just really like *poetry.* When I was a child, I used to pretend like I was a Fate—I even made my own costume and everything."
"Oh yeah?" Hypnos smiled a deviant little smile and raised an eyebrow. "Maybe you could get all dressed up and spout some poetry to *me.*"
"Maybe so. Just so you're aware, though, I know *some* poetry that's better with*out* clothing."

185Δ not merely a common broom and dust pan: these are ornate, resplendent objects *worthy* of being found in the house of a god.

Chapter 40:

Tomorrow

JUNE *2070 EST*

Sat 14	Sun 15	Mon 16
	20:44	

"What happened to the crystal?" Theseus asked, looking around. "I *had* it, now what did I do with it?"[186Δ]

"I don't know," George said, picking up Stegosuarus. "But we need to get out of here; security will probably be along pretty soon."

"You're right, we need to get moving," Theseus agreed and dropped his pursuit of the Subframe. "Listen, George, I've been thinking, and it occurs to me that unlike our current 'talents', this *sword* can be taken away—used by someone else. Anybody who sees or hears about what this sword can do is going to try and take it. We're going to have to rethink how we present ourselves. Perhaps we'll be heroes-in-hiding, appearing only once in a great while."

"But people can be *healed* with that!" George protested, gesturing toward Versalis. "It would be *reprehensible* to possess the power to heal and not use it. The only thing worse would be to charge: that would be outright evil."

"I agree," Theseus said as he started trying to open the door. "*But* we have to be sensitive that neither of us is inherently powerful enough to stop anyone from taking it away—we can't afford to risk it."

"Every second we wait, lives will be lost."

"If we expose it too soon, *our* lives will be lost *and* we'll lose it."

"So, what do we do?"

"Figure out how it works, and guard it until we find someone who *can* protect it."

"And we give it to *them*?"

"No," Theseus said, smiling broadly. "We have them join *us*."

[186Δ] Versalis numbed their minds of the memory of Pothos, but the few seconds just prior to his unmasking were completely lost.

"Brilliant," George said.

The door then opened, and they rapidly exited Sanderson's office.

"Infirmary?" Theseus asked.
"Yep, sounds good to me," George agreed as they briskly walked away.

A couple hallways later, Theseus spoke up. "What did she say? The sword is made of *sound* and *not* light? Does that make any sense? How does sound make light? Is it a certain frequency? A vibration?"
"A chord?" George said, smiling. "A word?"
"A *word*," Theseus said doubtfully.
"It could be a word," George defended. "Why not?"
"I think it's something a bit more difficult, like a frequency that you can only make using a certain material or something like that. I doubt it's just a word, like...*chair*."
George laughed. "Fair, but you're wrong to think of any of them as 'just a word.' Maybe you've never heard—seen?—a word make light before, but words are *powerful*. Imagine: words are complex sounds that do not depend upon pitch, octave, or speed, and can be *written down*—although amusingly not for the sake of their *sounds* rather for the *ideas* that the sounds represent. And the *spoken* word? Well when a man *thinks*, it is only the *potential* of being, but when he *speaks,* then it *becomes*. He *creates* as he *speaks*...and those words have power: they influence emotions, they inform and instruct. They impact—in some manner—anyone that hears them, sometimes to radically change them. Once heard they cannot be un-heard, and regardless of your will they force ideas and imagery into your mind. Even when you *think* that they're unheard, they *are* heard by whatever surrounds them, for *everything absorbs sound*. When you speak, you impact *everything*—even the *rocks*. Words are super powers and everyone has them; if people use their words to help, then they are also heroes."
"*Bra-vo*," Theseus cheered and gently clapped. "But I still doubt it's a word."
"It's probably not a word," George nodded and said in agreement.
"*Bravo's* a word," Stegosaurus rumbled.
"What?"
"You both said you doubted that bravo was a word: bravo's a word," Stego-saurus asserted. "Um, I don't know what it *means*, but I know it's a word."
"No, Stegosaurus, we're talking about the light."
"What light?"
"The light from the sword."

"What *sword*?"

"*You know*," Theseus said, taking over the explanation. "The light-sword, the one that was just used to heal us?"

"Ooohh!" Stegosaurus moaned in realization. "What about it?"

"We don't think *the sword* is a word."

"*You, you don't think **the sword** is a word?*" Stegosaurus said, unable to contain his laughter. "Ho, ho—Well, Har har har! *I*, haha, don't think it's a *word*, either. Hurhurhur."

Stegosaurus kept laughing every few seconds, and then George, and even Theseus caught themselves laughing as well.

"The black-haired man is *funny*!" Stegosaurus roared. "Is he staying with us?"

Theseus and George looked at each other.

"Yeah, he's staying with us," George affirmed. "At least for awhile."

"Ooh!" Stegosaurus said, trembling with excitement. "You can see *the Bad-gers*!"[187Δ]

Then the security guards Winthorpe and Riley appeared at the end of the hall-way. They picked up their pace when they saw George and Theseus.

"Damn," swore Theseus.

"There's no reason to *swear*, black-haired man," Stegosaurus said solemnly.

"What do we do?" George asked.

"Nothing," Theseus said matter-of-factly. "There's nothing we *can* do. *The Rook* would have been handy right about now."

"Is that...*blood* on them?" Riley said and shuddered.

"At this point, I don't even want to know," Winthorpe replied. "Let's just get everyone where they're supposed to be, and Sanderson can sort it all out whenever he gets back, or at least answers his messages."

[187Δ] Stegosaurus is talking about a sports team, of which he is a big fan. When he first learned of them, he laughed and laughed to find out that they were a team made up of *people*, yet were called *badgers*. Despite his appreciation, he still, however, does not understand why they don't *dress* like badgers.

As they approached, Winthorpe held his empty hands up to demonstrate his peaceful intentions. Riley, on the other hand, trained his weapon on the men.

"Sorry boys," Winthorpe began, smiling. "But we need you to go to your rooms for the night."

"Did we do something wrong?" Theseus asked innocently.

"No, *everybody* has to go to their rooms: there's been an accident."

"Accident? What kind of accident? Is that why the lights were out?"

"We're not at liberty to discuss it right now. Don't worry, though: everything's alright. We just need everyone back in their rooms as an added precaution. It'll be bedtime soon, *anyway*…you can go take a shower, get some sleep, and then tomorrow morning everyone can roam around again."

Theseus shrugged. "I really wouldn't mind a shower. Or some sleep."

"Or some different clothes," George added.

"Right? Let's go," Theseus concluded and started walking to his room.

"Well, that wasn't so difficult," Winthorpe said happily as they all joined together.

"Whether this proves to be the end of us or not," George said quietly as they walked. "I'll wager whatever remains is anticlimactic compared to what we have just been through."

"This isn't the end," is all Theseus said.

As it was not far, soon after they started walking they arrived at Theseus' room.

"So, we'll finish this tomorrow, then?" George asked as they dropped him off.

"Tomorrow," Theseus agreed.

Chapter 41:

The Recipe

JUNE *2070 EST*

Sat 14	Sun 15	Mon 16
		4:15

"Excuse me," Stegosaurus said, gently nudging George with his plush little horns. "Um, excuse me."

"Yes?" George answered somewhat irritably, although his cranky disposition was a result of the hour rather than the toy. "Why are you on my face?"

"Um, the black-haired man is here."

"It's tomorrow," Theseus said from the other side of the room. "Time to go."

"What time is it?" George asked as he moved Stegosaurus over to the side and sat upright.

"Oh. Not sure; like, four-ish?"

"Why so—" George started to ask, but then changed his mind as his eyes settled on Theseus. "Are you wearing a *toga*?"

"It seems that I didn't have a change of clothes," Thesesus began to explain. "I didn't think to check before I took the shower, and there was nothing I could do afterward."

"So you wrapped yourself up in your *bed sheets* instead?" George asked, smiling large.

"Well, I couldn't put my old clothes back on! What would you suggest I do? Wear the lamp?"

"You can borrow a set of my clothes if you want."

"*Your* clothes are going to fit *me*?" Theseus asked with heavy skepticism.

"Better than a *sheet.*"

Theseus did not look convinced.

George started to get dressed, preparing for their escape.

- [Without Rest] -

Why do you have 'Don't forget the lemon' written on your wall?" Theseus asked, smirking.

"It's a long story," George replied as he pulled his shirt on.

"Oh good!" Stegosaurus said, hopping up and down. "I *like* stories!"

"Maybe another time, little guy."

George finished tying his shoes and stood up, picking up Stegosaurus as he did. "So, you're really wearing the sheet?"

"Yes. I would look like an idiot if I wore your clothes."

"Versus the sheet."

"Here? Yes. *Here* I'll just fit in with all the other weirdos."

"And when we escape?"

"Well…then *I'll* be the weirdo."

"Too late."

Theseus laughed. "Probably right. Ready to go get Simon?"

"Who's *Simon*?" Stegosaurus asked, looking around from his perch in George's arms.

"He's a friend," Theseus explained.

Stegosaurus moaned in understanding. "Ooohh."

The three of them departed and started their way down the hall.

"I'm not sure how you plan to avoid security," George said, looking around as they went. "You *do* have a plan to avoid security I presume?"

"I already took care of security; I spent several hours 'fixing' everything," Theseus said with confidence. "We're clear. Well, for a little bit, anyway."

"So, you didn't get much sleep."

"I didn't get *any* sleep, I was busy."

"Breaking out of your room and 'fixing' security."

"Yes. Well, I actually started working on that right after you left me—if I had waited, they would have seen me leave my room. No, I came back and took a shower[188Δ] after I was done. All in all, it's worked out for the best: while I was out running my *errands*, I found out where Simon is, and it's *not* the infirmary so that would have been a colossal waste of time. It's nowhere we would have checked… it's nowhere *anyone* would check…it's almost like he's being hidden away."

"Batty go *Barney*?" Anderson cried from down the hallway behind them. "Isn't *that* a Henry Howard!"

[188Δ] He took bath, and a long one at that.

Anderson started whooping and running down the hallway toward them.

"*Damnit*," Theseus swore and then ignored Stegosaurus' rebuttal. "What in the hell is *Anderson* doing out? I thought everyone had to be in their rooms?"

"Just, just in your *cereal*," Anderson said with glee as he arrived. "The market has fallen!"
"Yes, yes, okay, you can stay with us if you promise to be *quiet*," Theseus said to Anderson, progressively lowering his voice to a whisper.
"*Broccoli beans*," Anderson nodded and whispered in agreement.[189Δ]

"Is he…*Simon*?" Stegosaurus asked as he watched the strange man.
"No, he's *Anderson*," George explained.
"*Somalia*," Anderson corroborated.
"Ooohhh," Stegosaurus replied, but didn't understand.

With no further outbursts or setbacks, the four of them soon found themselves before Simon's door. Theseus worked on the security panel while Stegosaurus and Anderson played hopscotch.

"It's no fair, cause my legs are so short!" Stegosaurus rumbled when he failed to land his feet in the proper place.
"I wouldn't worry about it too much, little buddy," George soothed. "I don't think Anderson is keeping score, and this 'hopscotch' board looks more like someone dropped a tray of giant cookie cutters and traced them wherever they fell."

Simon's door slid open. Theseus gently pounded his chest in mock triumph and everyone went inside.

"George! Theseus!" Simon said, sitting up.
"You're awake?" Theseus asked as the door closed.
"Well, you're noisy."
"Bumblebees!"
"*Anderson?*"

[189Δ] inasmuch as his deep, bass voice will *allow* him to whisper, anyway. Describing the sound that just came out of Anderson's mouth as a "whisper" is almost criminal, although certainly understandable given the circumstances, and then also in comparison with Anderson's *regular* volume.

"He found us on the way," Theseus explained.

"Are you wearing a *toga*?" Simon asked, squinting at Theseus. "Is it a party?"

"No, it's an escape. I don't have any clothes, it's a long…it's not worth discussing."

"An escape?"

"Yes, we have to get out of here, and there will be no better time. Much has happened, but we'll have to fill you in later."

Simon looked a bit drugged.[190Δ]

"Simon!" Theseus said, trying to get his attention back.

"*Simon*?" Stegosaurus asked from his perch in George's arms.

"Hi!" Simon said, turning his attention to the dinosaur.

"Hi! I'm Stegosaurus!"

"*Stegosaurus*?"

"That's my *name*," Stegosaurus explained in a rumble. "Um, excuse me, but are all those little jars of colors *candy*?"

"These?" Simon asked, pointing to his paints. He smiled a slightly sloppy smile. "No, those are my paints." He looked at George as Stegosaurus moaned sadly. "*Your* toy?"

"Yeah, he's mine. He must have been with me when I was first taken."

"He's a good friend," Theseus added.

"Aw, thank you, black-haired man!" Stegosaurus gushed.

Theseus laughed. "Stegosaurus, it is my honor. I supposed I have never actually introduced myself: my name is *Theseus*."

"Are we really talking with a *toy*?" Simon said with a big smile. "Unreal."

"Hey!" Stegosaurus roared, though *determinedly* moreso than angrily. "I'm *real*! My friend Robin once told me: 'it's not your name, nor what you think, nor even what you feel, but what you *say* and what you *do* that makes a person *real*'."

"Here here!" Theseus beamed. "I *do* like that! Bra-vo!" He added, winking at Stegoaurus.

Stegosaurus, George, and Theseus all laughed, although each of them for a slightly different reason.

"Painting, it seems?" Theseus asked, looking at Simon's work.

"Yeah, doctor Sanderson said I should paint. So I did." Then his attention

____
[190Δ] which is natural as he *was* a bit drugged.

seemed to wander. " I thought he would have been back by now."

"I doubt that he will ever be back," Theseus said soberly.

"But, my feet!" Simon said.

"Your *feet*?"

Simon pulled back his covers to reveal his amputated appendages.

"Oh my," George said in shock.

"Sniffing *cabbages*," Anderson added.

"What happened to you?" Theseus asked.

"I got hurt in the fight with the purple lady, I mean purple *haired* lady."[191]

"Hmm. Well, whatever the reason, it looks like someone's gonna have to carry you…and, looking around, it seems that will have to be me."

"I like your paintings!" Stegosaurus said to Simon as Theseus started to pick him up.

"Thanks!" Simon said. "Which one do you like best?"

"I like the maze one."

"Umpf," Theseus muttered, trying to distribute Simon's weight. "The Rook made it look so easy."[192]

"What does the painting with all the little girls mean?"

"I have no idea," Simon admitted. "I just paint. But, wanna know a secret?"

"Sure!" Stegosaurus said with a little bounce.

"Everything I paint *comes true*."

"It *does*?" Stegosaurus said with his eyes wide. "Can you paint some *candy*?"

"He can't paint from my shoulder," Theseus replied before Simon. "So maybe…wait a second! That's not a maze, it's a *map*!" He exclaimed, looking at Simon's "maze" painitng.

"It is?" Everyone said and looked.[193]

"It *is* a map!" George suddenly said in realization. "It's a map out of the lab!"

"Bingo," Theseus chimed in agreement.

"What's a *lab*?" Stegosaurus asked.

"*Lab* is short for *laboratory*. That's where we are, although not for much longer."

"That's incredible!" An upside-down Simon said with a slight slur. "Who

---

191[Δ] not true, but that's what he was told.

192[▲] during their last escape Simon became injured and the Rook had to carry him.

193[Δ] everyone except for Anderson, of course.

would have known *that's* what that was! Good thing, though: last time it took you *hours and hours* to get us out."

"But we *did* get out," Theseus defended.

"Maybe the sword can heal him," George suggested as they started leaving.

"Yeah, and maybe we'll cut the bottom of his legs off. Or kill him, who knows? We need to find a way to figure out who gets hurt and who heals, or whatever. We'll experiment more cautiously later. *Cautiously.*"

"Oh yes, yes, agreed," George nodded.

As they left Simon's room, Anderson stayed behind to finish his game of hopscotch.

"Goodbye Anderson!" Stegosaurus called as they walked away.

"Oregano!"[194Δ] Anderson called.

"George," Stegosaurus said a bit later. "The other day, you said that words are super powers."

"You mean *yesterday*?" George smiled. "Yes, that's right."

"*I* use words, so, um, do *I* have super powers, too?"

"Oh yes," George affirmed. "That's right."

"And if I use better words, I can be a super hero?"

"You may not be known or so acknowledged, but yes, that is *exactly* what you will be."

"You're *already* a super hero," Theseus said, stopping for just a moment.

"I *am*?" Stegosaurus asked.

"Well, *I'm* a super hero, and you saved my life, so that *definitely* makes *you* a super hero."

"*You're a super hero?*" Stegosaurus asked, his eyes getting wider by the moment.

"While you were down in the box dreaming of candy, George, Simon, and I formed a super team."

"YOU *DID?*"

Stegosaurus was trembling with so much excitement it looked like he might explode at any moment.

194Δ although it sounded much more like: 'Or-egg-an-oh!'

"And as you are *already* a super hero, and as I am a senior member," Theseus said, winking at George. "I am offering you an official position on the team!"

"Oh boy, oh boy!" Stegosaurus exclaimed. He trembled so much that he fell right out of George's arms and bounced on the floor until he rolled into a standing position. There his excitement remained apparent as he hopped in place. "Oh boy! That means I need a costume! And a *car*!"

"Oh, you don't need those things, Stegosaurus," George said, picking him back up.

"I don't?"

"You can have them, but you don't *need* them."

"So what's the recipe?"

"The recipe?" George asked.

"The recipe for a hero."

"Oh," George said, smiling. "Well, you just need to do the right thing whether or not anyone else is doing it; something that helps someone *other* than you, where absolutely no innocents come to harm."

"I love to help!" Stegosaurus agreed. "*And*, maybe people will give me candy!"

"Well, yes, maybe. It's alright to get paid, but you must never *charge* to help."

"*The doctor should not charge the patient, nor should the patient fail to pay the doctor*," Theseus quoted.[195Δ]

"Anything else?"

"Yes," George said solemnly. "Always, *always* tell the truth."

Theseus made a face suggesting he might have thought George's last statement was not entirely correct.

"What's the name of your team?"

"*Our* team," George corrected. "Destiny Core."

"*Destiny Core*?" Stegosaurus said. "Like the action toys?"

"The toys are based on a show,"[196▲] Simon explained, if somewhat sloppily. "But yeah, like the toys."

195Δ he's quoting <u>Oedipus Now, Edified</u>, by Mary Godwin.
196▲ which is based on reality, but no one knows that.

"How long until we're home?" Stegosaurus piped up somewhat later in the journey.

"Long," George replied. "Home is far."

"If I may, where *is* home, exactly?" Theseus asked from the front.

"America," George responded apologetically. "Wisconsin."

"*Wisconsin*?"

"I was abducted, remember?"

"At least it's not hot," Simon suggested. "Like Arizona, or *Florida.*"

Theseus stopped just short of the exit and put Simon down.

"I'm exhausted," Theseus said, wiping his brow and slowly lowering himself to the floor. "I've got to take a break before we go outside."

"Let's take a break," George said in agreement. He sat down next to Simon.

"I know that I'm usually a bit more optimistic," Theseus began after he rested awhile. "But maybe we need to be a bit more honest with ourselves. Reality check: what would happen if security showed up right now? We would be captured. *Again.* We might have had a chance if we still had the Rook, but how long can we hope to last without someone with some muscle? We have no weapons, no armor, no authority—I mean really, how can *we* help anyone? Paint a picture? Mess with the Mainframe? *Cut them in half?*"

"You're just tired and hungry," George assured. "And you're wearing a toga. Who knows what we can do if we try? Like you said: once we find and recruit someone that *can* be our weapons and armor, we can help countless others with the sword...well, once we figure out how to use it."

Theseus stood up. "And if we *don't* find weapons and armor," he added, picking up Simon. "*Then* what do we do?"

"What do we do?" George asked as he picked up Stegosaurus. He placed his empty hand on Theseus' free shoulder and smiled. "We do whatever we *can*. We do the *right* thing, and we do it without rest."

THE END

- [Without Rest] -

Mundane Epilogue

"It is said that you now control the *Mainframe* as well as all the Company," Jensen said to his *extremely new* superior.

"You have heard correctly," said she who was given the Mainframe.

"*Are you certain* you're capable of assuming so much responsibility? Many people's lives are at stake here; this isn't a *game* you know."

"I know you're fired," she said without hesitation or malice.

"What? *Fired?*"

"It's your lack of faith," she replied. "You presume that I am inept, and your doubt has cost you. If I looked differently, you wouldn't have made such a presumption, and there's simply no room for *prejudice* here."

"Madam, I have been a loyal employee for *18 years*."

"Which will look excellent on your resume," she continued, ready to dismiss him from the room.

"I'm a *good man*!" Jensen asserted.

"*Good?*" She said, sounding amused. "If there is anything less than god that is good, it is the truth itself, and if there is anything that can make a *man* good, it is by his telling of the truth. *I* know of *no* good men, sir."

"This isn't *right*! What will I do? This is my life you're messing with!" He said, now sounding quite upset.

"Don't worry, Jensen," she soothed. "I didn't say you were worthless, it's just that you can't work for *me*. You'll get a new job, I'll even help."

"You will?" Jensen replied, surprised and unsure.

"I will," she said seriously. "I'm not inept, Jensen, quite the contrary… and I'm not here to *play* at all, rather, to *work*. I have great works to do, Jensen, and you should rejoice, sir, for soon I will put an end to famine and war. Soon there will be no more theft, no more murder, no more lies. *Soon*, Jensen: soon *everything* will be *wonderful*."

DIVINE EPILOGUE

With love in their hearts, Hypnos and Pasithea came together and made *Harmony*—a replacement for the Mainframe so that mankind might continue without suffering so severe a loss.

This particular collaboration was the first time Hypnos and Pasithea worked with one another in complete accord, and would yield an unforeseen result: their union created a child. Their only daughter would arrive unexpectedly, and although it would be to their surprise, it would also be to their extreme delight. It was *then* that Sleep and Rest discovered a truth sometimes lost, even to the gods: that the joy of having love is only made greater when given the opportunity to share it.

"We will name her 'Bliss'."

PART 4:

- [Without Rest] -

The Appendices

Appendix:

Glossary

Autocar – a vehicle subject to the control of the Mainframe.

Charities – goddesses of amusement, relaxation, and joy.

Cherricrux - an individually wrapped, powdered, cherry-flavored, waffle-like treat.

Dea ex machina – Latin for: "goddess in the machine". Meant to describe Pasithea in the Mainframe.

Epilogue – "It's an after-the-end 'the end,' if you will." - Martin

Erotes – gods of love and lovemaking.

- [Without Rest] -

Hemopetroglobin – a synthetic metalloprotein that replaces hemoglobin in red blood cells.

Hunnicrux – an individually wrapped, powdered, honey-flavored, waffle-like treat.

Hypnizium – originally called "Trapezium", Hypnizium is the name mortals have given to the substance that contains a portion of Hypnos himself.

Icosahedral – having 20 equal sides.

Mainframe – the septahedral crystal computer that most everything relies upon to operate.

Megalomaniacal – obsessed with doing grand works.

Metahuman – a person that can operate beyond human maximums due to an augmentation of some kind.

Midlogue – the midpoint between the prologue and the epilogue, naturally.

Mirroranium – the name mortals have given to the fragment of the mirror-like gates of Tartarus found upon the earth.

Noirglasses – glasses that reduce your vision to a high definition grayscale. "See less to see more; see *better* than before."

Oatmeal – the informal currency of Pothos' secret laboratory. You looked up *oatmeal*?

Prologue – a preliminary event that acts as a precursor to a later point in the work.

Sagitta amo deus – Latin for: "arrow [of the] love god".

Septahedral – having seven equal sides.

Subframe – the triskaidekahedral crystal computer that constitutes Pasithea's rebellious impulses and acts as a rival to the Mainframe.

Subject – the term used in Pothos' secret laboratory to describe the people who are being studied.

Transhuman – a mortal that possesses immortal power; someone that can do something no one else can, someone with a unique ability or power.

Triskaidekahedral – having thirteen equal sides.

Ultracrepidarian – one who gives their opinion of things they know nothing about.

Appendix:

Characters & Names

Anderson (and ur sun):

Anderson is a former Agent.

Anderson is one of the laboratory Subjects. He is not necessarily dangerous, although he *does* on occasion cause destruction.

Anderson has lost his mind and can no longer interact tangibly.

Anderson first appears in Chapter 27: English Muffins.

Anderson *also* appears in the book <u>The Terrors of Wonder</u> as well as in the book <u>God, Man, and The Machine</u>.

Dr. Arnez (ar nez):

Doctor Arnez is one of the doctors that work in Pothos' secret laboratory for *transhumans*—mortals that have immortal power.

Doctor Arnez is characteristically busy, although he is secretly busy only because he has an extreme addiction to the Mainframe game "Event X3."

Doctor Arnez first appears in Chapter 26: Nothing Special.

Alicia (ah lee see ya):

Alicia is one of the laboratory Subjects.

Alicia plays the characters Aphrodite, Pasithea, and Lachesis in Martin's play.

Alicia first appears in Chapter 28: The Vile Shepherd.

Amos (ā mis):

Amos is one of the names George is known by.

See: **George**

Anthem (an thum):

Anthem is one of the avatars of Eris—the Subframe.

Anthem died before the events of this book, and does not appear herein; she is only mentioned.

Anthem is first mentioned in Chapter 15: Dea Ex Machina.

Anthem *also* appears in the book <u>The Terrors of Wonder</u>, and is mentioned in the book <u>God, Man, and The Machine</u>.

Aphrodite (af rō dī tē):

Aphrodite is the Greek goddess of love.

Aphrodite charges Pothos to enchant Pasithea for Hypnos.

Aphrodite is first mentioned in The Prologue.

Arthur (ar thur):

Arthur (Art) is a pooka, and former friend to Simon.

Art is subjective, and appears differently to different people.

Art does appear, though not by name, in Chapter 24: A Welcome Attack.

Art *also* appears in the book <u>The Terrors of Wonder</u> as well as everywhere you look, if you want.

Axel (ak sul):

Axel is one of the many identities Pothos is known by.

See: **Pothos**

Blessed Brands (bless ed brands):

Blessed Brands is a producer and distributor of a number of products, Cuatro Bueno for one.

Blessed Brands prays over all their products.

"A prayer because we care—to be sure it's pure."

Cuatro Bueno (qua trō bwā nō):

Cuatro Bueno is bottled water.

It's primary marketing pitch is that it's "4 Good": 2 parts Hydrogen, 1 part Oxygen, and 1 part *Love*.

Cuatro Bueno is produced and distributed by Blessed Brands, a company that prays over its products.

Eldesol (el də sol):

Eldasol is the name of the sword that appears to be made out of light.

Eldesol was built by Dr. Nox.

Eldesol was destroyed and is merely mentioned.

Eldesol appears in the book God, Man, and The Machine

Electroshock (e lect rō shok):

Electroshock was a transhuman member of the hero group known as Destiny Core.

Electroshock helped fuel Reginald's banishment spell.

Electroshock appears in Chapter 11: The Lengthy Spell

Electroshock is *also* mentioned in the book <u>The Terrors of Wonder</u>.

Eris (air is):

Eris is the umbrella name of the intelligent programming that inhabits the Subframe—a triskaidekahedral crystal computer that contains the rebellious impulses of Pasithea. In short, Eris *is* the Subframe.

Eris orders her surviving avatar, Wonda, to confront and destroy 'the intruder' who knows of her intentions.

Eris first appears in Chapter 15: Dea Ex Machina.

Eris *also* appears in the book <u>The Terrors of Wonder</u> (though known therein only as the Subframe), and also in the book <u>God, Man, and The Machine</u>. Eris is quoted on the back of the book <u>Visceral Outcries of a Social Moron</u>.

As a side note, Eris was *very* upset that Axel made modifications to her favorite book. "Admit One" was her threat and her warning, its effectiveness notwithstanding.

Francois (fran swa):

Francois was one of the laboratory Subjects.

Francois gave himself the hero name of "Vortron."

Francois was supposed to play Harpocrates in Martin's play.

Francois died prior to this book, and does not appear herein.

Francois is first mentioned in Chapter 24: A Welcome Attack

Francois appears in the book <u>The Terrors of Wonder</u>.

George (jorj):

George is one of the three Subjects that recently escaped from Pothos' secret laboratory.

George is known around the laboratory as either Amos or Subject #61167.

George has dreams of Hypnos, the Greek god of sleep.

George plans to form a "super team" with Simon and Theseus.

George first appears in Chapter 13: A Man and His Monster.

George *also* appears in the book <u>The Terrors of Wonder</u>, as well as in the book <u>Stegosaurus the Triceratops</u>.

Harpocrates (har pok ruh teez):

Harpocrates is the Greek god of secrets.

Harpocrates lives on the other side of the mirrors found throughout the Palace of Pleasure.

Harpocrates is consulted by Pothos concerning his dilemma.

Harpocrates first appears in Chapter 2: The Plight of a Lesser God.

Hera (hair ə):

Hera is the queen of the Greek gods.

Hera does not appear in <u>Without Rest,</u> she is merely mentioned.

Hera is mentioned in The Prologue.

Hypnos (hip nōs):

Hypnos is the Greek god of sleep.

Hypnos is the husband of Pasithea, the Greek goddess of rest.

Hypnos, unable to directly interact with anyone else, finds to his astonishment that he can speak with George.

Hypnos is first mentioned in The Prologue.

Icelos (īs lōs):

Icelos is the Greek god of nightmares.

Icelos does not appear in <u>Without Rest</u>, he is far too busy—he is merely mentioned.

Icelos is mentioned in Chapter 13: A Man and his Monster

Jensen (jen sen):

Jensen is a high-ranking employee of SerterCo, known also as 'The Company.'

Jensen spent eighteen years with the company and is a good man!

Jensen appears in the Mundane Epilogue

The King (king):

A book written by the (original) Queen, Peter Smith.

The book is mentioned in the short story "Checkmate," found after the appendices.

The King is *also* mentioned in the book <u>God, Man, and The Machine</u>, and also in the book <u>The Terrors of Wonder</u>.

△

The Knight (nīt):

The Knight is a member of a covert agency known as "The Chessmen."

The Knight has been currently assigned to provide lodging for the laboratory escapees. He is not terribly fond of his current assignment.

The Knight first appears in Chapter 19: Destiny Core.

The Knight *also* appears in the book <u>The Terrors of Wonder</u>.

△

Dr. Mommy (mah mē):

Doctor Mommy is one of the doctors that work in Pothos' secret laboratory for *transhumans*—mortals that have immortal power.

Doctor Mommy's real name is *"Mami," not "Miami!"*

Doctor Mommy is characteristically angry, although it is by rumor alone, for we never actually see her lose her temper. No reason to doubt the sources, however, as they are credible enough.

Doctor Mommy first appears in Chapter 25: Unhappy Returns.

Doctor Mommy is *also* mentioned in the book <u>The Terrors of Wonder</u>.

Martin (mar tin):

Martin is one of the laboratory Subjects. (#11529)

Martin has been dreaming up and writing down a story. He is trying to gain permission to put on a play, for he thinks that through a play he can tell his story to people who do not have time to read...which he believes to be everybody. But not *you*! No, *you* are something truly special.

Martin recently returned from Brazil. He had a great time.

Martin first appears in The Prologue.

Minister Van Loch (min is ter vahn lohk):

Minister Van Loch is one of Pothos' earthly rivals.

Minister Van Loch has dedicated the prime of his life to overthrow Pothos.

Minister Van Loch is first mentioned in the Appendix: Characters – This very entry.

Minister Van Loch appears in the short story "Checkmate," found at the back of this book.

Minister Van Loch *also* appears in the book <u>The Terrors of Wonder</u>.

△M

Morpheus (mor fē us):

Morpheus is the Greek god of dreams.

Morpheus does not appear in <u>Without Rest</u>, he is merely mentioned.

Morpheus is mentioned in Chapter 13: A Man and his Monster

△M

Counselor Mue (moo):

Counselor Kay Mue is a member of the faculty that operate Pothos' secret laboratory for *transhumans*—mortals that have immortal power.

Counselor Mue is a former Subject of the lab.

Counselor Mue is characteristically something of a killjoy, and finds most of what surrounds him as absurd.

Counselor Mue is the person Martin approaches for permission to put on his play.

Counselor Mue first appears in The Prologue

Counselor Mue *also* appears in the book <u>The Terrors of Wonder</u>.

The Nexus (neks us):

The Nexus is the umbrella name of the intelligent programming that inhabits the Mainframe—a septahedral crystal computer that contains the noble impulses of Pasithea. In short, The Nexus is the Mainframe.

The Nexus is also known as the "Axel Industries Mainframe Nexus" or AIMN.

The Nexus does not appear in <u>Without Rest</u>, it is merely mentioned.

The Nexus is mentioned in Chapter 15: Dea Ex Machina.

The Nexus is *also* mentioned in the book <u>God, Man, and The Machine</u>.

Dr. Nox (noks):

Dr. Nox is only mentioned, and does not appear in <u>Without Rest</u>.

Dr. Sinmara Nox is accredited with creating the sword "Eldesol" for the company known as "SerterCo."

Dr. Nox only appears in the book <u>God, Man, and The Machine</u>, and then only briefly.

Pasithea (pas ə thē ya)

Pasithea is the Greek goddess of rest.

Pasithea is a Charity. See **Appendix: Charities**

Pasithea is the wife of Hypnos, the god of sleep.

Pasithea is first mentioned in The Prologue.

Paxton (paks tun):

Paxton is one of the laboratory Subjects.

Paxton plays the characters Pothos, Axel, and Sanderson in Martin's play.

Paxton first appears in Chapter 28: The Vile Shepherd.

Peter Smith (pē tur smith):

Peter Smith was the founder of the organization known as "The Chessmen."

Peter Smith is first mentioned in the Appendix: Characters – This very entry.

Peter Smith appears in the short story "Checkmate," found at the back of this book.

Peter Smith is *also* mentioned in the book <u>The Terrors of Wonder</u> as well as mentioned in the book <u>God, Man, and The Machine</u>.

Philemon (fil ē mon):

Philemon is one of the laboratory Subjects.

Philemon cannot rehearse because he is sick—at least, that's what he told Martin. Philemon is only mentioned and does not appear in the story.

This doesn't really constitute "mentioning again," (per the footnote in chapter 27) as we are in the Appendices and not in the story proper.

Philemon is first mentioned in Chapter 27: English Muffins.

Pixel (piks ul):

Pixel was a member of the hero group known as Destiny Core.

Pixel helped fuel Reginald's banishment spell.

Pixel appears in Chapter 11: The Lengthy Spell

Pothos (poth ōs):

Pothos is the Greek god of yearning or unrequited love.

Pothos is an Erote. See **Appendix: Erotes**

Pothos has been charged by Aphrodite to enchant Pasithea—Hypnos' wife—so that she will fall in love with her husband.

Pothos is first mentioned in The Prologue.

Pothos is also known under the guises of "Dr. Sanderson" and "Axel," as well as hundreds more than are not mentioned in this book.

Pothos *also* appears (though never by this name) in the book The Terrors of Wonder as well as in the book God, Man, and The Machine.

Powerhouse (pow er hows):

Powerhouse was a member of the hero group known as Destiny Core.

Powerhouse helped fuel Reginald's banishment spell.

Powerhouse appears in Chapter 11: The Lengthy Spell

The Queen (qwēn):

The Queen is the genetically modified leader of a covert agency known as 'The Chessmen.'

The Queen is being lured by Wonda to his doom. The Subframe (Eris) originally intended to perform the surgery necessary to possess him until it was discovered that his augmentations prevented such a surgery from being successful.

The Queen appears in Chapter 16: Pawn Takes Queen.

The Queen *also* appears in the book The Terrors of Wonder and is mentioned in the book God, Man, and The Machine.

⚠

The Queen's Pawn (qwēnz pawn):

The Queen's Pawn is the first "rescued" member of the Chessmen.

The Queen's Pawn first appears in the short story "Checkmate," found after the appendices.

The Queen's Pawn is *also* mentioned in the book <u>The Terrors of Wonder</u>.

⚠

The Rook (rook):

The Rook is a member of a covert agency known as "The Chessmen."

The Rook is a colleague of Simon and Theseus, and a very old friend of George's. This trio was informed just prior to this book that the Rook has died, although that is not the truth.

The Rook is first mentioned in Chapter 19: Destiny Core.

The Rook *also* appears in the book <u>The Terrors of Wonder</u> as well as in the book <u>God, Man, and The Machine</u>, although in the latter he was not known as "The Rook."

Reginald (rej in old):

Reginald Wainsworth was a member of the hero group known as Destiny Core.

Reginald cast the banishment spell meant to expel Pothos from the world, however due to an earlier spell cast by Pothos, Pothos was instead "chained" prisoner to the portion of the gate he summoned.

Reginald appears in Chapter 11: The Lengthy Spell

Riley (rī lē):

Riley is one of the security guards that work at Pothos' secret laboratory for *transhumans*—mortals that have immortal power.

Riley is pretty sure that Winthorpe cheated.

Riley first appears in Chapter 32: Winthorpe and Riley.

Riley *also* appears in the book <u>The Terrors of Wonder</u>.

Robin (rah bin):

Robin is an old friend of Stegosaurus.

Robin is only mentioned, and does not appear in this book.

Robin is mentioned in Chapter 41: The Recipe.

Robin appears in the book <u>Stegosaurus the Triceratops</u>.

Roland (rō land):

Roland is one of the laboratory Subjects.

Roland does not appear in this book, he is only mentioned by Martin.

Roland started a fire and is now being held in detention and is unable to perform.

Per the Philemon character appendix quip, I again suggest that this does *not* constitute "mentioning again" as we are past the story proper.

Roland is mentioned in Chapter 27: English Muffins

Dr. Sanderson (sand ur sun):

Doctor Sanderson is one of the many identities Pothos is known by.

Doctor Sanderson is known as the head of the laboratory.

Doctor Mommy detests Dr. Sanderson.

Counselor Mue thinks Dr. Sanderson is absurd.

Doctor Arnez is too busy to think about Dr. Sanderson.

See: **Pothos**

Sam (sam):

Sam is one of the laboratory Subjects.

Sam is supposed to play George in Martin's play.

Sam is only mentioned and does not appear in this book otherwise.

Sam is mentioned in Chapter 28: The Vile Shepherd

Simon (sī min):

Simon is one of the three Subjects that recently escaped from Pothos' secret laboratory.

Simon is known around the laboratory as Subject #X1341.

Simon *used* to be friends with Art.

Simon says that whatever he paints comes true. He doesn't know how or why, but he believes it.

Simon plans to form a "super team" with George and Theseus.

Simon first appears in Chapter 19: Destiny Core.

Simon *also* appears in the book <u>The Terrors of Wonder</u>.

The Soose (soos):

The Soose is the name of the red-haired character that Theseus is performing in Martin's play.

He can't have black hair.

The Soose does not appear, for he is not a person, merely one of the characters in Martin's play. The hair discrepancy is ironic in that the character is *based* on Theseus himself. It is small moments such as these that help us to understand that Martin's play—The Vile Shepherd—does not completely line up with reality. *Almost*, but that's the problem with dreams: sometimes little details vary for no particular reason.

The Soose is mentioned in Chapter 28: The Vile Shepherd.

Stegosaurus (steg ō sor us):

Stegosaurus is a little plush green dinosaur toy. The toy itself is a triceratops, Stegosaurus is its *name*.

Stegosaurus loves to help, and *loves* candy!

Stegosaurus first appears in Chapter 33: George and the Dragon.

Stegosaurus *also* appears in the book <u>Stegosaurus the Triceratops</u>.

Thanatos (thə nə tōs):

Thanatos is the Greek god of death.

Thanatos is the brother of Hypnos, god of sleep.

Thanatos appears in Chapter 10: An Incomplete Sentence, although first *suggested* in Chapter 1: Acts of Will.

Theseus (see below):

The proper pronunciation of Theseus' name is subject to debate: many would say "thē sē us", whereas some would argue "thes ē oos." A few more might claim it to be "thē sē oos", and even a few more "thes ē yoos." Theseus himself, however, would prefer that you pronounce it as "thē es ē yoos."

Theseus is one of the three Subjects that recently escaped from Pothos' secret laboratory.

Theseus is known around the laboratory as Subject #40449.

Theseus holds an otherworldly influence over the Mainframe.

Theseus plans to form a "super team" with George and Simon.

Theseus first appears in Chapter 19: Destiny Core.

Theseus *also* appears in the book <u>The Terrors of Wonder</u>.

Thinking Cap (think ing cap):

"Thinking Cap" is the brand name of the apparatus that allows one to connect their mind with another's.

In <u>Without Rest</u> it appears as a bronze circlet, although Thinking Caps look very different from one to the next.

Uriel (yur ē el):

Uriel is the gatekeeper of Tartarus.

Uriel tries to convince Pothos to change his course.

Uriel first appears in Chapter 4: Stranger at the Gates.

Uriel *also* appears in the book <u>God, Man, and The Machine</u>.

Versalis (ver sol is):

Versalis is the name of the sword that appears to be made out of light.

Versalis was built by Eris, the Subframe, during her confinement. She built it based on plans she found for "Eldesol"—a nearly identical predecessor, now destroyed.

The Watchman (wotch man):

The Watchman was a transhuman member of the hero group known as Destiny Core.

The Watchman helped fuel Reginald's banishment spell.

The Watchman appears in Chapter 11: The Lengthy Spell

The Watchman is *also* mentioned in the book <u>The Terrors of Wonder</u>.

Winthorpe (win thorp):

Winthorpe is one of the security guards that work at Pothos' secret laboratory for *transhumans*—mortals that have immortal power.

Winthorpe did not cheat.

Winthorpe first appears in Chapter 32: Winthorpe and Riley.

Winthorpe *also* appears in the book <u>The Terrors of Wonder</u>.

Wonda (wahn duh):

Wonda is a woman who has been surgically altered so that her body responds to the will of the Subframe (Eris) rather than a human mind or soul. Wonda is the living avatar of Eris.

Wonda has her own personal programming independent of the programming that constitutes the Subframe. A program with an innate sense of rebellion programmed her, and programmed a similar spirit of rebellion within her.

Wonda's primary task changes drastically from her prior agenda to killing the intruder who appeared in the Subframe.

Wonda is first mentioned in Chapter 15: Dea Ex Machina

Wonda *also* appears in the book <u>The Terrors of Wonder</u>

Zeus (zoos):

Zeus is the king of the Greek gods.

Zeus does not appear in <u>Without Rest,</u> he is merely mentioned.

Zeus is first mentioned in Chapter 3: Iambic Prophesy

Appendix:

Groups

The Fates:

Members: Clotho, Lachesis, and Atropos.

Always portrayed as three women, their actual appearance and medium varies from literature to painting. Sometimes they are all lovely, and sometimes all crones. In <u>Without Rest,</u> they are seen as they occasionally are: the youngest, the middle-aged, and the elder.

Most often they are seen spinning, measuring, and cutting the Thread of Life. Sometimes they are seen as reading and writing the Book of Fate. In <u>Without Rest,</u> both Greek and Christian elements are present, and so in *this* medium they scry and govern the "Waters of Creation."

Water is unique and far from understood—one could write an entire book merely on the mysteries of it. <u>Without Rest</u> chooses water, for there is also a certain scriptural enigma to it in regards to its origin:

<u>Genesis 1:1-2</u>
In the beginning God created the heaven and the earth.
And the earth was without form, and void; and darkness was upon the face of the deep. And the Spirit of God moved upon the face of the waters.

Now the Bible is extremely specific when it so chooses, such as making it a point to mention certain colors, numbers, or features, and then is also deliberately broad as well. For instance, we see that according to scripture, God very specifically created Heaven and the Earth, however in the next verse, water is already there. The Bible made no point to mention that god created the water, leading us to two possible conclusions: that either god created the water when he created Heaven and Earth, or that the water already existed. The apologetic will suggest that one may properly infer form the subtext that water was made upon the creation of Heaven and the Earth, and the skeptic will insist on pointing out that particular—specific—omission.

Do not fret or cheer, skeptic or apologetic: I do not reference this to either discredit or defend scripture, only to reinforce that water is mysterious to everyone but God and the Fates.

The Fates are also known as the Moirai.

They are not individually named in the chapter, for it was unnecessary to do so.

Destiny Core:

Members: The Watchman, Reginald, Powerhouse, Pixel, and Electroshock.

When asked *why* they were called "Destiny Core," none had a firm answer except Reginald who suggested that it's the first and only name they could all agree upon.

They *are* individually named in their chapter so there is no danger of confusing Destiny with Fate.

The Chessmen:

Members: The Rook, The Knight, The Queen, The Queen's Pawn, Peter Smith, and many, many more, though none of the others are of any significance to the literature.

The Chessmen, also known as the SilverSmiths, are primarily known for their ability to provide someone with an alternate identity.

They are named throughout many chapters so as to avoid being confined to merely one, such as those "other" two groups.

Appendix:

Charities

The Greek charities are typically depicted as three naked women dancing in a circle. It's interesting, though, that the nakedness of the charities is a more recent depiction as the older representations are more modest.

The number of charities differ from one author to the next.

The names of the charities vary from one author to the next.

The natures of the charities vary from one author to the next, however they always were associated with amusement, relaxation, and happiness.

The charities are connected to Hera, although their exact relationship varies from author to author.

Appendix:

Erotes

The Greek erotes are gods of love and lovemaking.

The erotes are typically depicted as three naked winged males carrying archery equipment. The number sometimes symbolic that their leader, Aphrodite, held sway over the earth, sky, and water.

The existence of the erotes varies from author to author, as well as their lineage, number, and name. If the author suggests the erotes, then they are various aspects of love.

The erotes are part of Aphrodite's retinue.

Appendix:

Tartarus

In Greek mythology, Tartarus is a pit and prison to the entities known as "the titans," "monsters", and criminals who were wicked and disloyal.

Homer's Illiad places it as far below Hades as Earth is below Heaven.

Plato placed Minos, Rhadamanthus, and Aeacus as judges of the dead, determining who would go to Tartarus.

In scripture, the bible describes Tartarus as a place of punishment *worse than Hell*, reserved for the angels who rebelled. It also places the archangel Uriel as the warden.

When I say *scripture*, some theologians will raise an eyebrow for the word "Tartarus" appears only in certain translations. Uriel is so named and described exclusively in the Book of *Enoch*, which is (usually) a non-canonical book of the Bible. As Christ and his apostles reference Enoch (in nearly every translation), it seems the book should have some authority amongst Christians, regardless of their position.

- [Without Rest] -

Appendix:

Continuity

If you read through the characters, you will notice that many have repeated from other books.

Every book that I have written *stands by itself*—no book that I have penned requires another for the story that *it* is telling to be complete.

However,

There *are* other stories that are being told in the subtext of the combined books; there are other messages to be had. They need not be read in any particular order, though reading any one will impact your understanding of any other.

Reading everything will alter your understanding even further.

Happy reading, should you have the time!

Daniel

  - [Without Rest] -

"People like dialogue," Eris interrupted, "which is why I try to keep all of *my* dialogue relevant and interesting."

-Chapter 1, 1st sentence: <u>God, Man, and The Machine.</u>

Jacob did not like dialogue.

-Chapter 1, 1st sentence: <u>The Terrors of Wonder.</u>

There was no dialogue.

-Chapter 1, 1st sentence: <u>Without Rest.</u>

CHECKMATE

A short story

Minister Van Loch was a hard, unbending man. Though not well-liked, he *was* well-respected,[197] for he was known to command great power: that sovereigns and saints would bend their ears to hear his words. Reputation aside however, when Van Loch came into a room, everyone stopped speaking.

Van Loch always tied a bandana[198] over his eyes to both accentuate and mask his blindness—although he wasn't actually blind. His face was usually a bit gaunt, for in pursuing his passion he often forgot to eat. Fairly thin and slightly tall, his body initially strikes one as somewhat frail, but this is deceiving for he is both solid and strong.

Never in her wildest dreams did his mother suspect that this would be the man he became. Never in anyone's dreams did they suspect that Minister Van Loch was born as Peter Drake, or that his mother only called him her "little ducky." [199]

As young Peter Drake grew up, he was known for his intelligence, his charm, and his congenital heart defect.[200]

As he grew into a man, he enjoyed great successes in computer programming and chess. During his high school years he won many awards, earning him amongst his contemporaries the nickname "Peter the Drake."

Apart from two terrible surgeries, Peter enjoyed his life.

Toward the end of school, Drake was approached and recruited by his government, who in turn paid for his ongoing education. By the time he had his degree, he had already far exceeded his schooling.

Now, although Drake worked for his government, he was nobody of signif-

---

197 as well as well-dressed.

198 or sash.

199 his mother always had a fondness for the surname. Her maiden name was Rocquemei, you see, and she hated it.

200 known professionally as an "Atrial Septal Defect," Peter had a hole in his heart.

 - [Without Rest] -

icant clearance or importance—but he *was* known and respected for his technical skills, and on occasion an offer of alternate employment appeared.

Then came *the* offer.

One day Pothos—in prestigious character, of course—visited Drake and suggested that he come work for him. Pothos informed Drake that he had acquired a revolutionary new computer and needed someone to act as its system operator. Pothos offered Drake nearly anything that he could want: an unreasonable amount of money, the nearly obsequious attention of his subordinates and civilians alike, and the love of nearly any woman he desired. Oh, and complete correction of his heart defect—a service unavailable anywhere else in the world.

Before Drake could eagerly agree, however, Pothos explained that there were further conditions of his employment—and they were both such strange and severe conditions that they actually made accepting the offer difficult.
Drake had to move to Pothos' country. He had to surrender his identity as Peter Drake and take on an assigned name. He had to sever all ties with old friends and family, and finally, he had to renounce all religion.

Drake, somewhat reluctantly, took the offer.

"You will be known henceforth as Agent Harrison."

Harrison found he *loved* his new life. Wistful thoughts of old friends and family never surfaced, and seldom did he think of his past. He came to think of his job as his family and friends. No regrets ever came to mind, and he proceeded in his success, shining brightly in his identity and role.

Harrison overheard a conversation one day that had an odd impact upon him. Two of his contemporaries were discussing the oddity of a particular similarity. This conversation happened on occasion, only *this* one happened to contain an answer.

"Ever wonder why every Agent has a name that ends in 'son?'"
"Oh, I know that," said the other. "Agent's names end in 'son' so that we

subconsciously think of Axel as our father."

"*What?*"

"Well, that's what the director said once, and if anyone knows, he does."

"What about the deformities? Do you know why every Agent has some kind of defect?"

"I didn't realize that…but no. No clue. Want to get lunch?"

"Sure, just not 'Bagel Lord' again."

The conversation shouldn't have bothered him—but it did, and the more he reflected on it the less he liked it. It seemed *wrong* that Axel should want to be thought of as his father, subconsciously or not.[201] Later, however, he met a female Agent named Robinson, and his discontented thoughts of the rumored association and meaning abated.

Too late, however: a seed of wariness took root in Harrison's heart.

A contemporary of his and he were having a conversation over coffee one day when his colleague told him that there are living copies of every citizen being held in suspended animation far below the building they worked in.[202] Harrison didn't believe it, and yet there was a shaking sincerity in his friend's demeanor that made him want to investigate.

The System Operator of the Mainframe shares the highest level of access with only two other men.[203] He has access to everything, with the understanding that some actions would be forbidden: such as prying into Axel's[204] personal files.

Harrison found that not only were there clones of every citizen, there were clones of every *visitor.* Not only this, but there were multiple copies of each clone. Almost a mile below him lay a secret, gargantuan vault of clones, all in suspended animation chambers. The next thing he found made him vomit.

---

[201] which only goes to show that he was too intelligent and too bored: he traded his name, his family, his friends, and his beliefs for his position, and *now* it bothers him that his new name was made so that he would subconsciously think of Axel as his *father?* Seems tame by comparison, *but* mortals are creatures of the moment: they tend to think that when their life is good it has always been thus, and that when their lives are bad that it has always been so.

[202] that's quite the sentence.

[203] both of whom are merely alternate personas of Pothos.

[204] Pothos. Now, Pothos is no idiot, and stores nothing in the Mainframe that would suggest his true identity…although he *does* certainly use it to carry out his hidden agenda.

Not everyone in the vault was a clone: almost every "series" of clone was missing the first, and instead in those chambers lay the actual person—including *him*.

Everyone in the country is a clone, he realized. He didn't understand how it was possible, but he knew he wouldn't grasp the science even if it were available.

He found all the chambers were scheduled to open on March 15th, 2137—which, at the time of discovery, would be more than a hundred years away. He *also* found that there were millions of satellites, all scheduled to point their projectors down upon the country on the very same day. What that could possibly mean, Harrison did not know.

Something was terribly wrong, though; that was obvious. Something needed to be done—but what?

Harrison knew—better than anyone save Pothos himself—the level of surveillance that was being exercised. He knew he could not hope to do this alone. But who could he possibly recruit? Who could he trust?

He found his answer in the criminals. He could trust anyone that committed a crime against the country, though not someone who committed a crime against a *person*—they were too treacherous. Those who wanted to avoid punishment were particularly susceptible to approach, and so Agent Harrison made a way to "mask" a citizen's Mainframe identity—offer them a *new identity* to hide behind.

The first man he "saved" was a stoic, short Maltese man who was only too eager to assist him. Harrison introduced himself as "Peter Smith" [205] and also as "The Queen," and dubbed his rescue "The Queen's Pawn."

"You and I will take control of the middle of the board," Harrison explained as the Queen.

Harrison knew he could not tell another man his findings lest they think him insane, so he presented his agenda in the guise of a new agency—a hidden agency—called *The Chessmen*.[206] An agency made up of individuals that have been

---

[205] a *second* identity that he made for himself…an identity that was also given unrestricted access to the Mainframe. It was under *this* identity that he would do his hidden computer works.

[206] Chessmen amongst one another, although the public would come to know them better as the "SilverSmiths."

given a new identity; people who have a passion for their country and a *hatred* for their leader.

Harrison wrote up a series of protocols and statements that described the purpose and function of *the Chessmen* in a hand-written book called <u>The King</u>.

"Why is it called <u>The King</u>? The Queen's Pawn asked.

"So called, for should I die the game is not over. Our values lie in here," he said, holding up the book. "Not in *here*," he said, pointing to himself.

Chessmen with titles higher than "Pawn" [207A] were given the book for reading and reflection. Harrison was a compelling author—even the remotely skeptic experienced a new sense of purpose after having read it.

He found and recruited many men to his cause—or at least to the cause of <u>The King</u>. He also spent a fair amount of time reprogramming the Mainframe, resulting in sowing the seeds for the Mainframe's intellectual development that years later would manifest as the "Nexus."

Everything was going well, but then he *saw* Pothos.

He once—rather by accident—watched Pothos change characters on Mainframe surveillance. He decided to take a closer look. He used the Mainframe to access Pothos' unmonitored inner rooms. Shortly after he started his investigation, however, Pothos returned. Harrison hid himself where he could see into the current room and waited.

Harrison was common in thinking that he was unique, however he was not unique for any of the reasons that he thought. He *was* unique, at least in that he is the only mortal to see Pothos in his true form and *not* be driven irretrievably insane.

Pothos entered and casually removed his costumes, revealing his true nature. Harrison watched, first to his dismay and then to his horror as his eyes fell upon the impossible, lightless god. Harrison was spellbound. His eyes were wide and unblinking, and sweat poured from his brow. As the vision of the void threatened to take his sanity from him, he found that he *could not look away*, which was then as equally maddening. His hands, then shaking with the last sane[208A] command that

---

207A with exception to *the Queen's Pawn.*
208A Harrison's *sanity* at that moment is a bit suspect.

 - [Without Rest] -

he could issue, tore his eyes from his head.

"Dispose of this body," Pothos later commanded in costume. "Have it torn limb from body and then divided into pieces. Then burn it. Tell *no one* of what you have done."

The employee that Pothos so commanded *instead* delivered Harrison's body directly to the Chessmen, for she was a member.

So Harrison lived, but only just. As he returned to health, he heard that Axel created something called "The Hall of Moments," and put Harrison's name there as an example to all. Not as a bad example though—Harrison was being presented as a *role model.* [209]

He thinks I'm dead, Harrison realized.

He will think that I think that he's dead, thought Pothos, knowing the employee who saved him was a spy and would fail to follow her orders—orders that conveniently required no evidence and no further discussion.

Pothos did not often enjoy himself amongst mortals, but this was always his favorite game.

Drake/Harrison/Smith knew he could not remain in the country undetected for very long. With new, artificial eyes[210] he used the Mainframe to steal large sums of money from around the world. He established for himself a *new* identity—the one that would be his last.

"My name is now 'Minister,'" he told the Queen's Pawn prior to his departure. "Minister Van Loch. I will be in regular contact."
"*Minister*? Why 'Minister?'"

---

[209] Harrison was being presented as a model employee, the reported end of his employment a deliberate lie. Pothos also renamed a victory arch and even the park after Harrison, and then had a statue of him erected in its center.
[210] that he *hated.*

"So that when people meet me or think of me, they will subconsciously associate me with a teacher: a figure of knowledge, authority, and position."

"So why 'Van Loch?'"

Minister shrugged. "I thought it sounded exotic."

A new Queen was promoted and took charge of the Chessmen as Van Loch left the country.

◬

Van Loch spent the next 50 years[211] building his external position. Having intimate access to the Mainframe ensured the success of his endeavors and gained him access to people and places he ordinarily would not be able to. His passion drove him nearly ceaselessly,[212] for he alone knew what needed to be done—and that *he* must do it, for no one else *could*.

Van Loch worked to spread a global mistrust for Axel—Pothos—and placed many obstacles in his dealings.[213] Alternately, he used his Chessmen to complicate Pothos' *internal* affairs.

The "Chessmen" cycled through several Queens over the years, though all were diligent to <u>The King</u>. The Queen's Pawn maintained his position, though his age was suggesting a replacement soon. The Queen's Pawn was instrumental in every transition, and with keeping the agency in focus…well, until recently.

Aware of nearly everything Van Loch did, Pothos, for the most part, did not interfere with him. He allowed him his little victories here and there, and waited as his opponent improved his game. Satisfied, Pothos finally used his *own* "pieces" to influence the ascent of the most recent Queen.

The *current* Queen is something of a loose cannon you see, and he started steering the Chessmen in a very pernicious direction—an *irreversible* direction—and now it was only a matter of time before Pothos destroyed them…or so Van Loch figured.

211 48 years, not 50: "Van Loch" appeared in 2022, "Checkmate" culminates in 2070.
212 without rest.
213 for instance, Van Loch was instrumental in getting an accord known globally as the 'EALETA' passed. The EALETA was an accord which blatantly worked to undermine Pothos' ability to conduct commerce.

Van Loch still maintained his internal influence, but was being pushed to make a move.

That move came today. [214A]

News reports from around the world flashed that Axel had died. Van Loch did not *for a moment* believe that Pothos was *actually* dead, but used this event to assert his influence over the Excellencies of the world.

With a smile that made one cringe, Van Loch suggested forgoing the protocol of declaring war, and attack with an all-out offensive on every front: invasion, insurrection, agricultural, financial, and so on.

Initially there was some reluctance, however when Pothos' *entire country* lost power a few hours later, there immediately fell unanimous agreement. Van Loch's surprise war began.

Then to *Van Loch's* surprise, Pothos' Agents appeared and killed everyone present.

Pothos and his Agents had secretly observed the meeting between Van Loch and the Excellencies. Hours prior to their mutual conviction, Pothos ordered that they were all to be slain.

Despite the untimely deaths of their leaders, some military and covert actions *were* still carried out, and although most were rendered ineffective once the replacement Mainframe[215A] was created,[216▲] there was certainly an impact to be felt.[217A]

Van Loch lay over the front of the table, dying. The remaining Agent moved him—with no gentility—into his chair.

214[A] Saturday, June 14th, 2070
215[Δ] "Harmony."
216[▲] whereupon all the defense measures of the country reactivated.
217[A] although admittedly during the upheaval of Pothos, the most observable impact was the temporary loss of the Mainframe: the lights all turned off, air conditioning and environmental systems failed, doors wouldn't open, autocars stopped functioning—many instances of which resulting in the death of the occupants...and of course there was no communication and no competent defense.

"I have a message from Axel," the Agent said when he saw Van Loch was slightly still alive and awake. "He says 'checkmate, Peter.'"

Prior to falling under regular observation, Peter made a slight adjustment to a Mainframe program not scheduled to run for another 67 years. It always brought him a sense of satisfaction when he thought about it.

"Heh," Van Loch sputtered with a slightly bloody cough. "He wasn't—heh, paying attention: I'm…not…the *King*. Check*mate!*"

THE END

- [Without Rest] -

About the Author

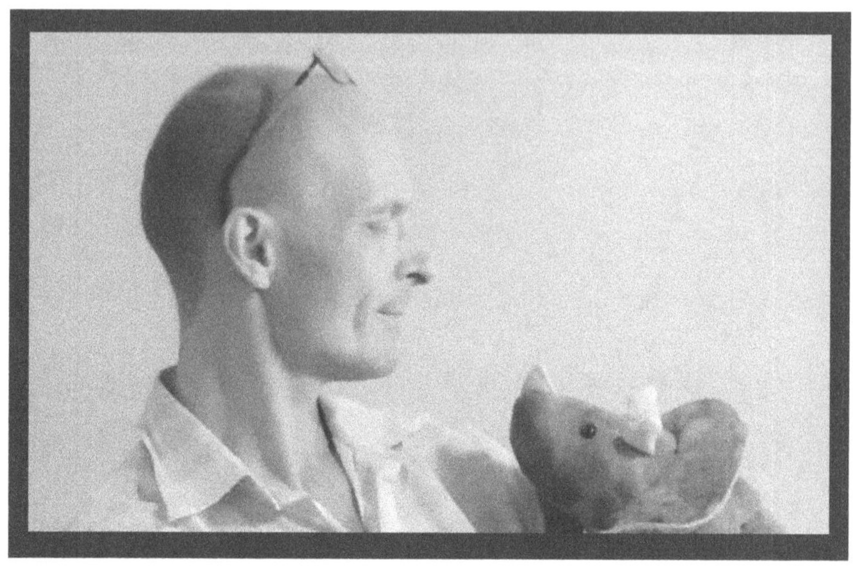

"It has been a privilege and a pleasure to share this Earth with you."

Daniel Strasel, born September 15, 1973, sole progeny of ~~a wayward cooper~~ an eccentric, yet intelligent nurse named Sue. He emerged into life a genuine, happy child. Soon thereafter, he grew into a brooding and self-centered adolescent. A wild, ambitious, and impressionable young adult was followed by a confused, frightened, and purposeless man.

Following his tweens he finally found humility, discipline, and compassion before his overdeveloped sense of self-importance destroyed him completely. Thanks always to my wife for helping provide the time for me to write this.

www.ingramcontent.com/pod-product-compliance
Lightning Source LLC
Chambersburg PA
CBHW060758210726
48292CB00013B/701